# Praise for *Between You and Me*

"Scott Nadelson gives us a true Gogolian hero in Paul Haberman, a small, yearning, middle-aged suburbanite in New Jersey, beset by vague terrors and also by a trembling awareness of all the world has to offer, while not knowing how to ask, most of the time, for any of it. Haberman is a radiant character and *Between You and Me* is a hilarious, poignant, darkly glittering gem of a novel."

—Suzanne Berne, author of *A Crime in the Neighborhood*

"What a wonderful and affecting novel Scott Nadelson has written. As is clear from the hilarious opening standoff in a New Jersey mall parking lot, the author has a talent for zooming in—with uncanny psychological precision—on the small, defining moments of individual experience. And yet the story that results, as we revisit Paul Haberman over two decades of his adulthood, becomes that of a universal everyman, whose equivocal life seems more and more resplendent as we follow him through the years."

—Frederick Reiken, author of *Day For Night*

"Scott Nadelson's novel, Between You and Me, grows on you, gains weight chapter by chapter as its hero, Paul Haberman—step-father, husband, lawyer, son and brother—stumbles his way through passive and passionless middle age to stand, finally, in his own skin as a man and to affirm his life. The ending is beautiful. The beginning and middle pieces add up, finally, like any good befuddling adventure, to something astounding. Something extraordinary. Yes, I said, when I'd read the last pages, yes."

—David Allan Cates, author of *Tom*

# BETWEEN
## YOU *and* ME

## ALSO BY SCOTT NADELSON

*The Next Scott Nadelson: A Life in Progress*

*Aftermath*

*The Cantor's Daughter: Stories*

*Saving Stanley: The Brickman Stories*

*For Chuck
+ Charlotte —
With all
best wishes —
Scott*

# BETWEEN
# YOU *and* ME

## SCOTT NADELSON

*Portland
11/30/15*

**Engine Books**
Indianapolis

**Engine Books**
PO Box 44167
Indianapolis, IN 46244
**enginebooks.org**

Copyright © 2015 by Scott Nadelson

All rights reserved. No part of this book may be reproduced or transmitted in any form or by any means, electronic or mechanical, including photocopying, recording, or by any storage and retrieval system, without the written permission of the publisher, except where permitted by law.

Every reasonable attempt has been made to identify owners of copyright. Errors or omissions will be corrected in subsequent editions.

This is a work of fiction. Names, characters, places, and incidents are either the product of the author's imagination or used fictitiously.

Also available in eBook formats from Engine Books.

Printed in the United States of America

10   9   8   7   6   5   4   3   2   1

ISBN: 978-1-938126-33-8

Library of Congress Control Number: 2015953148

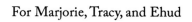

For Marjorie, Tracy, and Ehud

A man who headed no cause, fought in no wars, and passed his life unaware of the great public issues—it might be asked: why trouble with such a man at all?

—Wright Morris

# CHAPTERS

# GIRL MADE OF METAL

## 1981

THE ROCKAWAY MALL MOVIE theater still had only six screens, tucked between the Bamberger's and the video arcade. It would be a few more years before another six were built, in a strip mall annex beside the Sizzler that dropouts from Morris Knolls High School would later accidentally burn down during a burglary. Those new screens would have plenty of parking spaces, separated as they were from the main complex, but this afternoon, a rainy Sunday in early July, Paul Haberman had to compete for spots with every shopper in Morris County, every teenager playing Asteroids and smoking cigarettes and trying to look fearsome.

In the back seat of his Imperial sat his wife's two children. Joy was nine, a fast-growing twig with surprisingly fair hair—both her mother's and father's were black—and an unfortunate habit of staring with her mouth open, which made her appear less intelligent than she was and less pretty than she wanted to be. Kyle, seven, was the slower of the two, a dark runt with Cynthia's curly hair and dense eyebrows and a tendency to whine when he didn't get what he wanted. When he didn't know what he wanted, he invented illnesses for himself: stomachaches, dizzy spells, mysterious, invisible rashes. He was whining now—"Why don't you park already?"—as Paul tried to pull into a spot just as another car nosed in.

Sunday afternoon was Paul's time to bond with the kids, while

SCOTT NADELSON

Cynthia attended Hadassah meetings at the synagogue in Morristown. They'd been married just over a month, and on five Sundays he'd taken the children to five different movies. He'd never had kids and didn't know what else to do with them. Spending two hours in a darkened room without speaking seemed the safest option.

In his younger days, during college and law school and his first years living on his own, when he was awkward and in debt and women weren't attracted to him, he'd mourned the notion that he'd never have a family. He'd fantasized idly about his unborn children, thinking how fortunate they would have been to have him as a father. There was so much he could have taught them—how to ride the subway, how to score a baseball game, how to avoid panhandlers and men in trenchcoats selling fake or stolen Rolexes. He would have imparted wisdom and taste and culture, introduced them to books, music, film. In his imagination they were always grateful, full of the appreciation he felt he deserved but never received from anyone else.

But by the time he hit his mid-thirties, he'd settled into a comfortable bachelor's life, with a job as in-house legal counsel— one of a dozen—for a mid-sized insurance firm in Midtown and an apartment on the Upper West Side he shared with his cat Franklin, a docile tabby content to sit in the window all day, staring down onto 79th Street. He flew around the world and ate dinner at four-star restaurants and always had more money than he knew how to spend, tossing it at extravagances like the Imperial, which, before moving to New Jersey, he'd hardly ever driven. Age suited his face, which had become, if not handsome, at least dignified, with a stately widow's peak and a neatly trimmed mustache that partly compensated for his sunken chin. He'd discovered a means of appearing confident even when he wasn't, cloaking self-consciousness in a façade of cool indifference. To his surprise, women now found him appealing, responding easily to his advances, and sometimes the uncomfortable notion came into his mind that it could have been this way all along, that he'd wasted years of opportunity. But mostly he was grateful. He no longer thought much about having a family, content with sex, which, having eluded him for so long, he finally enjoyed in abundance.

He met Cynthia a week after his fortieth birthday, at a Passover seder his cousin hosted at her house in Randolph. His cousin was also a member of the Morristown Hadassah and had been talking to him about Cynthia for nearly a year, though nothing she'd said had sparked his interest. What did he want with a suburban divorcée, the mother of two kids, a woman nearly as old as himself, when he regularly went to bed with girls in their early twenties, carefree and unfettered, who often as not would disappear from Paul's life before he knew where they were born, how many siblings they had, what college they'd attended?

But his cousin was right. Cynthia was far sexier than most of those twenty-three-year-olds, who hadn't yet grown into their beautiful bodies, didn't know how to move them, as Cynthia did, in a way that made him gawk as she carried trays of food into his cousin's dining room, her loose dress sashaying around her hips, bare shoulders pearly under his cousin's gaudy chandelier. Her voice had a hint of rasp in it, especially when she laughed, and she asked questions about Paul's job in a direct, probing manner that startled him, her arms crossed on the table, eyes locked on his. When he described how he spent his days—negotiating contracts and filing briefs—she winced and shook her head. "God, that sounds deadly." She told him about her own job as a counselor at Morris Knolls, writing letters of recommendation for half the population, bound for college, recommending drug rehab programs for the other half, bound for prison. "It's pretty deadly, too," she said.

At the end of the evening, after they'd eaten their fill of matzah and horseradish and drank their four glasses of wine, Paul walked her to her car. He asked for her number and shook her hand, thinking it would be too forward to kiss her cheek—she was the mother of young children, after all, who were at a seder with their father—and in response she gave him a look of confusion, and maybe insult. "Aren't you following me home?" she asked. "Isn't that what all this was about?"

He found himself deeply, heedlessly in love. It astonished him to think he could have been content with anything else, and again he had the feeling that he'd wasted time, that he could have had what he'd wanted all along, if only he'd been brave enough to decide what that was. It astonished him, too, to find himself happily spending Saturdays in New Jersey, a place that before had been nothing but a wall of cliffs and dock cranes glimpsed through his office window. Cynthia's kids spent Saturdays with their father, a burly man with a military bearing, who, to Paul's surprise, had been a shaggy hippie when he and Cynthia had gotten together. "We were such kids," Cynthia said whenever she talked about her marriage, and though she said it to explain what a mistake it had been, her voice carried a longing that made Paul envious. He wished they could have been wild kids together, too—though he hadn't been much of a wild kid on his own—and not these adults with so many responsibilities, jobs and mortgages and car payments and children.

Children. Did he want them, after all this time?

When they discussed marriage, Cynthia was quick to say that she didn't expect him to be a father to Joy and Kyle. "They already have one reluctant dad. They don't need a second."

He just had to be himself, she told him, and whatever developed between them was fine with her. And this, he supposed, was what he'd really wanted all along. A family with no obligation, no responsibilities other than those he already had.

He proposed.


But now, more than a month after he'd rented out his apartment and moved Franklin into Cynthia's rambling suburban house, where the cat was made suddenly anxious by the choice of so many windows to sit in, pacing all night and crying for no reason, Paul faced these Sunday afternoons with trepidation. If he wasn't supposed to be the children's father, what *was* he supposed to be? He didn't want to be their friend, exactly, or some benevolent uncle figure. He wanted them to look up to him, to benefit from his experience and taste. On their first outing to the movies he'd taken them to see *Kramer vs. Kramer*—checking ahead to make sure it was rated PG—at a second-run theater in Montclair. Kyle fell asleep after the first fifteen minutes and was cranky for the rest of the evening. Joy said afterward that she thought the movie was "hyper," which Paul took to mean she found it melodramatic. She was the child of a divorce, she reminded him; she knew about these things firsthand. Plus, she didn't think it was an appropriate choice for someone her age.

Since then he'd let the kids choose the films, and they'd seen two inane pictures about a Volkswagen Beetle with a mind of its own and a ridiculous comedy about cavemen—with Ringo Starr, of all people, in the lead role—which, despite himself, Paul enjoyed. Now they were on their way to the new Muppets movie, running late because Joy decided to change her shoes just before they walked out the door, and because Kyle spent five minutes arguing about putting on his raincoat. Paul had circled the parking lot for another fifteen, squinting through his fogged windshield, occasionally glimpsing a spot the next aisle over and winging too fast around a corner, only to find it taken by the time he got there. His window was open a crack, but still he found it hard to breathe, and rain sputtered against his neck. He felt a touch of panic at the thought of Cynthia's exasperation when she came home from Hadassah to find everyone miserable and desperate for her attention. When he saw the empty spot only a few aisles from the theater's entrance, he jammed on the gas in spite of the car gunning for it from the opposite direction.

Neither car could get into the spot. Both Paul and the other driver leaned on their horns. In the backseat, Kyle whined louder, the only distinguishable words being "Muppets" and "promise."

Joy said, "This is just terrific."

The other car was a Camaro, with flames painted on its hood, and the kid who stuck his head out the driver's window had lank hair to his shoulders and a long pointed face, like a possum's. Paul had seen a possum for the first time earlier this month, pulling into the driveway late one evening after work. It had been flat on the pavement, dead, he thought, until he approached and nudged it with his foot. Then it hissed at him, baring its needle teeth, eyes hollow and chilling. Paul stifled a shriek as it ran away, its tail longer and more naked than any rat's, of which he'd seen plenty during his forty years riding New York subways. A week later he saw a raccoon while taking out the trash, and early one morning soon after, a deer defoliating one of the backyard shrubs. How he'd gotten himself into the wilderness he had no idea. The place was overrun with—or run by—animals and teenagers. In comparison, Manhattan was the tamest, most civilized place on earth.

In the Camaro's passenger seat was a pale, pimpled girl with a cigarette dangling from one corner of her mouth and hair that swooped in front of her eyes before feathering over her ears. He couldn't be sure she could even see him, until she lifted a hand lazily and gave him the finger. "Beat it, man," the kid beside her said, waving a hairless arm that was almost as slender as Joy's. "This one's mine."

"We missed the start," Joy said. "We might as well go home."

"I want Kermit," Kyle said, beginning to cry. He tried clambering over the front seat, but Paul blocked his way with an arm.

"We've got time," he said. "Sit until we're parked."

"You better find another spot, then," Joy said. "This could take all day."

"I was here first. I had my blinker on."

Paul hit the horn again, which sent the kid into a fury of throwing open his door, shouting, tapping himself on the chest. A possum playing ape. He wore a t-shirt with the sleeves cut off, the words "Iron Maiden" at the top, some kind of neon demon wielding a hatchet beneath. When he stood, he was taller than Paul expected, half a head taller than himself, though narrow across the shoulders, with almost dainty hands.

"Paul," Joy said, leaning over the front seat. "I think you should let him have it."

What did she want him to have, the spot or a punch in the nose? From her tone he couldn't tell, and he didn't ask. Instead he jerked a thumb over his shoulder. "Down," he said.

Kyle whimpered. "I want to go home."

"Get the fuck outta my way," the kid shouted, coming toward them. The rain made hair stick to his face, and now he looked like a wet possum, only his teeth were blunt and yellowed. "Or get outta the car."

Paul rolled up his window, locked the door, and hit the horn. The kid's nose and chin were red, eyes slits.

"This isn't getting us anywhere," Joy said.

"I was here first," Paul said again. He knew he was supposed to do something now, and that whatever he did would be a lesson for the children. But what lesson was the appropriate one? It was strange to think his actions could have consequences for anyone outside of himself. If he backed the car away, as he wanted to, wouldn't that teach them meekness, that the aggressor always wins? If he got out of the car and shouted the kid down, as Cynthia would have, or pummeled him, as the children's father might, they'd turn into loud, thoughtless brutes. Maybe the best course was to let the kid pummel him—likely, if he did get out of the car—and then lecture the children about Ghandi and nonviolent resistance and tell them stories about the protests of the sixties, which he'd watched on TV.

The one thing he knew they shouldn't learn was how petrified he was, though he suspected they could smell it on him as dogs did. He decided against doing anything, except to sit there with his hands locked on the steering wheel, eyes set straight ahead. The girl in the passenger seat of the Camaro looked bored or asleep, head resting against the window, cigarette still burning.

"I'll kick your fucking ass," the kid said. He pressed his possum face to the window, palms flat against the glass.

"My bladder hurts," Kyle said. "And I have a fever."

The demon on the black t-shirt was meant to be menacing, but if anything Paul found it mesmerizing. Its eyes were empty holes, glowing in their centers, its mouth set in an enormous skeletal sneer above a cleft, skinless chin. Hands grabbed its shirt from below, and its hatchet dripped blood, but there was a soft chartreuse shimmer to its teased hair, and behind it floated pearly clouds. He knew what an iron maiden was and supposed it was a clever name for a rock and roll outfit—it was no sillier, really, than The Beatles—but it seemed to have nothing to do with the demon, which was as lanky and feminine as the kid himself, who backed away a step now, and crossed his arms. It took Paul a moment to realize why.

Joy had stepped out of the car. She stood on the pavement, staring up at the kid, rain pattering her fair hair. In the last month she'd often seemed older than her nine years. On their second outing, when they'd gone to see *Herbie Goes Bananas,* she'd told him he seemed tense, that maybe he needed a cocktail, and Paul, mortified, sounded like Kyle when he answered, "I just have a little headache." But now she looked only gangly and innocent in her pink shirt and floral shorts, her head hardly coming up past the kid's waist. How had he managed to let her out of the house without a raincoat after fighting about it with Kyle? The kid seemed to be waiting for her to speak, maybe thinking she was an imbecile, gawking at him like that with her mouth open. Paul wished she would close it. He was waiting, too, to hear what she had to say. But she only stood there, getting drenched.

"Look," the kid told her. "I was totally here first. You were way down at the end of the aisle."

What was it that fascinated him about the t-shirt? That it failed in its attempt to seem sinister? That the demon looked like a crazed Muppet, more sultry than threatening, striking a harlot's pose on a dimly lit street beneath a beautifully striated sky?

"Shit, man," the kid said. "You know that spot was mine, and you come flying in and try to steal it." He turned to Paul and called through the window, "Why don't you get outta the car, man?"

The girl in the Camaro stirred, tossing her cigarette out the window, her head following. Her hair was still in her eyes, and Paul couldn't tell how she saw what was going on around her. "What's the hold-up," she called, voice high and abrasive, not at all what he'd expected from her lazy, languid smoking. "Get him to fucking move."

"I have an infection," Kyle said quietly, hunched down on the car's floor.

Joy was good and soaked now, and so was the kid. They were having a battle of wills, and Joy was clearly winning. She still hadn't said anything, hadn't moved, just stared at the kid with her mouth gaping, until he backed off another step. This was the lesson, then, Paul thought. Teaching the children that they could do things for themselves. The key now, he knew, was to keep Cynthia from finding out about it. He hit the horn, hard, and held it for five full seconds.

The kid threw up his hands and turned away. "Okay! Take the goddamn spot. I don't have time for this."

On the back of his t-shirt was the word "Killers" in shaky red ink, as if written in blood, and for some reason this had its intended effect, making Paul shudder. Joy watched the kid until he was all the way back to the Camaro, and only when his attention was taken up by the pimpled girl, who'd lit another cigarette and was questioning him with a skeptical, exasperated expression similar to the one Paul imagined Cynthia turning on him later this afternoon, did he roll down his window and tell Joy to get back into the car. "You're sopping wet," he said.

"Aren't you supposed to thank me now?" Her shorts made a squishing sound on the leather seat. The Camaro backed out with a screech of tires, and the girl gave Paul the finger again. He smiled and waved.

"If you catch cold, your mother won't forgive me," he said. "You'd better not tell her about this."

"I never get colds in summer," Joy said. "And I never talk to mom about her men."

"Let's go!" Kyle cried, standing on the seat.

"Down until we're parked." Paul had to maneuver the car back and forth three times before he could pull into the spot, which was a tight though satisfying fit. The Camaro would have had an easier time with it. "Watch the doors," he said, just as both Kyle and Joy slammed theirs into the cars on either side. He had to suck in his belly to squeeze out and then fought with the umbrella that stuck halfway open. Kyle started to run ahead, and Paul shouted at him to wait. Joy, to his surprise, took his hand and pressed close to him, shivering.

"Paul?" she said. "Iron's a metal, right?"

"That's right."

She nodded but didn't say anything more, instead dodging a puddle that Paul saw only as he stepped in it. They hurried the rest of the way to the theater, passing the video arcade spilling out cackling teenagers—doped, he thought, and neglected by their parents—but of course they were too late. The Muppets had begun ten minutes before. Kyle muttered something about chest pains. "We might as well go home," Joy said. Paul scanned the board and checked his watch.

There were two possibilities, but one was sure to get him into trouble. *A History of the World: Part I* sounded innocent enough, educational, even, but it was rated R. "*Raiders of the Lost Ark*," he told the girl at the ticket counter. "One adult, two children."

The kid in the Iron Maiden t-shirt and the pimpled girl with hair in her face were ahead of them, arms around each other's waists. They were all going into the same theater, and Paul had an intimation of his mistake. "Killers," he read, before walking the children into the gloom.

"Why did God melt their faces?" Kyle asked, blanket pulled up to his chin, though it was steamy in the house now, humid after the rain.

"God wouldn't really do something like that," Paul said. And he explained for the tenth time that it was just a movie, a made-up story by twisted people who somehow decided that "PG" included heads exploding on screen. He was perched at the end of Kyle's bed, feet on the floor. He'd stood twice already, and twice Kyle had kept him there by asking about details of the movie's plot. It was half an hour past Kyle's bedtime and getting close to Paul's own. Cynthia had been in the bath for as long as he'd been in here, and he imagined her skin first growing pink and angry, then puckered.

Tacked crookedly above Kyle's bed was a New York Yankees pennant. Paul tried not to look at it. He'd grown up within walking distance of Ebbets Field, where his father and uncles had season tickets, and the thought of someone in his house being a Yankees fan made him mildly nauseous. But he couldn't convince Kyle to root for the Mets, one of the worst teams in baseball. The current strike was a blessing. He hoped it would last the whole season, so Kyle wouldn't start begging again to be taken to a game. In his entire life, Paul had never once set foot in the Bronx, much less in Yankee Stadium.

"Why did ghosts come out of the box?" Kyle asked.

"They were supposed to be angels, I think," Paul said. "The avenging kind."

"Why did angels melt their faces?"

"Because they were Nazis," Paul said. "That's what always happens to Nazis."

"Will angels do that to me?"

"Of course not. You're not a Nazi, are you?" Kyle shook his head. "I didn't think so."

"Why did Indy want the box?"

"I told you already. He's an archeologist. It's his job to find ancient things."

"Can I be an archeologist?"

"You can be anything you want to be," Paul said, hoping not only that this was the right answer but the one that would end the conversation.

"I don't want to find any ghosts."

"Most archeologists don't have such exciting lives as Indiana Jones, I bet. Or as dangerous."

"Can I be a baseball player?"

"Well," Paul said. He'd watched one of Kyle's Little League games, and Kyle had hardly been able to hit the ball off the tee. "Sure you can. You'd have to practice a lot. And there's always the question of natural ability—"

"Can I play for the Yankees?" Kyle asked. His voice was quieter, and his eyes were beginning to close. Paul eased himself off the bed.

"I don't think you get to choose your team. It depends who picks you. You might get to play for the Mets, though. Wouldn't that be great?"

Paul was standing now. He took a step away. But then Kyle's eyes went wide, and he sat up. "Are there ghosts in here?"

"None. I promise."

As soon as he said it he heard rustling behind him, and the curtain moved, though there was no breeze. He whirled, and Kyle ducked under the blanket. But it was only Franklin, making his nervous rounds from one window to another, his tail flicking against the screen.

"No ghosts," Paul said. "No such thing."

"I feel pale," Kyle said, his voice coming from where Paul expected his feet to be. "And my elbow hurts."

"You'll feel better after a good night's sleep," Paul said, hurrying to the door and turning out the lights. "And remember, it was only a movie. None of it was real."

He said the same thing to Joy when he checked on her, but she only gave him that blank, open-mouthed stare that was entirely disconcerting, and he understood why the kid in the Camaro had run away. She was reading a book about cats, and her walls were covered in posters with kittens on them—one hanging from a tree, another spinning on a turntable, a third standing in the middle of a collapsed birthday cake—but never once had he seen her pay any attention to Franklin. After a moment he asked if she also wasn't afraid of angels or ghosts who might melt her face.

"Don't be silly," she said.

"But I'm so good at it."

"Paul?" she called when he was at the door, and her puzzled squint sent a chill through him. Why? What could she ask that he wouldn't be able to answer? "A maiden's not the same as a maid, is it?"

"No," he said, breathing shallowly. "It isn't."

"That's what I thought."

He waited for her to ask more, and when she didn't, said good night and closed the door behind him.

"It's outrageous," he said, pacing in front of the bed. "Faces melting? They call that PG? I'm going to write to the ratings board. You better believe it. And to the movie academy, or whatever it's called. And to Spielberg."

Cynthia lay on top of the comforter, her robe open at the throat, hair wrapped in a towel. Her skin was flushed, and her neck glistened with sweat. She watched him as he paced but said nothing, giving him the same disconcerting, silent stare Joy had fixed on the kid in the parking lot. Only Cynthia's mouth was closed, and Paul thought he could see a muscle in her jaw jump as she clenched it.

"I mean, what's the point of having a ratings system if it doesn't mean anything? I would have been better off taking them to *History of the Earth*. They would have seen a cavewoman's breasts, maybe, but they might have learned something, at least. They wouldn't have nightmares until they're twenty. I mean, I think *I* may have nightmares. It was really traumatic."

Cynthia fanned herself with her hand, and Paul stopped pacing to push on the window sash, though it was already open as far as it would go. It was hot enough to turn on the air conditioning, but Cynthia didn't like it running all night; it dried out her eyes and made her cough all morning. She was three years younger than Paul, a small woman but solid, with thick ankles and heavy hips—peasant stock, she joked when she wasn't feeling self-conscious about her weight, though her ancestors had been merchants, in Vilnius and then in New York. Her father was a jeweler, with a storefront on 47th Street he'd inherited from Cynthia's grandfather and a wholesale business that supplied fittings to diamond dealers up and down the Eastern Seaboard. Cynthia had her father's smart, scrutinizing eyes, and a smile that was always the slightest bit skeptical, as if she expected to be disappointed by whatever amused her. Paul still found her raspy voice seductive nine months after he'd heard it for the first time, and wished he could hear it now, or see that smile. She fanned herself with her other hand, pulled the robe's hem up over her knees, uncrossed her legs.

"I know what you're going to say," Paul went on, taking a seat at the end of the bed, with his back to her. The window closest to him looked out on their backyard and the intersection of Union Knoll Drive and Crescent Ridge. To the right, just across Union Knoll, the ridge dropped away abruptly, and in daylight they had a view of roofs and treetops all the way to Dover, and beyond, to the Rockaway Mall. He gestured at the mall now, though all he could see outside was a streetlamp swarmed by moths, and what he thought was a shadow crossing the lawn. Another possum, maybe, or a raccoon, or a bear cub, or a baboon—who knew what was lurking in the strip of woods between this neighborhood and the next one down the ridge? "I should have done something else with them when we were too late for the movie. But what was I supposed to do? Kyle was ready to throw a fit. It was raining. I couldn't take them to the park. What could we have done? Walk around the mall and let Joy try on every pair of shoes in the

Thom McAns? Or play games in the video arcade, with every stoned teenager in the county?"

He paused, waiting for her to answer, though he knew she wouldn't. When he glanced over his shoulder, her robe was open at the waist, and now she was fanning her chest. He turned away. How was he supposed to defend himself when she was mostly naked, her skin flushed and gleaming? How could he come off as anything other than irrational and bullying? "I know, I should have found out more about the movie before I took them in, but I didn't have time, and I—I was rattled, I'll admit. The parking lot. You wouldn't believe what a madhouse it was," he said, and then told her about the kid in the Camaro, only leaving out the part about Joy getting out of the car, and the part about the kid getting out of the car, too, and even the part about him honking his horn. All he did tell her, really, was that just as he was pulling into a spot another driver raced in and tried to steal it from him, but that he'd held his ground until the other driver backed away.

He got himself worked up telling it and was soon off the bed again, pacing. He wanted the kids to learn something, he said. He wanted them to understand that pushiness shouldn't be rewarded, that some principles are worth standing up for. He felt a swell of indignation, and also of pride, though when he saw that Cynthia had her robe all the way open now, her hand flapping over her perfect triangle of pubic hair—had she just trimmed it?—he was quickly deflated. "I'm going to write to the mall people, too," he said. "If they don't open up more parking, and keep those kids from pouring out of the video arcade into the theater lobby, they're going to lose some customers." He went to the window once more and watched the moths careening stupidly again and again into the streetlamp's glass cover. A car came speeding down Union Knoll, taking the turn onto Crescent Ridge too fast, fishtailing, kicking up loose gravel, and then screeched past the house. Another teenager, Paul thought, let loose by negligent parents to terrorize the neighborhood. Everywhere he turned, wild animals and drug-addled kids. His one obligation, he knew, was to keep the children from harm, but in a place like this, how was it possible? He felt his shoulders sinking. He was resigned now. "It was a mistake," he said. "I'm sorry."

"Paul," Cynthia said, that rasp making him turn and take in the full sight of her, the robe covering only her arms now, her towel gone, hair loose and damp to her shoulders. "You have exactly thirty seconds to get your clothes off, turn out the lights, and get on top of me, or I'm not talking to you for the rest of the week."

He had everything off but his socks when there was a scratching at the door. Avenging angels came to mind, and ghosts, and the cat, but it wasn't any of those. It was Kyle, whimpering. Paul pulled on his shorts and opened the door. By then Cynthia had the robe wrapped around her again. "Your face isn't going to melt," she said, as Kyle clambered onto the bed, blubbering, and snuggled against her. Paul was left without much space to lie down, but he managed to settle himself on the edge of the mattress. He was nearly asleep when Kyle said, "Paul? Why was that man yelling at you in the parking lot?"

"He was a Nazi," Paul said.

"Is his face going to melt?"

"One can only hope."

"No one's face is going to melt," Cynthia said.


In the morning, only Joy and Franklin were awake before Paul left for work. It was a relief to have made it to Monday, to know that soon he'd be on a train heading toward the safety of Manhattan, and it relaxed him to think about facing the busy week ahead. He fed the cat and offered to pour Joy some cereal, but she was already toasting herself a frozen waffle. She studied him as he ate, hair sticking up in back, face still puffy and sleep-dazed, mouth hanging open. He tried to guess whether she, too, had had a nightmare, or had thrashed around all night, as Kyle had, but her grogginess seemed to be of a calm, peaceful sort. Paul's own nightmare wasn't of avenging angels or melting Nazis or even of menacing teenagers with possum faces, but oddly, of leaning out the window of his old West Side apartment so far that he went tumbling out, twelve stories down onto 79th Street.

"Sleep okay?" he asked.

She nodded and took a bite of waffle. Then nodded again and said, "I think this is going to work out just fine."

"Oh yeah?"

"We've got some fine-tuning to do," she said. "But that takes time."

"You weren't sure before?"

"It's a big adjustment."

"That's true. But now you think we'll manage?"

"Well enough."

"Glad to hear it."

Franklin jumped onto the counter, walked across the stove, and hopped onto the windowsill above the sink. The first time he'd done it in Cynthia's presence, she'd hollered at him and tossed him down and then asked Paul if he'd ever tried to train him. "You can't let an animal walk around where you make your food," she'd said. Since then she kept a spray bottle full of water on the counter and gave Franklin a squirt whenever he thought about jumping up. She told Paul the cat was more likely to respond if he did it as well, but as yet he hadn't been able to bring himself to pick the bottle up.

This morning, he felt comfortable with his permissiveness. His own parenting instincts leaned toward allowing for freedom and self-discovery, he decided, though that was the opposite of how he himself had been raised. His mother had walked him to school until he was fourteen and had done his laundry—ironing even his underwear and socks—until he'd gone away to college, and again when he'd lived at home after graduating. He'd never had to fend for himself, and as a teenager he'd been an outcast, lonely and miserable, while his peers wreaked havoc all over the city.

"Paul?" Joy asked. She gave him the same thoughtful but puzzled expression she'd had the night before, and again he was made uneasy by the dip in her ordinary confidence. "An iron maiden's a girl made out of metal, right?"

"That's right," he said, and immediately wondered if he should have told the truth. Why try to protect her from the ugliness of the world, from its cruelty, from knowledge she'd gain sooner or later? She seemed satisfied with his answer, wiping waffle grease from her fingers onto her pajamas. It amazed him to think she'd take his word so easily. He had too much power, too much capacity for harm. "I think that's right," he added. "But you might want to look it up."

The cat hissed and growled on the windowsill, its fur raised in a line down its back. Paul went to the window and found himself facing a deer, only inches away, its moist eyes taking him in with modest concern, its huge comical ears swiveling, flank twitching. When it saw that he and Franklin were safely contained, it went back to munching pansies in Cynthia's planter.

"Are they at it again?" Joy said behind him. "For crying out loud."

He couldn't take his eyes from the creature, wondering how it carried such bulk on its twiggy legs, how something as insubstantial as flowers could sustain it. He heard Joy push back from the table and head for the door and knew he should stop her—this was a wild animal, after all, four times her size—but he didn't move. Franklin hissed again, and the deer flicked its tail. When the back door slammed, it raised its head once more, looking first at Paul with something like accusation, as if the two of them had struck a bargain on which Paul had reneged. Then, glimpsing Joy running toward it, it sprang away with an impossible lightness, weighing no more, it seemed, than the blossoms it had swallowed.

"Shoo," Joy called, chasing it across the lawn, her lemon pajamas flapping around her, until it hopped a short fence into a neighbor's yard. On her way back she turned a couple of cartwheels, her bare, oversized feet flinging into the air, and Paul felt himself, too, go light as those blossoms, dizzy and choked up to the point of tears.

How could he have wasted so much time? How could he have so little left?

In a few short years Joy would be a teenager herself, with hair in her eyes and demons on her clothes, and nothing he'd say would touch her at all.

# THE MEASURE OF A MAN

## 1983

IT WAS A MILD Saturday in late October, and Paul was raking leaves. He'd never raked before. His previous experience with leaves was to watch them blow off the park and get sucked into mechanized street sweepers. In the two years since he'd moved to the suburbs, he'd consistently avoided outdoor chores, always finding an excuse to go to the office those weekends Cynthia decided it was time for spring clean-up or summer planting. He would have avoided them this time, too, except she'd caught him unprepared, saying at breakfast that she'd like his help cleaning the gutters. "You mean on the roof?" he'd asked from the counter, where he was pouring coffee. Dizziness came with a sudden chill in his groin, and he had to close his eyes. When he opened them, Cynthia was standing next to him, in her robe, giving the closed-lip smile that always flushed his head of reasonable thoughts. For that smile he'd moved to the sticks. He supposed he would have climbed roofs for it, too. Or jumped off of them.

"No, I mean at the bowling alley," she said, and flicked his earlobe with a finger. "You can stay on the lawn and pick up what I chuck down."

She was on the roof now, in a kerchief and a pair of faded overalls he hadn't known she owned—holdovers from her emaciated counterculture days, maybe, though even now that her body had filled out, they drooped on her and left her shapeless—wielding a small shovel with which she tossed down soggy, half-rotted mounds of leaves that Paul raked along with those freshly fallen. And to his surprise, he enjoyed the movement of his arms, the sound of metal tines scraping earth, the sun on his neck, even the sweat dripping down his back. There was satisfaction in seeing grass reappear strip by strip, and in making multicolored heaps at the curb. He thought he could go on raking all day, pleasurably mindless, in a sort of half-trance, until Cynthia's kids came home in the early evening. And if he weren't thinking about the kids, off with their father God-knows-where, he might have felt as relaxed as he'd ever been.

But the thought of Kyle and Joy hurtling down country roads in Russell Demsky's Mustang convertible distracted him, and more than once he found himself staring up Lenape Road when a car came racing down. "That rake isn't going to move itself," Cynthia called, and for the next fifteen minutes he fixed his gaze on the ground. It wasn't that he believed the kids were in danger—not physically, at least— but Russell's influence troubled him. They were with their father most Saturdays, when he took them on excursions in the opposite direction from those Paul preferred, fishing in Lake Hopatcong, hiking at High Point, canoeing in the Delaware Water Gap. Kyle and Joy came home sunburned and so exhausted that half an hour of TV and a bowl of ice cream were all it took to get them to sleep, when normally they'd negotiate for hours, promising to keep their rooms clean and make their beds every day for the rest of their lives if only this once they could stay up till midnight.

Their enthusiasm for Russell's outings stirred unexpected jealousy, and to make himself feel better, Paul organized Sunday trips to the circus or the Ice Capades or the Museum of Natural History, where Kyle gawked at dinosaur bones and Joy scrutinized gems in the hall of minerals. He waited for them to express excitement, and even more, gratitude, and always found himself dejected when they weren't forthcoming. His stepkids went strangely silent when they emerged from the Lincoln Tunnel to find the world so altered in front of them: sharp angles of stone and brick, steel and glass, framing segmented patches of sky and clouds. Neat containers, Paul had always thought, for childhood dreams. He wanted to take their silence for awe, but he knew fear too well not to recognize it in their faces as they stepped over sleeping bodies in the Port Authority or grabbed onto his coat as they crossed Eighth Avenue. He hoped, at least, that they were impressed with the energy and grit, or if nothing else, with his ease in navigating the crowded sidewalks. But only when a streetwalker in red vinyl shorts waved a lit cigarette at him, asking if he wanted a date, did the kids look up from their shoes. He knew better than to make eye contact, but still the woman followed them to the end of the block. Joy giggled into her sleeve, and Kyle kept asking what she wanted. Eventually Paul answered, "Money for clothes. Wouldn't you be cold out here without long pants?"

Joy, who knew too much for her age, mimicked the woman's sultry voice, her own just above a whisper. "Looking for love, honey?" Then she laughed so hard she doubled over and lost her grip on Paul's coat. He walked on a few steps without her, and when she realized it, her face went white with panic. He held his hand out to her, and though she ran to it, she also gave him a look of such injury, lower lip sucked into her mouth, brows pinched together, that he knew it would take days for her to forgive him this moment of abandonment. To make up for it, he bought each of them a hot dog and cotton candy the moment they stepped into the Garden, and on the drive home he was gratified when Joy laughed with him over one of the figure skaters' outfits— "She looked like a rotten strawberry"—and even more so when Kyle fell asleep just shy of the Meadowlands.

Still, the next morning, when he asked if they'd like to visit South Street Seaport the following Sunday, or ride to the top of the Empire State Building, neither of them responded, and he left for work in a sour mood. On the train, he tried to reassure himself that, looking back later in life, they'd appreciate his effort and value these adventures together at least as much as those with their father—though jostling his way onto the overcrowded Path, he had his doubts. One day, when they were old enough, he'd ask outright.

•

In the two years he'd been married to Cynthia he'd come to accept the complex role he played in the kids' lives. He spent far more time with them than Russell did, and his presence—assuming it lasted—would inevitably color their view of the world and impact their future. But he had to work with a light and steady hand. If he tried too hard, they'd rebel; if he feigned indifference, they'd drift in the direction of their father, an amiable though inconsistent figure in their lives, who spun elaborate stories about his travels and brushes with the law but who often canceled visits at the last minute or, when he didn't cancel, occasionally forgot to feed them lunch.

Paul saw himself as an antidote to Russell Demsky: serious, predictable, conscientious, and forthright where Russell was silly, erratic, thoughtless, and dissembling. He didn't intend to undermine their father, or make them love him less, but he hoped to guide the children toward adulthoods in which they weren't scarred by Russell's influence, always wishing for some alternate model of male responsibility. For Kyle, the danger was less a threat to himself than to his future family. More worrisome was the possibility that Joy might marry an asshole.

At dinner he told stories about growing up in Brooklyn. Not at length, and not every night, but just often enough to give them a sense of what they were missing in this placid neighborhood where sidewalks led only from one lawn to another, and where the closest newspaper was a ten-minute drive away. He tried to provide enough details for them to visualize: his family's apartment five stories above Crown Street, stickball games in a lot behind Empire Boulevard, his father Manny—born Menachem, and whom the children called Papi—standing at the counter of his pharmacy on Utica Avenue, or on the sidewalk out front, greeting neighbors, arguing about baseball—"Ruth never coulda hit Newcombe. Not with a bat the size of a tennis racket"—yelling at drivers to slow down. But he purposely left out anything unsavory, including the two times his father had been robbed coming out of his store, once with a knife, once at gunpoint. He didn't tell them about the friend who, chasing a rubber ball into traffic, ran straight into a Ford Deluxe and died in the hospital two days later. Nor did he describe the way his mother bullied the local grocers, questioning the accuracy of their scales, in order to get discounts on produce for which she could afford to pay full price. If his version of Brooklyn was idealized, it was at least honest in its broad strokes, and it accomplished what he hoped: giving Joy and Kyle a picture of childhood that didn't include constant complaints of boredom and fights over who would sit in the front seat of the car.

The problem was, their father had had a similar childhood, but in the Bronx, where he'd gone to the nefarious Yankee Stadium instead of Ebbets Field, and he told similar stories, except that rather than leave things out, Russell embellished. Not even the toughest neighborhoods in the '50s had as many fights or gangs or underworld criminals as the kids reported hearing from their father, and the Demskys couldn't have been so poor that Russell went one entire winter wearing a scavenged bathrobe as a coat. But that was how Russell told it, and that was what the children believed. Most afternoons they didn't want to leave the backyard, where Kyle searched for salamanders under rocks and Joy practiced moves she'd learned in dance class, kicking up her legs, flinging her arms over her head, landing in splits—none of it quite graceful, with her long bony limbs and big wobbly head, a body that would soon, Cynthia kept warning him, explode into puberty. "Don't you mean blossom into womanhood?" Paul asked, to which Cynthia replied, "That won't happen until she gets her first vibrator."

Paul had heard enough stories about Russell to know that lying wasn't beyond him. Nor was crime. When they were in their early twenties, living upstate with friends who'd bought a dilapidated farm, Cynthia and Russell had been so broke they'd sold their car and record player and the few pieces of jewelry Cynthia had inherited from her grandmother. But they burned through that money—dope, dope, and more dope, Cynthia said—and could afford to eat only once a day. The friends owned six acres, but all they managed to grow was a handful of peas and a field of wormy potatoes. "I thought about turning tricks," Cynthia said, in a sardonic voice that left Paul wondering whether or not she was pulling his leg. "I kind of liked the idea, but Russ wasn't too keen. Why do I always end up with such possessive men?"

Late one night Russell snuck out with a pillowcase over his

shoulder. An hour later he returned with a load of beans and squash. The next night he came back with a bucket full of eggs, and a week later, a slaughtered chicken. He wouldn't tell where he'd gotten any of it. Their friends started calling him Russell Hood, and then just The Hood. "He kept us from starving," Cynthia said. "But I swear I'll never eat squash again." She said it with a short, dismissive laugh, but Paul heard the wistfulness in it, the nostalgia for the craziness and freedom of youth, and admiration for the man who'd shared her bed for a dozen years. "He could surprise you, that's for sure," she said. "Most of the surprises I could have done without. But every once in a while he'd just make you scratch your head and go along. It was best not to do too much thinking." When the farm was foreclosed, Russell borrowed the friends' car, siphoned gas from a neighbor, and took off—without Cynthia. She caught up to him a month later, in Virginia Beach, where he was living with another woman. Three years later she was pregnant with Joy.

In the one photograph Paul had seen from that time, Cynthia was a stick in a short, flimsy sack, her body hardly more developed than Joy's, long fingers gripping a trowel, dirty feet turned inward like an infant's. Russell's hair was a woolly mass that fell past his shoulders, and his long mustache cut his entire face in half, flaring out from his nostrils and connecting to his sideburns. He wore fringed leather trousers and cowboy boots. If not for the loose embroidered shirt and string of beads around his neck, he could have played an outlaw in a Peckinpah bloodbath.

Now, aside from the Mustang—a '67, which he'd bought in '79—and his irritating habit of quoting, or misquoting, famous figures of the era—"Ask not what Demsky can do for you, but what you can get Demsky to drink"—Russell had left the sixties behind. The mass of hair was cut almost as short as a Marine's, receding in front and thinning at the crown, and he'd traded leather trousers and cowboy boots for golf slacks and boat shoes, beads for an outrageously expensive antique Swiss watch: a 1929 Patek Philippe, he liked to tell everyone, with a solid gold base and a porcelain dial painted with radium. "Some poor girl in Geneva nuked herself so I can tell time in the dark," he'd say, and laugh. He'd been married and divorced once more since he and Cynthia had split, and now he was engaged to a woman Joy referred to as Her Highness, the Princess of Roxbury, whom Paul had glimpsed only once, from the bedroom window, sitting stiffly in the Mustang, wearing sunglasses and a silk headscarf. Russell had traded his part in a Western for one in a film noir.

But as much as Paul wanted to ridicule him, he couldn't help being fascinated by Russell, or at least by the idea of Russell, who lived a life unencumbered by ordinary notions of right and wrong. He made his living as a dealer in antique oriental rugs, and most of his stock came into the country illegally from Isfahan. "The blessed State Department," he'd say, when new sanctions were imposed on Iran. "They just doubled the value of my stock." Then he'd start a lecture about the history of Persia, explaining, as if anyone cared, that the Islamists had co-opted what had started as a Marxist revolution. "They did me a big favor," he'd say. "If the Commies had taken over, I'd be out of business. They'd be using kilims to cover the floors of factories."

By late afternoon, when the lawn was nearly free of leaves, Paul was anxious to know that the Mustang wasn't overturned in a ditch or at the bottom of a ravine. But mostly he was picturing the kids' wide eyes as Russell paddled a canoe through rapids or reeled in a flailing fish. There was no reason to be envious; he was the one married to Cynthia, the one living in the house with Joy and Kyle. Still, he had to work hard to keep himself from pacing in the yard as the time Russell had promised to return the kids approached, arrived, and passed.

"He's always late," Cynthia called from the roof, her overalls filthy now, her neck and face spotted with muck. The slope pitched her at an impossible angle, and two stories up she loomed against the bright sky, the ends of her kerchief sticking up like horns. "You should be used to it by now."

When the Mustang did finally pull to the curb, it rolled over one of his leaf piles. The kids poured out of the front and jumped in another pile, and then tore into the house, trailing leaves across the lawn. "Hey!"

Paul cried, but before he could say anything else, Russell clapped and called to him.

"The measure of a man," he said, raising a hand triumphantly over his head, "is not where he stands in moments of comfort and convenience. So get off your ass and help me unload the goods."

Paul took his time setting aside the rake. The words weren't accurate—he hadn't been on his ass at all—but they bothered him most because "measure of a man" sounded like a crack about his height. Russell had four inches on him, and at least two neck sizes, though as far as Paul knew Russell never buttoned a collar or wore a tie. His clients wanted what he had to sell badly enough that they put up with his open shirt and tufts of chest hair, which were a good inch longer than the hair on his head. In the back seat were two enormous pumpkins, leaning together like an additional pair of fat, warty children. "Watch the leather," Russell said as Paul got his arms around one. It was heavier than he'd expected and knocked against the door before he could pull it free. "That stem's got sharp edges."

The kids had reappeared. Kyle dove at the leaf pile again, this time scattering it halfway across the street. Joy made a show of helping Paul carry the pumpkin, but mostly she wanted to examine it more closely, moving from one side to the other, and in the process added extra weight that nearly yanked it out of his hands. "Isn't it beautiful?" she asked, flinging a braid out of her face, and answered herself before he could respond. "I think it's a particularly nice pumpkin." Paul didn't blame her for wanting to throw herself at it. Russell's gifts were sporadic— they almost never came on birthdays or Hanukkah—but were usually elaborate, in questionable taste, and often didn't fit anywhere except in the garage. Where Paul would have parked his car, there was a prancing carousel horse, bought from the owner of a defunct amusement park in western Pennsylvania and shipped on a flatbed truck. It mostly collected dust, though every so often Joy would go out and polish it, petting its mane and flanks as if they were hair and flesh. She touched the pumpkin with the same reverence, no longer pretending to help as they got closer to the door. "I think the face should go on this side," she said, sticking her hand between the pumpkin and Paul's chest. "Don't you agree?"

"I hope you paid for those," Cynthia called from the roof. She was standing at the edge, leaning casually on the shovel's handle without any thought, it seemed, that it might slip out from under her arm and send her crashing down. Paul didn't like the smile she gave Russell, which looked too much like the one she'd given him this morning, head cocked, lips pulled to one side.

"Rosie the Roofer," Russell said.

"You didn't steal them, I hope," Cynthia said. "You're not turning my children into criminals."

"Liberated, babe. Remember? Liberated. I never stole anything in my life."

"They cost twenty dollars," Joy said.

"Dad said he'd carve mine with fangs," Kyle said.

"Staying for dinner?" Cynthia asked.

"Only if you cook it," Russell said.

"After I shower."

Russell closed his eyes, raised his chin, and smiled a dreamy smile. "That I can picture," he said, and his boat shoes scraped their way inside.

At the door Paul had to readjust the pumpkin, propping it up with his knee to keep it from slipping out of his hands. Joy made a move to help again, this time giving a look of sympathy that made him turn away. "Do you want to carve mine?" she asked. "I don't care about fangs."

"Your dad'll do it," Paul said. "I've got to finish raking the leaves."

In the kitchen, Kyle was waiting for them, holding up two knives, one as long as his forearm, the other brand new, with a glinting edge. "Which do you want to use?" he asked, and even before Russell answered, Paul knew it would be the sharper one, the easier to cut out his heart.


He stayed outside until the sun dropped behind the hills, taking his time clearing stray leaves and remolding his piles. From the kitchen he heard the kids' laughter, and then Cynthia's. No one came to check

SCOTT NADELSON

on him. The ladder was still propped against the house, giving burglars easy access to the skylights, but he couldn't move it on his own. The blunt handle of Cynthia's shovel peeked over the edge of the gutter. If it rained, the blade might rust, and though the morning's weather report predicted clear skies for another day, he took hold of the ladder's rails and put his foot on the first rung. One step up was easy. Five made sweat leak onto his forehead. Soon he was on a level with the bedroom windows, and his breath came quicker, but he didn't stop. Another bout of dizziness made him close his eyes as he turned and lowered himself onto the roof shingles. The kids didn't appreciate him. Cynthia had married him only because she didn't have to worry he'd shack up with another woman. He could rake leaves all day, and still people told him to get off his ass.

There was enough light on the horizon to make out other rooftops and the crowns of oaks sloping away on the western flank of Union Knoll, a kidney-shaped section of Lenape Lake peeking through a gap, the water a flat silver in the dusk, reflecting nothing. Far below were the plains of Dover and Rockaway, marked by a haphazard array of streetlights, nothing grid-like or orderly about it, and beyond, the hills of Sussex County rising toward High Point and the Water Gap, the wilderness into which Russell and the kids disappeared most summer Saturdays. Paul had spent the better part of his life higher off the ground than this, in apartments above Crown Street and West End Avenue, in his office south of Columbus Circle. But without walls or windows to hold him in, he felt as if he were dangling over the vista that surrounded him, as if the world could tip at any moment and roll him off the roof. He tossed the shovel down, hoping to spear it blade-first into the grass. But he couldn't bring himself to look over the edge as he let go, and after a moment metal clanged on concrete.

Yes, he was the one who saw Cynthia's wry smile every day, her impatient frown, her naked body, no longer a stick, stepping out of the shower. He was the one who knew that Kyle had flunked two of his last five math quizzes and that Joy had recently replaced the kitten posters on her walls with figures carefully cut from magazines: not only movie stars but politicians, criminals, models from fashion advertisements, all

arranged in a clever tableau, Faye Dunaway carrying on a conversation with Henry Kissinger, a bikini-clad model shaking a finger at a mobster in handcuffs. Russell could charm them all he wanted, but in a few hours he'd be gone, and Paul would have them for the rest of the week, with their complaints of boredom, their fights, their demands on his time and energy, their indifference and ingratitude. He didn't have the luxury of driving off to the hills in a convertible, not today or ever. The light had faded now, the trees and rooftops losing their shape, and any moment Paul expected someone to come looking for him. The moment passed, and so did the next. No one did.

When he went inside, potatoes were boiling on the stove, the sink was full of pumpkin guts, and Russell was wiping the Patek Philippe with a dishtowel. "Forgot to take it off," he said. "Only cost me three months' profit." The two pumpkins sat on the counter, one with sharp fangs, as promised, the other with a gap-toothed smile and curlicues spinning out from its eyes. Kyle had put on his Halloween costume, a tattered shirt stuffed with rags and a rubber Frankenstein mask whose eye-holes didn't quite line up with his sockets. He stomped around the kitchen, groaning and flailing his arms, bumping into a chair and then into Paul's legs. At the kitchen table, Joy, who was going to her first co-ed party the next weekend, practiced her apple-bobbing skills with an orange sunk in a salad bowl. She winced every time she bit into the rind. Cynthia chopped vegetables at the counter, only a foot or so separating her from Russell. Her hair was wet, the skin of her neck pink from the shower, the smell of her shampoo strong even across the room. Russell watched her and grinned.

"The leaves are done," Paul said. "Just need to bag them. We should move the ladder before it's too dark to see." No one seemed to hear him but Kyle, who roared and stomped close enough that Paul had to do a little shuffle to save his toes. He made a break for the hallway, where he announced, louder than he meant to, "I'll get the nice tablecloth." When he turned back, Cynthia was holding up a spoonful of gravy for Russell to taste, and Russell's mouth—wide and slick, lips lewdly spread—was heading in the direction of her chest. Paul hurried away.

At dinner, he tried to describe Halloweens in Brooklyn, where

Jewish kids scoured the neighborhood for gentile households, gathering homemade cookies and cakes without worrying they were filled with poison or baked with razor blades inside. But before he got very far, Russell cut him off with a story of his own. "Speaking of cookies," Russell said, and then, after a long dramatic pause, started telling about a gang fight he'd witnessed one Halloween, between Italian boys in baseball outfits and Irish boys dressed as pirates. The story was violent and unseemly, and Paul didn't believe a word. "Those pirates had little swords," Russell said. "But they were really only kitchen knives. Couldn't do much against baseball bats."

Paul didn't see where cookies came into it, but before he could ask, Russell moved on to a new story, this one about sneaking into Yankee Stadium for a Sunday double-header. "Tickets cost a buck fifty then," he said. "That doesn't sound like much to you, but for me, it was a whole week's lunches, and a dinner, too." It was a convoluted story involving incredible risks and close-calls, run-ins with menacing ushers, encounters with beautiful women, connections to organized crime. Kyle, whose mask was now propped on top of his head, was so rapt he forgot to bring food up with his fork and instead bit down on metal. Cynthia smiled nostalgically, and when Paul caught her eye and winked at one of Russell's more outrageous embellishments, she seemed startled to see him there, first blinking and then giving him a puzzled, impatient look before turning back to Russell. Only Joy was indifferent, baseball being a subject for boys, and Paul admired her independence as she made patterns in her potatoes by pressing them with the back of her fork. The whole time Russell spoke, Paul was aware of the gold watch flashing on his wrist, the radioactive face already glowing faintly in the dim light. Its presence, more than anything, offended him enough to make him break into the story for clarification. "What did you say the guard looked like?" he asked.

"I didn't," Russell said, squinting at him, his square head tilted slightly to the side, his scalp, where the hair had receded, red and waxy. "Big guy. Like a guard."

"Dark hair? Light?"

"He was wearing a hat. More importantly, he was carrying a night stick."

"Did guards really carry night sticks then?"

"This one did," Russell said. "Can I finish, please?"

When young Russell finally made it into the stadium, he didn't sit just anywhere, but right above the dugout. During the bottom of the sixth inning, he had a long conversation with Joe DiMaggio, telling Joe that his grandmother was sick, but that he was sure she'd get better if Joe hit a good one for him. And Joe did, a double that knocked in the winning run. "Best day of my life," he said, and reached an arm in Cynthia's direction, leaning so far forward his chest hair nearly dunked in his gravy. "That is, until I met your mother."

"Didn't DiMaggio retire in '51?" Paul asked.

Russell turned to him slowly. "I don't memorize statistics," he said. "And you're younger than me, right? Born in what, '44, '45?"

"And? What's your point?" This time he turned to Kyle, raised his eyebrows, and jerked a thumb in Paul's direction. "Is this guy a lawyer or what?"

Paul knew he shouldn't go on. It wasn't his place to shatter the children's illusions about their father. But he was tired of illusions, especially the one that made him invisible. "So you must have been only six or seven when it happened," he said.

"I was mature for my age," Russell said, sitting up straighter, forcing a smile no one could have mistaken for genuine.

"And isn't the Yankees dugout on the first base side?" This time Russell didn't answer. He had his arms crossed in front of his plate, wrist bulging around watchband. Cynthia's look now wasn't impatient but plainly irritated, and Kyle pushed food around his plate, his eyes growing red. Joy went on eating her food as if the conversation still didn't concern her, and now Paul wished her independence would give way to a newly adjusted loyalty. Why couldn't they all see he was doing this for their benefit, exposing the emptiness of Russell's charm, the danger of his influence? Didn't Cynthia know the harm he was capable of better than anyone? Didn't she want Joy to avoid her mistakes, when she finally did blossom into womanhood? "You said Berra waved to you when he rounded third," he went on, in a casual, musing voice, as if he were in the process of puzzling out a significant mystery. "But if you were behind the dugout, you must have been on the other side of the field…"

He waited for Russell to admit his lies. Or better yet, to deny them and disclose the depth of his deceit. But Russell just stuck a bite of chicken in his mouth and chewed. Kyle left the table without being excused, and soon TV voices replaced the protracted silence. After a minute, Joy started telling her father about her Halloween costume, which she was making herself out of old curtains. She was going as Miss Havisham from *Great Expectations*, an abridged version of which she'd read in school. "I'm going to be just like her when I grow up," she said. "Rich and powerful, and I'm never going to get married."

Cynthia's eyes flicked up to Paul and then down to her plate. "That's the best idea I've heard all day," she said.


Soon Joy joined Kyle in front of the TV, and Cynthia began clearing plates. "Delicious as always," Russell said, following close behind. "Let me do the washing."

Paul returned the good cloth to the hall closet, and when he came back into the kitchen, Cynthia and Russell stood close together at the sink, hardly enough space between them to see the cabinet behind. Both their feet were bare, Russell's boat shoes left behind under the dining room table, and there was something inappropriately intimate about their nearly mingled toes. Dishes were piled on the counter, but the water wasn't running yet. A few feet away the two jack-o'-lanterns alternately scowled and laughed.

Russell and Cynthia were speaking in low tones, eyes fixed on each other. They seemed to be in some kind of communion: a married couple, Paul thought, who knew each other better than anyone and whom no one could pull apart. They were discussing something that went beyond words, that rose up from their deepest well of desire, that encompassed their long past together, that projected all their hopes for the future. Paul was quite certain that he and Cynthia had never had a conversation like this and never would. After two years, they weren't much more than acquaintances who shared a bed, and he decided, not for the first time, that everything he did was a mistake, every step he'd taken in his life a wrong turn.

They didn't face him when he came in, not even when he cleared his throat. He took a step closer, but still their eyes didn't leave each other's faces. Impending loss gripped him, at once dark and enlightening, and with it came an odd curiosity. What would it feel like to fall from a roof? How many times would he tumble? On what vital organ would he land?

He was close enough now to hear their words: "You told me you would," Cynthia said. "And now you're saying you won't."

"That's not what I said." Russell did glance at him then. He gave a surprising little grin—a look of collusion, it seemed, one that asked for sympathy, that anticipated a mutual understanding. In his confusion all Paul could do was stare back blankly. Russell turned to the counter and started moving dishes into the sink. "I said I'd have to check the books and make some arrangements. It might take some time."

"I'm not paying late again," Cynthia said. "I did it last year with their Hebrew school fees. It's embarrassing."

"Hey," Russell said, turning on the faucet and giving Paul another look over his shoulder, this one desperate, a plea for help. "Ask not what Demsky can do—"

"Your watch!" Paul cried, just as Russell was about to plunge it into the suds.

For a moment Russell froze above the water, his hands clawed, shoulders hunched, and Paul thought he could see the outlaw in him, or the petty thief sneaking through a moonlit field stuffing a pillowcase with squash. The look of relief on his face went beyond antique watches. He thanked himself every day, Paul guessed, for having unburdened himself of family and obligation, for having freed himself from one trap after another. But the question remained: why did he always find new things to trap him? He thanked Paul and handed him the Patek Philippe. "Saved me some bucks," he said. "I owe you one."

Cynthia had moved to the stove, where she scrubbed a spot of gravy beside the largest burner, her feet now closer to Paul's—in socks—than Russell's. "You know this isn't about money," she said. "We can afford to do it ourselves. But she's your daughter, too."

"I know she is," Russell said. "Didn't I just get her a pumpkin?"

"It's not the same as paying for bat mitzvah lessons."

"It's Beth," he said, quieter now, his voice going hoarse. "The wedding. The goddamn dress. She's bleeding me dry."

"People who don't have money for their kids don't honeymoon in Fiji."

"Give me a break, Cyn," he said, all the swagger gone from his voice, his arm stripped of gold and radium, covered in nothing but soap bubbles.

"You've had more breaks than one person deserves. I don't have any left to give. Not to you," she said, and shot Paul a quick, furious glance, "or anyone else."

Paul had done enough work for one day. His leg muscles were sore from raking, his hands beginning to cramp. He joined the kids in the family room, where they were watching *The Godfather*, edited for television. The scene cut away just before Sonny's assassination, and Paul said, "They ruin it with the advertisements," but neither of the kids looked up. They were both asleep, Kyle stretched out on the floor, Joy with one long leg dangling off the couch.

From the armchair he watched a car speeding along winding mountain roads, then a family eating fast food burgers, then a man shaving: two blades, apparently, were more effective than one. Moments later James Caan pulled up to the toll booth. Paul was still holding the watch. It was a pleasant weight, smooth to touch, glowing eerily when he cupped his hands around it and peeked between his fingers. Bullets rained on Sonny's car. Joy stirred but didn't open her eyes. The Patek Philippe slipped easily into Paul's pocket. For bat mitzvah lessons, he thought, picturing a pawn shop and a roll of cash, hearing his wife's and stepdaughter's words of gratitude.

While Al Pacino and his associates plotted to avenge Sonny's death, Russell popped his head in, saw that the kids were asleep, gave a little wave with one finger, a half-salute that suited his Marine's cut, and left. Cynthia came in soon after and sat at Paul's feet. "He's impossible," she said. "He always has been." Paul considered showing her the watch but decided against it. He wanted to believe he really would sell it but couldn't be sure he wouldn't just stick it in a dresser drawer and wait for Russell to ask for it back. Did Cynthia find him impossible, too? He would have liked to ask, but it was best to keep quiet, he thought, to remain out of view until her anger subsided. But she glanced up at him anyway. "You," she said, as if reading his mind, and he braced himself. She let out a heavy breath. "You're just challenging." And then she leaned back against his legs.

Challenges, at least, sometimes brought rewards. He laid his hands on her shoulders and with a thumb worked at a knotted muscle. On TV, criminals cut each other down.

# NOCTURNE FOR LEFT HAND

*EVERY NIGHT, AFTER THE kids have gone to bed, he searches for their shoes. They might be anywhere: under the couch, in the middle of the kitchen floor, on the basement landing, or if it's warm enough, out on the lawn, damp with dew. This is one of his contributions to the efficient running of the household, maybe his most important contribution, though not the most visible. If anyone has noticed, none has said a word. He performs the task quietly, without announcing himself, and takes private pleasure in knowing how useful he has been.*

*He does, of course, have selfish reasons for doing it. To keep the morning from starting with kids shouting up the stairs and Cynthia shouting down, with Joy begging him to drive her to school because she's missed the bus and doesn't want to walk, with Kyle saying he hates school anyway and why doesn't he just drop out and start his own business like his father did. "Your father dropped out of college, not grade school," Paul told him. "And the only way he started a business was by borrowing money from all his friends and never paying them back."*

*But even more important, he likes the feeling of quiet accomplishment. Neither child has to ask, where are my Keds or my Reeboks or my ballet slippers? After breakfast they just walk into the laundry room and find them lined up beneath their coats, a generous assortment, left foot and right arranged in proper position. The only mornings they miss the bus now are those when Joy spends forty-five minutes in the shower, undeterred by the water going lukewarm and then frigid; or when Kyle, having forgotten to study for a geography test, hides in his closet, or in the basement, or in the shrubs by the back fence, until Cynthia, exasperated, finally cries, "Fine! Stay home and watch the soaps. What do I care?"*

*The job is easiest from April through September, when Joy mostly wears sandals or slip-on flats and even Kyle occasionally spends the day in flip-flops. Tonight, though, mid-November, temperature dropping to near freezing, he's guaranteed to find two pairs of sneakers. The first, Kyle's high-tops, he discovers quickly enough, toppled against each other beneath the kitchen table, along with three shriveled green beans and a stale challah crust. Locating the second takes more effort. He passes through all the rooms downstairs twice before spotting one of Joy's running shoes: yellow with blue stripes, poking out from beneath a throw pillow on a living room armchair, where earlier she sat cross-legged, crouched over math homework. Its mate is nowhere in sight.*

*He spends another half hour searching, twice creeping into Joy's bedroom and listening to her sleeping breath until his eyes adjust to the dark. Then he checks around and under her bed, in her closet, and even lifts the end of her blanket to make sure she isn't still wearing it. Only when he's ready to give up, to accept the chaos of the coming morning, or else to leave for work before anyone else wakes up, he thinks to look in her backpack. And there it is, along with her math homework, a sheet of meticulously written long division problems, three digits into four, extensive strings of decimals. He doesn't wonder how the shoe got in there but whether the kids are aware of his efforts after all, whether they intentionally set up obstacles for him. And if so, are they impressed by his persistence?*

*The real challenge with sneakers, however, isn't tracking them down. It's that neither kid unties the laces before kicking them off. And though Kyle quit Cub Scouts after a year and Joy refused to even consider joining the Cadettes because their uniforms, she said, were "utterly demoralizing," what experts they are at knot-tying. Double, triple bows, pulled so tightly it's hard to distinguish one strand from another. He imagines how they must strain when yanking those loops away from each other, the laces resisting, the muscles of their forearms clenching, fingers holding the red impression of woven cotton and nylon. His own fingers ache as he sits on the couch working at each knot in turn. He has let his fingernails grow long enough that he has something to pick with, and sometimes he uses the tip of a pen or the tine of a fork for leverage.*

*Tonight Joy's laces, hideously chartreuse, come free without much trouble. But Kyle's might as well be welded. Again he wonders if the children know what they're doing, if they have conspired to make things difficult: tonight you hide yours, Kyle might have said to Joy, and I'll make impossible knots in mine. But he knows they are as conscious of others' work on their behalf as they are of gravity. And he knows, too, that it's better this way. Obliviousness to the lives of adults is the gift of childhood, its crucial freedom. It has taken him three years of step-parenting to understand this, or to stop resisting it, and now he has come not only to accept but to savor it, wishing he could preserve their freedom forever.*

*So he wrestles with Kyle's laces, digging, tugging, teasing. He gets part of one loop free, but then something catches, and he has to ease it back and try a different angle. From upstairs comes the sound of the sink, Cynthia getting ready for bed. Outside, the first flurries of the season bounce against the window. The lace tangles. He feels sweat sliding down his sides. His knuckles grow stiff. He reminds himself that he should buy replacement laces, stock up with every color and length. If he had a pair now, he'd cut the goddamn things off and start fresh. But all he can do is keep pulling, as patiently as possible, while big wet snowflakes catch light from his lamp on their descent.*

# OLD WHAT'S HIS NAME

## 1985

PAUL WAITED AS THE image slowly emerged. Here was the backyard, a late summer afternoon, idealized inside a white frame. Cynthia, in shorts, hair loose to her shoulders, was frozen mid-hop above a shovel, the muddy start of a flower bed just visible beneath her feet. Kyle sat on the lowest porch step and held a leash, at the end of which Franklin slept on a bumpy rock. Joy, in full pubescent awkwardness, head teetering on gangly body, braces reflecting sunlight, picked at a freckle on her arm. And out of sight, behind the Polaroid, Paul sat in a canvas chair, a book in his lap, brown loafers burrowed in grass.

He was preparing to fly that evening to Zurich. He'd already packed and confirmed the car service, double-checked his passport and traveler's checks, written down phone numbers for Cynthia, who'd inevitably misplace them as soon as he left—he'd find the sheet with his carefully written note buried under a stack of magazines two months after he returned. Four and a half years into his marriage, he still traveled routinely for work—brief trips, four days, a week at most, packed full with meetings and dinners, discussions of contracts, negotiations, and an afternoon to slip into a museum to gawk at paintings he'd seen reproduced in books. At most he took two extra suits, a second pair of shoes, slippers for evenings, and a small pillow for the airplane. This time he might bring the picture, too, to keep home in his thoughts— an unnecessary gesture, maybe, and sentimental, but one his business associates seemed to expect when they asked about his family.

When he'd still been single he used to spend these last hours before a flight sitting in his darkening living room, eating the simplest meal he could think of—rice with beef skewers, usually, sent up from a hibachi restaurant around the corner—staring out the window onto cabs lunging downtown, the doorman across the avenue blowing smoke into an awning. Even when he was traveling to a place he'd been a dozen times before, he had the feeling of heading into uncharted territory, and though he knew his return flight information by heart, there remained in his mind the small possibility that he'd never find his way back.

If this had made him fret, it was only because of Franklin, who would shun his cat sitter and mope around the apartment, eating almost nothing, for at least three days after Paul came home. His sister Reggie had promised to take Franklin if anything ever happened to Paul, but he knew Reggie had no interest in cats, and even more, that she never kept her word. At best, what she really meant was that if something happened to Paul she'd take Franklin to the pound rather than let him starve to death in the empty apartment.

Now Franklin was over twelve, and either age or the suburbs had subdued him. He no longer seemed to notice when Paul was gone, and though Paul tried to give him extra affection when he came back from a trip, pulling him onto his lap and sneaking a few treats into his kibble, Franklin mostly wanted to sleep on the crack between the couch cushions, leaving a fur-covered indentation that had Cynthia grumbling about covering all the furniture with plastic. Even with the kids to look after him, Paul worried about the cat during these final hours before a flight, and after putting the camera aside he couldn't keep himself from saying to Kyle, "Indoors only when I'm gone, okay? Even with the leash."

"He likes it out here," Kyle said.

"He might get loose. He doesn't know his way back."

"He never goes farther than that rock," Cynthia said, jumping on her shovel and shimmying back and forth.

"He's just as happy inside," Paul said. "And he doesn't have claws, remember? He can't defend himself if something attacks him."

"What kind of something?" Cynthia asked, glancing at the narrow strip of woods that separated their yard from the neighbor's. "A coyote? A bear?"

"A wolf," Kyle said.

"Maybe a werewolf," Cynthia said.

"I saw another raccoon last week," Paul said. "They're vicious."

"He's only got a few years left," Kyle said. "He might as well enjoy himself."

"He enjoys himself inside. And he's got plenty of years left." On the rock, Franklin was a lifeless lump, head sunk on paws, tail wrapped around his haunches, only his ear occasionally twitching, and Paul fought off an urge to run to him and sweep him into his arms. "He could live to twenty or more."

"Not if you keep feeding him so much," Joy said, clapping, swinging her arms over her head, jumping with her legs spread apart. She was trying out for the freshman cheerleading team next month, and though she had the moves down, her sense of rhythm was so inconsistent, her chants so out of synch with the flailing of her limbs, her smile so painfully inauthentic when she cried, "Go Mallards!" that Paul had already begun to imagine consoling her when the team turned her down. Now she put her hands on her hips, flung her head to the right and then the left, ponytail whipping one cheek and then the other. "Look how fat he is," she said, gesturing at Franklin. "He can hardly clean his tail." So skinny herself—her thighs indistinguishable from her calves—she'd recently decided everyone else was overweight. She'd suggested both Paul and Cynthia go on diets and even warned Kyle to watch how much ice cream he ate if he didn't want to get called a pudge when he started junior high in the fall. As for herself, she could eat anything she wanted and never gain an ounce. "Are you bringing back chocolate bars this time?" she asked.

"Chocolate isn't good for your skin," Paul said. So far she'd had only a small streak of acne on her chin, but he remembered the pain and humiliation of blemishes only too well, even thirty years later. If he ever forgot, he had the scars on his cheeks to remind him.

"I don't like the dark ones," Joy said, ignoring him just as her mother did when she wasn't interested in what he had to say.

"No nuts," Kyle said.

Cynthia bent down to the hole she'd dug and yanked out a chunk of root, eight inches long and as thick around as Paul's wrist, severed at either end. "Plenty of dark nuts for me," she said, and then put on a look of offended innocence when the kids snorted and laughed.

"I'll miss you," Paul said, and tried his best to mean it. He slipped the photograph onto the porch step above Kyle. On the rock, Franklin stretched out a paw and turned his chin up to the sun.

The truth was, as soon as he settled himself on the plane, Paul felt only relief. What he might have missed about his family he experienced only vaguely, or rather intellectually, knowing he couldn't live without them but not thinking about what living without them would actually mean. Even when he imagined Franklin getting loose when Kyle inevitably brought him outside, running into the woods and getting flayed by a rabid raccoon while flailing his impotent paws, Paul could get himself worked up only to the point of mild irritation. It was as if as soon as the plane's doors closed, he was shut off from Cynthia, from the kids and the cat, and also shut off from the part of himself that felt responsible for them and their well-being.

The firm still flew him first-class, and he enjoyed the way the stewardess smiled at him when she handed him a drink, though he knew she was paid to do so. She was supposed to make him feel important, and with a scotch and soda in hand—something he drank only on airplanes—his attaché case open on his lap, the wide expanse of leather behind his back, he felt his importance universally, if briefly, acknowledged. The stewardess wasn't as attractive as he might have hoped, or as young, but her smile was warm, her lips naturally pouty and painted dark red, and when she spoke he found her voice pleasant, her accent mild and musical. He liked the way she said his name—with "a" sounding like "ah" in "Mr. Haberman"—and when she asked if she could hang up his jacket, he stood and let her slip the sleeves from his arms. She pouted genuinely when he declined the cheese plate she offered as an appetizer. "You must find hunger for dinner," she said. "I do not accept no for an answer."

He promised he would, though he knew hunger wouldn't find him for some time yet, because despite all his protests, Cynthia had prepared an elaborate meal with which to send him off, a baked chicken dish with a lot of cheese and a side of pasta that left him feeling bloated and nostalgic for his rice and skewers. What he'd really wanted instead of a big family dinner was to ship the kids off to their father's for the evening so that he and Cynthia could make love and lounge in bed for the two hours before the car service came to pick him up.

But dinner took longer to prepare than Cynthia had anticipated, and then she insisted he eat a piece of the peach pie she'd bought, and the car service showed up before he'd finished. He had to run upstairs to grab his bags, and the best he could manage was a quick peck on Cynthia's lips before rushing out the door. On his way, he ruffled Kyle's hair and gave Joy a hug, and to his surprise she crushed her skinny body against him, pointy bones and too much perfume and the breasts that had seemed to spring, fully formed, from the flat front of her in the last year. "Remember not to eat too much," she said in his ear, and then he was heading down the front steps to the driveway, where a driver was holding open the door of a shiny black Lincoln. But the embrace stayed with him all the way to the airport, the suddenness of it, the pressure of her long slim fingers against his back, the bump of her knee into his thigh.

And now, buckled into his seat for takeoff, his attaché case stashed underneath, a contract to review on his lap, it wasn't Cynthia's body he found himself picturing, nor Joy's, but that of his last lover before getting married, a young woman who waited tables at a restaurant around the corner from his office, where he often took meetings with co-workers and clients. For months she'd flirted with him in a breezy, unserious way that he understood as a means to bigger tips, but one afternoon, on his way out, she handed him her number and said, "You've been wanting to ask for that, right?" They saw each other for two and a half months, and during that time Paul took secret pleasure in watching her scramble dizzyingly through the restaurant, always, it seemed, on the verge of a breakdown. She was a terrible waitress, constantly writing orders wrong, forgetting to bring ketchup or fresh coffee, fumbling soup bowls and spilling half their contents down her legs. While he chatted calmly with his lunch companion, he'd picture the way she threw off her clothes when they came into his apartment after dinner or a movie, not even waiting for him to kiss her before unbuttoning her blouse and dropping her skirt, always in a hurry to get on to what they'd both been imagining all evening.

On the plane, it was a particular image that came to mind: the young woman leaving his bed, her body in shadow, then backlit in the frame of the bathroom door, then gone behind it. For just a moment her silhouette was frozen in front of him, and woozy with sex and fatigue, Paul was struck with the notion that he was glimpsing something he could call perfect. The curve of shoulder and hip, the narrow V of parted thighs, the lift of heels off the cold floor. Combined, these things left the impression of something less than solid, the phantom of a woman he'd never met rather than the outline of one whose body he'd felt beneath him moments before, whose skin had been slick against his, whose breath had steamed the side of his face.

And somehow the thought that he'd never meet this woman, never *could* meet her, disappointed him so deeply that he wanted only to be alone in the apartment, and when his lover came back to bed he couldn't speak. She snuggled against him, and though it was the same curve of hip that pressed into his side, the same V of thighs now closed around his hand, he felt only the odd rubberiness of her chilled skin and the unpleasant texture of goose bumps. She kissed him on the ear, on the cheek, but he didn't respond. After a minute she asked what was wrong. "Tired," he muttered, and though he could feel her stiffen beside him, her hip pulling away, he did nothing to keep her close.

After they broke up, he worried that he wasn't unlucky in his attempts to connect with other people but unable, that genuine intimacy was beyond his reach. And it wasn't because he was shy or bumbling or afraid of rejection, but because he didn't like people enough to let them into his life. Why else would he recoil from their quirks and idiosyncrasies and harmless flaws? Why be so bothered by the waitress's snoring, her constant griping about her mother, the sour smell of her shoes after a long shift? Maybe he wasn't capable of generosity or compassion, and this crime would sentence him to loneliness forever.

These fears subsided, of course, as soon as he met Cynthia. There were plenty of things about her he might have shied away from—her age, her tendency to carry weight in her thighs, the way spit gathered at the corners of her mouth when she laughed, the fact that she had two kids who weren't his—but love, coming as it did in a sudden, unexpected flood, drowned most of his concerns. Still, all these years later he couldn't quite shake the image of his ex-lover backlit in a doorway, stepping out of reach. For a year he'd stayed away from the restaurant where she worked, though it was awkward explaining the change to clients and co-workers. "I heard someone got food poisoning from their chicken salad," he'd say. He returned only when he was sure she'd moved on. She'd probably forgotten him long since, had a dozen other lovers, fallen for an artist and moved into a SoHo loft where she nursed a baby in a window above Prince Street, her small breasts now engorged with milk, her frenetic energy occupied by motherhood.

He had these two images in mind, side by side, of his ex-lover, whose name, for the life of him, he couldn't recall—Dana? Adrienne? both sounded familiar but he couldn't connect either with her face—in a doorway and in front of a window, two women who in fact didn't exist, when the plane leveled off and the stewardess returned to him, squatting in the aisle, her head just higher than his lap. "You are hungry now?" she asked, and he might have been, except that her lipstick had smeared onto her teeth, and there was a bluish birthmark beside her nose, and all he felt was the chicken and pasta lying heavily in his stomach.

"Sorry," he said, but this time she didn't pout. She just stood without a word and went to the passenger in the seat ahead of him, bending down with the same smile, the same submissive nod of the head. Eventually she disappeared behind a curtain, and for the rest of the flight, whenever he woke from his fitful sleep, he saw one of her feet moving beneath the end of the fabric, dipping down and bobbing up, as if kicking something he couldn't see.

If the woman weren't blocking his way, he doubted he would have noticed her legs. Given an open path he would have bolted past without a glance. As it was, his eyes were fixed on them, in black nylons, dark over her calves, sheer where they stretched over the first flare of her thighs, more so, he imagined, the higher they rose under her skirt. She walked the way models did down a runway, heel to toe, but she did so lazily, with no urgency, weaving gently through the crowded terminal, unaware, it seemed, of people streaming past in either direction. She wasn't as tall as a model, or as thin, and when he allowed his eyes to rise above her waist, he saw that her posture was slouched, her neck squat, brown hair dull despite a fashionable cut, sheared high in back and molded into points on either cheek. Still, her face in profile had a casual austerity he found appealing, her jawline prominent, chin protruding just slightly past her lips, which were full and gently parted. Her nose, slightly upturned, he could live with.

He'd fallen in behind her on the way out of the plane, which meant either she'd pushed up to the front as soon as they'd landed or she, too, had been in first class, though he hadn't noticed her during the flight. He'd slept through much of it, rising out of a panicked dream an hour before arriving, imagining he'd brought the wrong contracts, or that he hadn't drafted them all. Of course he had drafted them—he'd looked them over a dozen times—but still he pulled his attaché case from beneath his seat and scanned them again as the plane descended over the Alps, accepting with gratitude from the stewardess—who, now that her lipstick had worn off, struck him as matronly and sexless—a hot towel to mop the sweat from his neck. But still the panic lingered as the plane touched down and followed a circuitous route to the gate, and by the time the doors opened he was in a hurry to get off, though he had nowhere to be for hours. The car would wait for him as long as it took to get his bag, and the hotel wouldn't have his room ready until afternoon. He'd have all morning to stroll the banks of the river or sit in the pews of the Fraumünster and study the Chagall windows. But even knowing all this, he couldn't keep himself from standing as soon as the seatbelt sign turned off, draping his jacket over a shoulder and sliding into the aisle before the man across from him—with a lumpy, cretinous forehead—could step in front.

He'd intended to pass the woman in the gangway, and then again when they stepped into the terminal, but every time he tried she swayed in the direction he was moving, and to get around her he would have had to bump her out of his way. She carried an overstuffed purse, which stuck out a good ten inches from her shoulder, and whenever her body wasn't in his path, the purse was. A familiar irritation rose up in him, along with the feeling of being ignored when he was in plain sight, which in turn made him think of Cynthia in the bedroom as he'd packed his suitcase. He'd waited for her to acknowledge the eyes he was making at her, meant to convey his desire and mild frustration, to let her know what he looked forward to when he came home. But she only smiled a distracted smile, half-turning to hear something Kyle was shouting from the kitchen, and when she turned back, she said, "Don't forget Joy's birthday's the day after you get back. Pick up something nice. Not another watch. Or one of those army knives." In her expression, there was no acknowledgment that he'd be gone from their bed for the next five nights, that they wouldn't make love in all that time. In fact, they hadn't made love for far more than five nights already, and when they last had, Cynthia had seemed utterly surprised to find Paul nuzzling her neck, his fingers fidgeting at the end of her nightgown. Afterward she said, "We should do that more often," and he'd agreed, though every night for the next week she was asleep before he finished brushing his teeth.

Now, slowed by the woman's meandering, the heavy bag pulling her to the side, he eased his pace. And slowed himself, he could study her legs, the sight of them slipping across each other calming his anxiety. He did his best to keep from imagining them freed from skirt and nylons, wrapped around him or partially draped with sheets, fabric and skin alternately catching light from half-drawn shades. And because he tried not to picture it, he didn't hold it against himself when the images came unbidden. He was groggy enough to forget momentarily what he was doing here, or to make himself believe he'd forgotten, instead recalling the exhilaration of being single and let loose in a foreign country, open to whatever adventures might present themselves. What did it matter that none ever had? His palm was suddenly slick on the handle of his attaché case, and he had to switch it to the other hand. The woman turned her head again, and again he caught her profile, stately and sensual, with a hint of prurience he associated particularly with Europeans.

His suitcase came off the carousel first, but he lingered until the woman got hers. Now, weighed down on both sides, she walked even slower, her steps less certain. He followed her through immigration, where she took her time digging through her crowded purse to find her passport. She hadn't acknowledged him directly yet, but at each stop she showed her profile again, and rather than stare at her he gazed into the distance, smiling dreamily, as if amused by some private thought.

When they were clear of customs he had a chance to pass her again, this time in a wide enough spot that she would have had to dive in front of him to keep him from getting past. But he didn't try. Before them rose an enormous glass wall, the gray sky brilliant, glittering, behind it, a suggestion of mountain peaks jutting through the tops of clouds. For a moment he so lost himself in trying to distinguish them that he didn't notice the woman had stopped in front of him. He pulled up just before kicking over her suitcase, one of his feet ending up tucked under its edge. She'd turned all the way around, facing him directly, and from straight on her face was narrower than he would have guessed, a sunken quality to her cheeks that made her eyes seem too large for their sockets, slightly bulging.

"You're still following me?" She did have an accent, but not the one he'd imagined. It was husky, nasal, exasperated, pure North Jersey. They might have been neighbors. She waved an arm across her body, sweeping him away. "Go already! Go!"

He had to take a step backward to extract himself from her suitcase and then skirted her in a broad arc, fighting an urge to glance behind, to apologize, to get one last glimpse of her legs. A few yards away a black-clad driver stared ahead somberly, holding up a sign: HABERMANN. Paul had another urge, to keep walking, to pretend he wasn't the one being summoned, to step out into the mostly strange city and make his way somewhere he'd never been. But without any acknowledgment on his part, the driver lowered the sign and reached for his bag. "It's spelled with one n," Paul said, but either the driver didn't hear him or didn't understand.

"Velcome to Zurich," he said, and started walking away with the suitcase. Paul had to jog to catch up. When they were outside he saw that what he'd mistaken for mountains were clouds piled on top of clouds.

He saw the woman a second time two days later, in the Flemish room of the Kunsthaus. By then he was happy to be alone; he was tired of his hosts' chilly politeness, their strained efforts at small talk, their obligatory gestures of revelry, which meant keeping him out late and sending him back to his hotel room with a stomach engorged with heavy food and a head reeling from strong beer. This afternoon, one of them had offered to take him on a boat ride up the lake, but Paul knew him too well to accept. Johann Becker couldn't resist working even when he was supposed to be relaxing, and he'd push ahead with negotiations while Paul was trying to clear his head, staring down at the water and listening to the rumble of the boat's engine. Plus Johann stood too close when he was talking, and his breath was sour. So instead Paul begged off, claiming to need the time to find a birthday present for Joy.

He'd been to the museum before, several times, and took in the paintings with cursory glances, his eye grazing a van Dyck virgin and child, a Snyders fruit bowl, a Brueghel woodland, hardly noticing more than a blur of color before moving on. The woman came in after him, this time wearing a suit with slacks, and without her legs to look at, Paul didn't know what he'd seen in her. She was in her mid-thirties, he guessed, with tired eyes and sallow skin, walking stiffly, with none of Cynthia's casual, hip-swinging charm. He pretended not to recognize her, though she gave him what looked like a rigid, embarrassed smile from across the long gallery. He studied the leaves of Brueghel's trees, hands behind his back, and listened to her heels clicking across the wooden floor, coming closer and then retreating. She'd veered off to a side gallery, and Paul wondered what would happen if he followed her again, whether she'd let him pass this time or turn and scold him, staring him down until he slinked away.

He made his way to the Impressionist gallery, where a blur of colors was all he was supposed to take in. Monet's water lilies were hardly more distinct than the pulses of light on the backs of his eyelids when he rubbed them with the heel of his hand. When he opened them, there was the woman, not three feet from him, looking at the same painting, arms crossed over her chest. The sculpted point of hair on her cheek seemed even sharper today, her face in profile more severe, and again Paul thought hers was a European look, a quality of wan stateliness that went deeper than haircut or pallor, that charged the air around her with a low-frequency erotic buzz. He caught a hint of her perfume, and that kept him from moving away, though by now he'd looked at the painting all he needed to and more.

"They don't look much like lilies to me," the woman said, and stretched out an arm not in the direction of the painting but toward Paul, her extended fingers just shy of brushing his arm. Once again he was startled by the accent, expecting it to have somehow corrected itself, to have taken on the appropriate German inflections. But it was still an American voice, still nasal, though gentler than in the airport, chummy. "More like fungus," she said. "Or cheese mold."

"He made a cheese mold series, too," Paul said. "It's not as well known."

She didn't laugh as he thought she would, but she did slide a step closer, and this time when she reached out her hand fell briefly on his shoulder. "I don't know shit about art," she said. "But at the hotel they told me to come see the Jacko statues, or whatever."

Since his first visit to the museum, more than a decade ago, he'd avoided the Giacometti galleries, which had so depressed him the one time he'd walked through that he'd gone straight back to his room and called his mother. He wanted to tell her how lonely he was, how much he hated the food, how frustrating he found it that his career required him to smile and nod at people whose speech sounded like truculent gibberish. But before he could say a word, his mother started right in complaining about his father—did Paul know how crazy it made her to live with a man who wore the same socks three days running?—and when he finally managed to tell her he was calling from overseas, she gave a shriek, asked if he was in the hospital or in jail, then scolded him for wasting his employer's money before hanging up. When he came home he found his apartment unbearably drab, signs of aggressive decay everywhere he looked—scuff marks near the front door, built-up grime along the baseboards, loose caulk around the bathroom fan— and that week he hired a painter to redo the entire interior.

Still, he agreed to take the woman to the galleries now, letting her pass first through a doorway that was wide enough to accommodate both of them and then falling in a step behind. Even without skirt and nylons her legs caught his attention, her odd walk, heel to toe, and the way it shaped and re-shaped her small backside. They passed Cézannes and Gaugins without stopping to glance at them, and it seemed the woman wasn't aware there might be something to glance at, so straight did her head remain above her sloping shoulders, offering not even a hint of profile now. They descended a set of stairs, and the sound of her heels was muffled by the cries of children rising from below, speaking Italian, Paul thought, or maybe Portuguese.

It must have been jetlag and two restless nights, as well as a touch of hangover, that made his surroundings seem stranger than they should have been and distorted his sense of time. Cynthia's house— his house—the backyard, the kids, Franklin, all seemed impossibly far away, part of a life he'd left behind so long ago he could no longer be sure it was real. And the life he'd lived previously, in his hushed apartment on West End Avenue, where he sat in the dark eating beef skewers and rice, where for a time he'd bedded young women and then turned away from them in fear and disgust, seemed more recent in comparison, the life he'd return to if he ever left this place. At the bottom of the stairs the woman paused to wait for him, turning without moving her feet. Whatever children he'd heard yelling were no longer here. "I went to the Grand Canyon once," the woman said. "Before now that's the farthest I've been from home." He expected her to say more, but she didn't. She stayed where she was, feet planted, until he passed her and held open the door. And then she walked through it as slowly as possible, as if camera bulbs were waiting to flash on the other side.

The Italian or Portuguese children had beaten them to Giacometti. There were maybe two dozen of them, running between the pedestals, standing on benches, shouting. A pair of adults stood in their midst, one of them clapping her hands over her head, the other whistling with his fingers in his mouth, but Paul couldn't tell whether they were trying to quiet the kids or add to the din. Neither could he be sure whether the face the woman made—nose scrunching as if she'd caught a whiff of something foul—was directed at the children or the sculpture. He explained Giacometti's work to her, summarizing what was on the placards she had no interest in reading, quickly moving her past the early surrealist work to the mature pieces she was most likely to see on postcards. "He was trying to capture the essence of the human figure," he said, after glancing at another placard.

"He got it right here," she said, standing in front of the famous emaciated dog, ears drooping, nose close to the ground. "The essence of my ex-husband."

It was hard to be depressed, hard to be affected at all, with children shouting and jostling him, but still he would have preferred not to see the sculpture again, the elongated walking men with hollow eyes and nothing that looked like skin—an image, he thought, of how he might look in twenty, thirty years, when his body began to give way to whatever would linger after it was gone. And maybe it was happening already, his flesh going not only soft but indistinct. Why else would Cynthia look so surprised those nights when he nuzzled her neck and ran a hand down her side, as if she'd forgotten he had hands and lips, as if she expected his touch to be weightless. He was a month shy of forty-five. He wasn't yet ready to give up the body, not his own or others. If he didn't experience desire as often as he once had, it was only because no one encouraged it. Could he blame himself if it was now stirred by this stranger standing beside one of Giacometti's tall female figures, arms stiff at her sides, lips pursed?

"I look just like her, don't I?" she asked. "Except my feet aren't so big. And I don't have such nice hoots."

On the way out of the museum they stopped in the gift shop, where Paul bought a miniature replica of the scrawny dog for Joy's birthday. Joy wanted a real dog, but so far Paul had put her off by saying she'd have to wait until Franklin was gone, by which time, he hoped, she'd be away at college. The woman picked out several postcards, including one picturing Monet's cheese mold and another showing the Giacometti figure she supposedly resembled. The latter she filled out in the museum's lobby, after retrieving her purse from the coat check and digging through it a good three minutes to find a pen. When she finished, she showed it to Paul. "Dear Sis," it read. "This is what I looked like after flying all night. Next time I'm taking sleeping pills. Heehaw, Trish."


It was Paul's suggestion to take the boat ride on the lake, and he made it, he told himself, because he had no idea what else to do. By the time they left the museum it was clear they would spend the rest of the afternoon together, though neither of them had said so out loud. And unless he walked her through the old part of the city, to the historic churches full of tourists, or to a beer hall he'd been taken to the previous night—either of which would send their footsteps in the direction of his hotel—he couldn't think of any way to pass the time. He had two and a half hours until a scheduled dinner with his hosts, and that gave him just long enough, he figured, to tire of Trish's voice and her habit of grabbing his arm, gasping, and pointing whenever something caught her eye. She did it in the middle of the street after they left the museum, gesturing, he thought, at the towers of the Grossmünster, but what she saw, as it turned out, was a bird sitting on a cable as a tram approached. She didn't want it to get electrocuted. Couldn't they do something? Throw a rock and scare it away? With her hand on his arm, Paul dragged her the rest of the way across the street. The bird flew off long before the tram reached it.

Trish worked for a bank in Weehawken, administrative assistant to the chief operating officer. He was in Zurich for a conference on international lending practices and had insisted she join him. He needed someone to take notes and keep his appointments. He also gave her his camera and told her to take pictures of him with anyone who looked important. She pulled it out of her purse—an expensive Minolta with a massive lens—and snapped a shot of the boat before they boarded. "How could I say no to a free plane ticket?" she asked as they stepped onto the gangway, and then answered herself, shaking her head. "I should have known better." Her boss had flown over, first class, on Friday, so he could spend the weekend skiing. He'd sent Trish on Monday, coach. For the past two days she'd snoozed through presentations in a windowless room, but today she'd skipped out after the morning session. She was around bankers all day at home, she said. Why do it halfway around the world? "He can kiss my ass if he thinks I'm coming back for the last day." She didn't ask what Paul did for a living or what he was doing here. In fact, she didn't ask him anything—not where he was from or whether he had a family, though he made an effort to keep his wedding ring in plain sight.

"My honeymoon was on a boat," she said, leaning far enough over the railing to watch the wake they were cutting through the lake's choppy surface. "A cruise ship to St. Thomas. Back then I could put on a bikini without a second thought."

A strong breeze stirred the water, but it did nothing to ruffle Trish's hair, those spikes on her cheeks staying put. It whipped her slacks around her legs, sometimes tracing a perfect outline, sometimes making them appear shapeless, empty spaces disguised by rustling fabric. It was cold enough on deck that most of the other passengers were inside, looking out through tinted windows, but except for a small patch covering the sun, the clouds had mostly lifted. The Alps made a ragged line against the sky. Paul knew from one of the museum placards that Giacometti had grown up among those peaks to the south, his village set high in a narrow valley that lay in perpetual shadow. It was no wonder his figures had no skin and hardly any flesh. Paul wished the clouds would blow a few degrees to the left, to let down a little more light.

"It was romantic enough," Trish said. She had her boss's camera out now, snapping indiscriminately at the water, at the mountains, at Paul. "You know, the sun and beaches and good food. We had a cabin with a balcony. Spent plenty of time in there. But I haven't been on a boat since."

Only one other couple was left on the small aft deck, but the woman began rubbing her arms, and in a language Paul didn't recognize said something to her companion, whose face was stony behind mirrored sunglasses. The two of them ducked inside, leaving Paul and Trish alone.

"We talked about doing a raft when we went to the Grand Canyon," Trish said, turning her back on the water, peering at Paul through the camera's viewfinder. "That was a year and a half ago. But it was so expensive, and too dangerous with the kids. Three boys. Oldest just turned ten. Should have left them with my folks. That's where they are now."

This was Paul's chance to talk about Cynthia and the kids, how far he felt from them, how easy it was to put them out of his mind. He might have told her that he couldn't have imagined how much Joy and Kyle would feel like his own children, and how crushing he sometimes found it that they would never be all the way his. He might have said that what he had with everyone in his life was at best a tenuous connection—with everyone except for Franklin, who had only a few years left, who might at this moment be loose in the raccoon-infested wilds of northern New Jersey—and all it took was a few days for him to feel those connections stretch and fray.

The clouds had moved as he'd hoped, a beam of sunlight striking the painted wooden boards of the deck. Trish turned her face to the sky, eyes closed, lips parted. When she spoke again, she kept her head that way and barely moved her mouth. "It could have been romantic, too," she said. "The sunset over the canyon. The whole place turning some crazy orange. But the boys kept getting close to the edge, and I got tired of chasing them away. It was gone before you could take it in. You get married young, and then you're thinking about the kids for years, and the whole thing…I don't even think I looked at him for five years. I mean, really looked at him. And then he's standing there like a fucking idiot in the sunset, with no clue what to do when his three-year-old's getting ready to pitch into the Grand-goddamn-Canyon." She lowered her head and opened her eyes, blinking and then shading them with the camera. "You think divorce'll solve everything. But then you're working for a guy who's been trying to fuck you since the day he hired you. You let him buy you clothes and fly you across the world, and every time he looks at you with those little pigeon eyes you're trying to figure out how you're going to keep him off you, or maybe you decide to just give in because it's easier. And you get a crazy fucking haircut, you get on a boat with a complete stranger who picks you up in an art museum of all places…"

The sun was all the way out now, and the other couple came back outside. Trish seemed to be waiting for just this moment to give him the insulted, accusatory look she'd turned on him in the airport, a mixture of scorn and challenge. She made an odd movement, crouching down and taking one step in his direction, arm flinging out as if to smack him. But then it swung up over her head, toward the water, and only after a moment did he realize she'd lobbed the camera. He caught sight of it on its descent, surprisingly far from the boat, a little black mark against the blue sky and then the gray mountains. It made no sound when it hit the lake. As soon as it disappeared, Trish ran past him, climbing the stairs to the upper deck. It was the fastest he'd seen her move. He smiled at the other couple apologetically and followed. Her back was to him, head tilted against a pole that propped a canopy overhead. He expected to find her crying, as he'd found Joy on multiple occasions over the past year, curled up on a couch or chair in a dark room he thought was vacant, and then shouting about never having any privacy, about everyone constantly getting in her face. But Trish was dry-eyed, staring out at the dark water, two fingers pulling at the point of hair on her right cheek.

"Shit on toast," she said when he reached her.

"You can say someone stole it."

"He had pictures of his kids on there."

Only now did he realize the boat had turned around, the city growing again on the horizon. He checked his watch. In less than an hour he was due to meet his associates for dinner. He'd likely be late, for the first time in his career.

Johann Becker, drunk, red-faced, showing off the brown grooves in his teeth, embraced Paul in the hotel lobby and then held him at arm's length, a meaty hand on each shoulder. "We'll miss you, my friend. Come back and see us soon." Paul didn't believe him for a moment, but he returned the smile anyway, assured him he'd be back as soon as he could, and when the embrace came a second time, he patted Johann's jacket, careful to turn his head away from the exhalation of tart breath.

Paul wasn't quite as drunk as Johann, but for the first time since he'd arrived he was caught up in the festive spirit of the evening. He'd laughed as loudly as his associates during dinner, hadn't put his hand over his glass when they poured a third serving of wine. He was, in fact, going to see Johann again soon—early tomorrow morning, for the final round of negotiations before his return flight—but he acted as if this were their leave-taking, as if he didn't know that Johann would spring some new demand on him at tomorrow's meeting, a surprise for which Paul had been prepared since he'd first known he was taking this trip. Still, he was giddy as Johann pulled him to his chest, as he took in the smell of cigarettes and oily skin, giddy to think he'd soon be heading home.

What cheered him most was that he'd be leaving nearly unscathed. After the boat ride he'd delivered Trish to a taxi, in front of which he'd squeezed her hand and wished her good luck, saying meaningless things about how life had a way of turning around when you least expected it, and as if to shut him up she kissed him, just briefly, and then folded herself in the most exquisite way into the back of the cab. His lips tingled where they'd been brushed by hers, the rough chapped edges grazing his chin as they moved away. He'd needed a cab, too, and could have shared hers. He could have asked for the name of her hotel, suggested they meet later. He was proud of himself for his restraint, and proud, too, that he'd have something, even something as immaterial as that kiss, to take home with him. And unlike Johann, Trish was someone he'd never have to see again.

Except that here she was, sitting at the bar in his hotel lobby, sipping white wine. He caught sight of her legs first, no longer in slacks, crossed and angled toward him. She didn't smile when she saw him, didn't wave or raise her glass, just turned a hard gaze on him so there was no way he could pretend he hadn't seen. She'd changed into a cocktail dress, dark purple, short and sleeveless, and wore open-toed shoes, no nylons. The haircut looked ridiculous to him now, a fashion advertisement superimposed on the image of a beleaguered mother of three.

"You're staying here, too?" he asked, not wanting to know if she'd somehow followed him, or searched him out. Or had he accidentally let the name slip? Had he invited her to meet him for a drink after all and then forgotten the invitation?

"I've eaten fondue every night I've been here," she said, swiveling her legs so he could slip past them and take the stool beside her. "Never had so much cheese in my life."

He ordered a scotch and soda, his airplane drink. What did it matter that he was on solid ground, since it felt so insubstantial beneath him? He might as well have been thousands of feet in the air. This was a notion he'd enjoy if he could convince himself to believe it: that he was adrift on haphazard or whimsical currents, indifferent to where he might land.

"If old what's his name—Jacko? If he'd eaten this much fondue his statues wouldn't be so skinny, I tell you that much."

"That's right," Paul said. "He would have been a tub, like Cheese Mold Monet."

She laughed—for the first time, now that he thought about it—a delighted, open-mouthed, but nearly silent ripple that rocked her body back and ended with her hand falling on his knee. "Cheese Mold Monet," she said.

With that laugh a deal had been sealed. Or maybe it had

happened with her kiss at the taxi, or with her throwing her boss's camera overboard. Or maybe with his invitation to take the boat ride, or with his following her through the airport, staring at her legs.

There was little left to say—for him, anyway—but they ordered another round, savoring the anticipation, he thought, putting off for just another moment what had been inevitable all along. Trish complained about the bankers at the conference, their arrogance, the new trend among the men to wear old-fashioned watch chains dangling from their vests. "They might as well have their dicks hanging out of their pants," she said. Then, scrunching up her nose, she added, "I'd give up men altogether if I wasn't afraid of eating clam."

When he still had half his drink to finish, he excused himself and stood in front of the bathroom mirror for a long minute, examining his hair and mustache, recently speckled with gray. Here was a man on the verge of crossing a threshold over which he couldn't return. And yet he looked ordinary enough, his face flushed, suit and tie a little rumpled, but otherwise composed. Anyone seeing him, if they bothered to glance in his direction, would have noticed only a foreign businessman slightly bewildered by his surroundings, unused to drink, aging just less than gracefully. He took a breath, straightened his tie, ran fingers through his hair.

The bar was busier when he came back through the lobby. A group of twelve or fifteen men—bankers from Trish's conference?—had taken up several tables in back. A few were looking over their shoulders at Trish, her body in profile on the barstool, legs on display. They were thinking nasty thoughts about her, maybe making nasty jokes—they might have mistaken her for a local prostitute—and Paul found himself mildly indignant on her behalf. Couldn't they recognize her for who she was, someone for whom life had taken unexpected turns, who felt her time running short?

He thought he saw, for the first time, how lovely she was, one leg hooked over the other, foot dangling above the floor, kicking gently, long slender arms folded on the bar, gaunt face and full lips set off against rows of multicolored bottles stacked above soft amber light. He lingered at the edge of the lobby, where she couldn't see him. He wanted to appreciate her as much as possible now, in case he wasn't able to do so when she lay in bed beside him.

One of the bankers called out to her in German, something Paul didn't understand, and the rest laughed. But Trish didn't turn away. She finished her wine, played with her hands in her lap. And then her movement was just as abrupt as on the boat. She snatched Paul's drink, tossed her head back, gulped twice. The glass came down hard on the bar. Her mouth made a series of strange movements, lips sucking inward, chin tucking toward chest. She pulled her big purse onto her lap, stuck her face into it, and came out paler than before. None of the men behind her seemed to notice. She closed the purse, hung it from the back of her chair, wiped her mouth with a bar napkin. And then, as if nothing had happened, went back to playing with her hands, kicking her leg.

It wasn't revulsion that made Paul take a step backward. It wasn't even sorrow for a woman halfway around the world, trying to get on with her life, puking into her purse. Rather it was the knowledge, as clear to him now as it should have been all along, that she, like most people, was better off without him. He staggered to the elevator and made his way to his empty room.


Late the next afternoon, when the car service dropped him off at home, he found everyone where they'd been before he left: Cynthia in the flower bed, Kyle on the steps of the back porch, Joy throwing her skinny limbs around the yard. Only Franklin wasn't where he was supposed to be. Instead of stretched out on the rock, he was sitting in the middle of the lawn, without a leash, looking sleepy and satisfied, a little black mound under an extended paw. "It's a *mole!*" Kyle cried when he spotted Paul. "You should have seen him. He chased it all the way around the house. I didn't know he could move so fast!"

Cynthia hugged him and whispered in his ear, "Can't wait to get you alone tonight." A few hours later she slipped into bed, in a negligee, while he went off to brush his teeth. When he came back, her eyes were closed. He sat for a long time on the edge of the bed, listening to her whistling breath, just shy of a snore, and staring at the bathroom's darkened doorway. There were some things love couldn't make up for, some things it would never entirely quell. It was love all the same, though, and after a while he slid under the sheets and let his body—so heavy, so burdened by skin and flesh and bones—sink into the mattress and then into sleep.

In the morning, he dug through his suitcase and handed Joy her birthday present, wrapped loosely in hotel stationery. She opened it carefully, pushing her hair behind her ear and giving him a curious glance, dreamy and sanguine and full of a yearning that made him want to warn her. But it was too late. She took a long look at Giacometti's dog—skeletal legs, pinched waist, mournful snout—before bursting into tears.

# COULD BE WORSE

## 1987

FOR A WEEK IN the middle of March, Paul felt increasingly out of sorts. Not much appetite, lousy sleep. In meetings he'd find himself absently chewing a knuckle. If the phone rang after nine at night, he braced for calamity. The wind blew hard against his bedroom window, and he imagined his neighbor's oak tipping onto the roof. Lying in bed, with Cynthia huffing peacefully beside him, he asked himself what could be the matter and then did his best to answer. Maybe he'd been working too hard. Maybe he was troubled by the state of the world. Maybe by the fact of his stepchildren growing up too fast. Or maybe it had been four months since he'd taken his car to the Baron. As soon as it grew light outside, he picked up the phone and dialed.

"Dr. H!" the Baron shouted on the other end of the line. "Why's it been so long?"

"Lost track of time," Paul said.

"You, maybe. But not that big beauty of yours. She needs a man who's regular."

"Any chance I can bring it—her—tomorrow?"

"Tomorrow, huh? Pretty busy, doc. But for your sweet lady, sure."

The Baron always called Paul doctor, and Paul never corrected him. At first he'd held back out of caution; maybe all the Baron's clients were doctors, and if he found out Paul was only a lawyer, he might turn him away. Paul had since crossed paths with others of the Baron's clients, and among them were a pharmaceutical executive, a stock analyst, the president of a pest company. But now they'd known each other more than three years, far too long to set things straight without embarrassment. Still, Paul hadn't quite gotten used to the idea of the Baron picturing him in a white coat, peering into people's ears. When the Baron said, "Better cancel all your patients before noon," it took Paul a moment to answer, and when he finally did, he could only murmur, "They won't miss me."

"I doubt that," the Baron said. "But it's what I appreciate about you, doc. Most of these guys, they think a medical degree turns their turds into bonbons."

The misunderstanding had likely come about because it was a doctor who'd first sent Paul to the Baron—a podiatrist, who'd talked for an hour about his Alfa Romeo while digging a plantar wart out of Paul's heel. As it turned out, he had a hard time talking and working at the same time, and he'd often pause to make a point, bloody scalpel jabbing the air above Paul's toes. "I thought the whole transmission was blown. But the Baron talked me down. Cost me a couple grand, but she runs better than ever." Paul worried the novocaine would wear off before he finished so refrained from asking questions. But after the third mention of the Baron he couldn't resist. The Baron of what? By then, in any case, the doctor was cauterizing the hole in his foot, and he wanted distraction from the smell of his burning flesh.

"You don't use a dealership, do you?" the doctor asked. "Might as well have my two-year-old change your oil." Then he lowered his voice and glanced over his shoulder to be sure the nurse wasn't lurking in the doorway. "Don't tell him you're a patient. Just say I sent you."

He slipped Paul a card. *The Flarin' Baron*, it read. *Italian and American cars only!* Underneath the phone number was a drawing of a hot-rod with flames bursting out of its rear. Was this meant to inspire confidence? After the doctor finished, Paul hobbled across the parking lot on his still-numb foot. He had no interest in Alfa Romeos that could take a hairpin turn at eighty miles an hour without braking. But all the way home he thought he heard something rattling under his Imperial's hood. That afternoon he called the number.

•

The truth was, he always believed something was wrong with his car. Within a few weeks of having it serviced he'd imagine his tires were going bald on one side, or his brake pads were wearing thin, or his radiator had cracked. The more time passed, the more convinced he became that a complete breakdown was imminent. Not having learned to drive until he was in his late thirties, he was still amazed that a person could sit behind the wheel of a metal box and careen down the freeway without exploding into flames. Every so often he'd open his hood and gaze into the tangle of pipes and wires, belts and filters, and understanding nothing of what he saw, experience an odd palpitation in his chest, along with a flash of heat in his face. How could this mess get him down the street, much less across state lines? How could it keep him from stalling on the Turnpike or from skidding into a semi on the George Washington Bridge?

Driving into downtown Denville, where the Baron's garage was tucked between the old library, abandoned for a larger and less convenient space to the north, and an imposing Methodist church, Paul already noted a loosening in his neck muscles and jaw. The blustery weather had calmed, and though the sky was still overcast, through the dashboard vents he caught an anticipatory whiff of spring. He breathed it in and promised himself he'd come here more often. So what if it meant taking a morning off work every other month? The garage was a nondescript building made of cinder blocks painted blue, with two sliding aluminum doors that were always closed, and set to one side, a fiberglass garden shed that served as an office. There was no sign to mark it, nothing in the way of advertising or welcome. Paul knew to pull around back, where a pair of pick-up trucks from the fifties sat on blocks, rusting beside a metal fence topped with sagging barbed wire. There, he honked three times, and with the engine still running, waited. Five minutes passed, ten. Finally, a windowless door—too small, it seemed, for the size of the building—sprang open, and out stepped the Baron, in dark blue coveralls and safety goggles, unruly tufts of black hair above both ears and centered over his forehead, clear scalp everywhere else.

"Dr. H!" he called, arms spread, palms up, as he made his way across the yard, a void of cracked concrete and discarded exhaust pipes. "Why you treating this baby so bad? She needs some lovin'."

When he reached the Imperial, he stroked its hood and cocked an ear to listen to the hum of its belts. Then he walked around it twice, kicking tires, signaling Paul to turn on headlights and blinkers, pointing to indicate he should step on the gas. "Shove over," he said, and Paul slid into the passenger seat. With the Baron came the smell of singed hair. For another few minutes, he fiddled with turn signals, wipers, heat controls, radio knobs, frowning the entire time, and Paul readied himself for bad news. But the Baron only nodded, caressed the steering wheel, leaned close to the dashboard, whispered something Paul couldn't hear. Then he straightened, smacked his hands together, tipped his head to the side. "Off you go." Paul slipped out and watched him roll the Imperial around to the front of the building. By the time he made it there himself, the car had already disappeared inside, and the sliding door was closed. In three years he'd never once glimpsed what went on behind it.

He waited in the little office, on the only chair, a stool on wheels in front of the folding table that served as the Baron's desk. The only other furniture in the shed was a filing cabinet, stacks of papers leaning against it. On one wall hung two flags, Italian and American. The others were covered in posters of cars—Maserati and Mustang, Fiat and Firebird—none of them framed, several hanging loose at one corner, a smudged loop of tape showing. The only image not automotive was a photograph of the Baron, whose real name was Ronnie Gianella, with his wife and three mostly grown boys, the oldest twenty-three, the youngest seventeen. The photo, also unframed, had been shot on a cruise ship. In the background, calm Caribbean water an impossible blue, a ragged ridge of coral visible in the distance. On deck, everyone was looking in a different direction, one of the boys leaning over the railing, another scowling at the camera, the youngest laughing at something out of sight. When it was taken, the Baron, five years younger, had had more hair but looked otherwise unchanged, broad squashed nose and skin the color of smoked pork, little eyes that seemed to have trouble peering out of too-deep wells.

Of them all, only his wife appeared content, a few steps removed from the group, smiling serenely at her boys, head covered in a silk scarf that didn't hide the bare scalp underneath. When Paul had first come to the Baron she'd just finished her second round of chemo. "Seems to be doing the job," the Baron had said. But then, slicing both hands down his chest, added, "Didn't save her beauties, though. Went from Delray curves to flat as a Caprice."

It was half an hour before the Baron joined him in the office, and when he did, he was frowning again, shaking his head, safety goggles reflecting the overhead light. Before he could open his mouth, Paul stood and said, "I know I should have come sooner—"

"You got that right."

"It's been a busy time."

"No excuse," the Baron said. "Great girl like that, you shouldn't neglect her."

"I didn't mean to."

"She needs attention. You know how it goes—she starts feeling like she's being taken for granted, then she gets cranky."

"Is it bad?"

The Baron's expression shifted from disapproval to sympathy, and he put an arm around Paul's shoulder. "Could be worse," he said. "Could be a lot worse. Be thankful for that."

He led Paul to the table, where he penciled out a list of services, adjustments, replacement parts. Paul understood little of it—didn't tires rotate automatically whenever he drove?—but he agreed to each of the Baron's suggestions. Cooling fan? Okay. Oil pan gasket? Sure. Wiper blades and fluid? Yes, yes. Only when the Baron mentioned an evaporator coil for the air conditioning did Paul hesitate. "Something's wrong with the air?" he asked. "Seemed to be working just fine."

The Baron frowned again and took a step away. "Sure it works," he said, voice inflected with insult. "But efficiently? Hell no. Chews through all our girl's gas. Notice how often you been filling the tank?"

Paul hadn't. Nor had he turned on the air since last summer. But he gave an apologetic shrug and gestured at the list. "Whatever you think it—she needs."

"Can't do things halfway," the Baron said. He leaned back on his heels, thumbs tucked into cloth loops on the coveralls. Pinched brows shadowed the whole of his eyes. "Not here."

"You're right. I know."

"Come to me, it means you're all in."

"Of course," Paul said.

"She worth it to you?"

"Absolutely."

"Okay, then," the Baron said. His brows relaxed, and he touched the tip of his pencil to his lips. "So. We finish off with some new spark plugs, grease the drive shaft, and she's a girl who feels pampered."

For a minute the Baron scrutinized the list, tapping the pencil on the tuft of wiry hair above his right ear. Then, without itemizing anything or making any calculations, he came up with a number, scrawling it quickly at the bottom of the page. He circled it, slapped the pencil on the table, shoved the paper at Paul, and turned his back, attending to a piece of mail he pulled from the top of a nearby stack. Paul knew to wait a moment before picking up the pencil and adding his initials. After he did, he cleared his throat and asked, "How's Janelle?"

When the Baron faced him again, he was grinning a tired grin, the goggles propped on top of his head. "Thanks for asking, doc."

"Last time I was in she was getting ready for radiation."

"Seems like it took. We'll know more next month."

"I'll be thinking about her."

"Could be worse, you know? Two years, total remission. And they got it early this time."

"And the boys?" Paul asked. "Doing any better?"

The Baron blinked his little eyes and wiped his palms on the front of his coveralls. "Up and down, I guess. Mike's working again, but his marriage, forget it. John and me, we just do better when we don't talk at all. He's good to his mom, anyway. And Jeremy, I think he's learned his lesson. He'll stay out of trouble, for the most part. But he'll never have a normal life, not now. I'll be taking care of him until they put me in the ground. But you know, could be—" He ran a hand down his face, recharging the grin, and let out an awkward little shout of laughter. "How 'bout you? Aside from your beauty out there? Things been good?"

Paul rubbed a thumb over his knuckle, chapped where he'd bitten it. "No complaints," he said.

"I'd swap places with you in a heartbeat, doc," the Baron said. Then he backhanded the air in front of him, as if swatting away clinging fingers. "Now get lost so I can take care of your girl."

For an hour Paul walked around the little town center, poking his head into a magazine and cigar shop, a jeweler's, a bakery where he came away with a cheese danish. He ate it on a bench in the riverside park, watching mallards paddle around the shallows, dipping green heads into murky water. The sun had begun breaking through clouds, and though the air was still crisp, he was comfortable enough to lean back and stretch an arm across wooden slats, two fingers picking idly at flaking paint.

No complaints. Wasn't it true? Sure, there were the long hours at work, the traveling that wore him out, the sore throat that had nagged him much of the winter. There was Joy, fifteen, spending afternoons with a rodent-faced boyfriend—her first—who lived with his grandmother in a dilapidated bungalow just off Route 10. Where the parents were Paul had no idea. He wore shirts that hung lopsided, jeans rolled above filthy sneakers. Whenever Paul answered his calls, which always came at odd hours—ten-thirty on a weeknight, seven on a Sunday morning—he didn't say hello or announce himself but just grunted, "Can you put her on?" A month ago Joy had come home with mouth-sized bruises on her neck. Last week, while folding laundry, Paul picked up a pair of silk underwear, blue and trimmed with lace, far too small for Cynthia.

And then there was Kyle, recently hammering sheets of plywood into a sprawling maple at the edge of the back yard. Wasn't he too old for a treehouse? Paul asked, and in response, Kyle spit in the grass and said, "It's not a treehouse. It's a fort." To keep out marauders? "Man, I just need my own space," Kyle said. The wood, it turned out, he'd swiped from a construction site at the top of the ridge, and a few evenings later a contractor knocked on the front door. He'd been up and down half the streets in the neighborhood so far and had found his supplies at every house with a kid in junior high. Paul led him out back and helped him carry away what wasn't already nailed down. He wrote a check for the rest, while Kyle sulked in the half-built fort, a pair of boards leaning crookedly across two limbs, a rickety ladder of two-by-fours spiraling up the maple's trunk. "He's not really mine," Paul told the contractor, who tucked the check in his pocket and said, "Know what you mean. I've got two. Most days I'd happily sell them to the fucking circus."

These were things he might have complained about, but not to the Baron. They weren't the same as having a son unemployed and wrecking his marriage, another who wouldn't speak to you, a third who'd broken into a liquor store and gone to jail. They certainly weren't the same as having a wife who'd lost breasts and hair to cancer, who was having radiation treatment after a two-year remission. They were things he could keep to himself, though now they seemed to drift with the ducks crossing to the far bank, the current carrying their opalescent heads and sooty backs a dozen yards downstream. Janelle Gianella. It was a lovely name, one of the loveliest he'd ever heard. He'd always wondered if she'd married the Baron just so she could have it. On his third or fourth visit, the Baron had insisted Paul call him Ronnie, but Paul had never been able to, not even in his thoughts. It sounded too silly for an adult. Why not go by Ron or Ronald? A few visits later, he'd asked Paul if he might take a peek at his wife's latest PET scan, see if he agreed that she needed another round of Cytoxan. "We like our doctors fine," the Baron said. "But you know, sometimes it's good to get another look." He'd be happy to, Paul muttered, but it wasn't his specialty, and he didn't know if he'd really be able to help—

"I understand, doc. You're a busy man. Forget I asked."

Janelle Gianella. He found himself repeating the name silently, the sound of it as lulling as that of the water easing past. What had he been so anxious about all month? Why chew on knuckles and fret over kids whose mother only shrugged and said, "They're not half as bad as I was at their age."

Overhead, crows squawked at something nearing their nest—a squirrel? a hawk?—and leaves rustled though there was no breeze. It was warm enough now to take off his jacket, which was scattered with flakes of paint and pastry. He checked his watch. Two hours had slipped by as swiftly as a sign on the freeway. When he made it back to the garage, the Imperial was outside again, parked on the street in front, hubcaps shining in the fresh sunlight. The Baron was waiting for him in the office, sitting on the stool, arms folded across his chest. If he had any other cars to work on today, they didn't seem to be here now. Paul had his checkbook in hand but had learned not to have filled anything out ahead of time, or at least not to have entered the figure the Baron had written down.

"You look relaxed," the Baron said. He picked up the pencil again and began tapping it once more on his lips.

"I don't get too many mornings off."

"Patients don't give you much of a break, I bet."

"I'll pay for it later," Paul said. "But it's worth it."

"Good to put yourself first every once in a while."

"Everything go smoothly?"

"She's a tough girl. Hardly any tears."

"No complications?"

"There's always something."

"Nothing too bad, I hope."

"Well, doc," the Baron said. His sympathetic look was back, though this time he didn't put an arm around Paul's shoulder, didn't rise from the stool. "Considering the possibilities, no, not too bad."

"What was it? What did she have this time?"

"Course I couldn't know until I got in there. Not just the evaporator coil, but the housing, too, and the housing cover. But you're lucky. The condenser, that's the big one. No problems there. Be grateful for that."

He wanted to be. There was plenty to be grateful for. But hearing the Baron say so irritated him, and he couldn't keep himself from remarking, "I never noticed any trouble with the air."

This time the Baron's expression wasn't insulted but injured. Without goggles on, his eyes had a precarious quality, on the verge of weeping, it seemed, and usually the sight of them made Paul turn away. But now he found himself waiting to see if tears would really fall. "Any time you want a second opinion—"

"I trust you," he said, more sharply than he meant to. "What's the damage?"

The Baron, looking no less hurt, squinted and tapped the pencil. He thought for a minute, two, and then wrote. The number he finally passed along was three hundred dollars more than the original. Paul filled in the check and handed it over without a word. "She did just fine," the Baron said. "Treat her well, and she'll take care of you a long time."

"Appreciate it, Baron," Paul said, catching sight once more of the photograph of Janelle and the boys, her smile less peaceful than chilling, he thought now, so removed from the distress of everyone around her. Why couldn't he call him Ronnie, just this once? After all he'd been through, why not give that one small thing, instead of begrudging him a few hundred bucks? "I'll be thinking good thoughts," he said, and then, knowing he shouldn't, added, "When the results of the next scan come in—"

"All right," the Baron said, standing abruptly and waving the check at the door. "Now get back to your patients before they start thinking you skipped out to play golf."

He followed Paul out to the curb, watched as he opened the Imperial's door and slid inside. The sunlight set him blinking, and he couldn't seem to stop. He had Paul rev the engine several times, run the windshield wipers, press on the brakes while he checked the rear lights. Then he patted the trunk and said, "You've got a keeper here. We should all be so blessed."

He stayed where he was as Paul put the car in gear and rolled down the street. He was still there, in the rearview mirror, by the time Paul made it to the intersection and began to turn. There was no question the Baron was taking him for a ride. He'd known that for some time now. What bothered him wasn't going along with it so much as realizing how badly he needed it. He couldn't wait to hear the Baron say, "Your life sounds all right, doc," only then believing it. It didn't matter that the Baron knew nothing about him, not even what he did for a living. Why couldn't he decide his life was all right for himself, without having to compare it to one that wasn't?

Nevertheless, he enjoyed gliding down the quiet, late-morning freeway, floating on rotated tires, all parts greased and slipping across each other without friction. Before he made it to the train station, he turned on the air conditioning and bathed in the cool breeze, knowing that for a short while—the rest of the day, the next week or two—he'd trust metal and rubber and the mostly smooth pavement underneath.

# NOCTURNE FOR LEFT HAND

SHE GRABS HIS HAND *and pulls him onto the dance floor before he can think to stop her. He has a glass in his other hand, the last sips of a Tom Collins Cynthia passed him more than an hour ago, the ice melted now, the gin and sweet-sour syrup watery and warm. He doesn't know what to do with it so clamps it against his chest and tries to move as little as possible to keep its contents from sloshing over the sides onto his shirt. But this isn't music that allows for stillness, with its hammering drums and barked lyrics, not to mention Joy thrashing in front of him, all sharp elbows and knees and shiny thick-soled boots stamping the floorboards by his feet. She might not mind a drink spilled on her shirt, black as it is and tattered, slices of skin showing through ragged slits over her belly, the sides drenched with sweat and stuck to her ribs. Her eyelids are black, too, bruised-looking, and so are the leather arm bands that circle both wrists and forearms. The only color she wears are patches of red, white, and blue on her skirt, which she has sewn together herself out of hacked wedges of a Union Jack. Her hair, recently clipped and dyed, is a dark shade of mauve.*

*Paul is the only one on the dance floor not wearing black, though some of the others have words written in radioactive-bright lettering on their t-shirts—"The Exploited," "Misfits"—along with screenprinted skulls. Most of the boys have hair spiked solid, with pomade, he guesses, or glue; a few have shaved heads or shaggy bowl cuts. The girls wear ripped tights and pointy silver rings on every finger, and they all stomp boots as heavy as Joy's.*

*He has seen this set of fashion choices for long enough now—glimpsing his first mohawk ten years ago, on Eighth Avenue—that they no longer seem strange to him, or dangerous, though he doesn't know if he'll ever get used to seeing them on Joy. Instead, the kids' clothes and makeup strike him as quaintly earnest, as do their grunts and howls whenever the music stops.*

*These are Joy's new friends, accumulated over the past six months or so, but the party itself is a holdover from her days as a ponytailed cheerleader on the Morris Knolls freshman squad, when she wore high-heeled pumps, lace-trimmed socks, and polo shirts with the collar turned up. Last year—a different geologic epoch in teenage time—she begged her mother to throw her a sweet sixteen party like those to which she'd been invited by older girls she admired and envied, something as elaborate and expensive as her bat mitzvah three years before. And though Cynthia held out for a while, on both economic and feminist grounds—why should sixteen-year-old girls be told they're sweet? she asked—she eventually relented, in part due to Paul's intervention. "Is it really worth making her resent you for the rest of her life?" he asked, and assured her his annual bonus would cover all the costs.*

*Joy since rejected, or abdicated, her old life and all its trappings, and a few months ago tried to get Cynthia to cancel the party. It's so bourgie, she said, which Paul took to mean embarrassingly ordinary. But Cynthia wasn't having any of it. Paul had already paid a deposit for the room and the catering. "You wanted it, now you're going through with it." Fights ensued, shouting and slammed doors, until they finally came to terms when Cynthia agreed to can the cheeseball deejay and let Joy and her friends take care of the music themselves.*

*So here they are, in the ballroom of the Madison Hotel, with forty-five of Joy's sweating, scowling comrades, and a buffet table spread with sliced cheese and whitefish and marinated peppers and miniature bagels, now plundered of all but a few scattered pickings. Cynthia has spent the evening ducking out to the lobby bar and returning with drinks she half-drains on the way, asking Paul each time if he needs a refill, though until now he has been content to sip the same Tom Collins for much of the night. Why didn't he ask for at least one more? He kept himself out of sight, or thought he did, in a corner of the ballroom, watching the fevered dancing, which has increasingly turned to groping, and admired Joy and her friends for their spirit, their willingness to turn what could have been a humiliating event into an ironic occasion, no opportunity for idealistic expressions of rage or defiance wasted.*

On the dance floor, he continues to admire them, is flattered to have been invited—or compelled—to join them, at least briefly, and when the song ends he pumps his fist in the air along with the others. He expects to see Cynthia laughing at him from the sidelines and plans to ham up his enthusiasm, sneering and stamping and bucking his head. But she's slumped in a chair, chin on chest, her own cocktail glass, empty, on the floor beside bare feet. He makes a move to join her, but again Joy grabs his hand and holds him where he is, and this time another of her friends, a girl with two tiny orange pigtails sticking out like blunted horns from the sides of her head, stretches out her arms to block his way.

The next song starts, even louder than the last, and somehow brasher, starting with a chant, "Hey, ho! Let's go!" He begins to shuffle his feet again, but this time instead of thrashing arms and heads, the kids are all bouncing straight up and down, the floor thumping beneath him, nearly buckling his knees. Joy has a serious look, of concentration, maybe, or anticipation, her black eyelids half shut so that for a moment he imagines he's looking through dark holes into the mysterious regions behind her skull. Why does she want him here? What is it about her life she hopes to show him? He gives a little hop or two of his own, forgetting his glass and the liquid inside, a few drops of which splash onto his fingers. But even then Joy doesn't smile, her mouth set firmly as she springs not quite in rhythm with the chant, the mauve hair looking almost natural as it flops across forehead and brows.

When the chant ends and the song starts in earnest, a fast simple beat and almost jauntily sung lyrics too rushed for him to understand, the kids keep leaping, only now rather than up and down, they're bouncing to all sides. The girl with orange pigtails bumps into his arm, and this time he can't keep the Tom Collins from spilling. Most of it lands on the leg of a kid who doesn't seem to notice, too busy is he flinging himself toward another boy jumping from the opposite direction. They knock shoulders, twist, land unsteadily, and bounce away. Paul excuses himself to the girl, but she only bumps him again, harder, with her hip, sending him sideways into Joy, who, grinning madly now, gives him a rough shove with her forearm.

"Excuse me," he says again, though by now it has dawned on him that *the bumps and shoves aren't accidental. The kids are throwing themselves at each other on purpose, shoulders, chests, backsides colliding. Some of the boys and girls slam together and kiss at the same time, lips grazing or mashing, tongues sliding across cheeks and chins, and all Paul can think is that they have gone insane. He is standing amidst raving, violent, black-clad lunatics. He tries to leave once more, but this time a limber pimpled boy lurches into him, knocking him backward. He holds his balance and then loses it, going down on one knee. It's all he can do to keep from dropping the glass. The last thing they need are shards scattered beneath them as they jostle one another. Worse than having kids barrel into him would be to spend the rest of the night explaining to an outraged mother how her child ended up with twelve stitches in her face.*

*He isn't down long before Joy yanks him up, and then it's only a moment before the girl with orange pigtails comes crashing into him, this time chest to chest. And when she hits, her arms go around his neck, her legs in torn tights around his waist, her tongue flicking out and sweeping across his lips. He is so astonished that he reaches around to grip her to him, but just as quickly she bucks off and careens into someone else. His lips are sticky, tasting of some sweetened sharp alcohol, vodka, maybe, or rum, something cheap and diluted with cola. The girl is drunk, he recognizes that now. They are all drunk, of course they are, of course they've been sneaking sips from bottles hidden in backpacks lined up behind the buffet table. Yes, drunk, not crazy, though he can't help believing still that they have willfully abandoned their senses, that he has been brought in to witness an ecstatic ceremony, primitive and mystifying. He doesn't think Cynthia will believe him when—if—he describes it to her.*

*And just as he thinks so, he glimpses movement in his periphery, black and mauve and the white of pale skin. It's Joy, charging at him, not for a kiss but a tackle. Head down, shoulder cocked, boots lifting high. He doesn't have time to brace himself. He catches the blow on the ribs. The glass flies out of his hand, and he waits for it to shatter. But if it does, he can't hear it over a new round of shouting as the song abruptly cuts off.*

*In its wake comes relative quiet, talking and laughter and clomping feet. He is on his back on the hard floor. Joy is on top of him, head resting on his chest. Her breath is boozy, her speech slurred. "You know what I always dug about you?" she asks. "You're game for whatever." He's mostly sure she has mistaken him for someone else.*

*The lights come on. Waiters are clearing the buffet. He sees Cynthia's feet move, then hears her groan. "Paul?" she calls, groggily. "Are you still here?" Joy stays where she is. Maybe asleep, maybe just enjoying the movement of her head, lifting and dropping as he breathes. Where her hair separates along a jagged seam, he can see sandy roots. The party, a success, is over.*

# SOME MACHER

## 1989

PAUL WAS COUGHING INTO his napkin when the comedian singled him out. "Excuse me? Sir? Would you please die of consumption on your own time?" At first Paul didn't register the comment, or at least didn't register that it was directed at him. He'd just gulped a mouthful of white wine—not cold enough and far too sweet—and some had gone down the wrong way. Several people at his table pressed water glasses on him, and he waved them off. He closed his eyes, mashed the cloth hard against his lips, and almost had the cough under control, when Cynthia, sitting to his right, elbowed him in the ribs. This set him coughing harder. "Sir? Sir? Excuse me? Should I call 911?" Now that his eyes were open, Paul realized the comedian—and everyone else in the room—was looking straight at him. With two fingers, Cynthia made an urgent slicing motion across her neck. "This is an emergency!" the comedian shouted into his hand, thumb and pinky spread to make it look like a phone receiver. "Come quick! Some macher's choking on a chicken bone and ruining my show!"

Paul occasionally had dreams like this, though in them he was always at a business conference and not the annual fundraising gala of the local Jewish Federation, harangued not by a comedian but an enraged executive. And of course he was always missing an important article of clothing—socks, tie, belt, pants. In the best of them, those he didn't consider nightmares, he managed to wish himself invisible and sneak out through a hotel kitchen. In others, the desire to disappear ended in nothing but desperation, which usually woke him with a gasp and often, to his puzzlement, an erection.

Already he felt the stirrings of panic, though at least now he was fully dressed. Too fully. He swallowed the next cough before it escaped and felt it stick in his throat, tickling, as did sweat that seeped onto his forehead. He shot Cynthia a glance. If she'd listened to him, they would have been sitting at the back of the room, out of view, where he could have coughed in peace. It was her fault he was left so exposed, just to the side of the stage. It was her fault, too, that he was one of only three men in the entire place dressed in a tuxedo. For that matter, it was her fault he was here at all, in the gym of a suburban synagogue decorated to look like a Harlem nightclub, with red curtains hanging from basketball hoops.

What else could he blame her for? That he lived in New Jersey and commuted an hour each way to work. That he'd vacationed the last three winters in Fort Lauderdale so her kids could visit their grandfather, who made Paul sit through Yankees spring training games and claimed that sunburns were good for the immune system. He wanted his look to remind her how much she owed him.

But if that was the effect it had—or if it had any effect—he'd find out only later. At the moment, her bottom lip puffed out, eyes bulged, cheeks reddened, as she tried to keep from busting up. Laughter stabbed him from the front, back, and both sides. All the way around the table, nothing but teeth and tongue.

"I could wait him out," the comedian said, still speaking, it seemed, to the imaginary dispatcher on the other end of his hand. "But they only gave me a half-hour slot. I know, I know. They wanted Joan Rivers but couldn't afford her."

Even with the red curtains, the flower vases and candles in glass globes, the portable stage draped with glittery streamers, the gym still looked like a gym, Paul's table set on a free throw line, the nearest hoop, netless, a short toss to his right. Only the comedian was dressed for the space, wearing high-top sneakers, purple, under black jeans. Covering much of his face was a pair of glasses as big as motorcycle goggles, thick black frames hiding his eyebrows. They were as much a part of his costume as the purple shoes and the silver sport coat he wore over an orange t-shirt, the outfit of a clown. And already Paul could see what purpose they served: every so often, without warning, the eyebrows would leap up from behind the frames, startlingly bushy, belonging, it seemed, to someone heavier, gruffer, more cruel. Behind the absurd getup lurked a secret, mean-spirited self who'd occasionally step out of the comedian's shadow to select an unsuspecting victim—whichever innocent dope made the mistake of coughing or sneezing or scratching his scalp.

"Ladies and gentlemen," the comedian said now, eyebrows popping, "the Surgeon General warns that interrupting the show is hazardous to your dignity and may result in copious humiliation."

One last cough came ripping through Paul's chest, so quickly he didn't have a chance to clap the napkin over his mouth. It rocked him against the table, and he had to reach out to keep his wine glass from toppling. Ice jounced in water pitchers. Another roar of laughter filled the gym, and now even Cynthia couldn't hold back, head tipping up, two silver crowns showing, eyelids closed and squeezing out tears. The tickle had disappeared, but Paul picked up his water glass anyway and took a long drink. His collar had constricted around his neck. His jacket felt tight, too, though he'd already unbuttoned it.

"You're wearing that?" Cynthia had asked earlier, when she'd come downstairs to find him in the same suit he'd worn to work, light gray, with pinstripes so subtle you could see them only in sunlight, plenty of room in the shoulders. "It's the gala. The biggest event of the year." She hustled him to his closet and made him put on the tux, though he hadn't had it cleaned or pressed since Kyle's bar mitzvah. On the left sleeve was a smear of gravy, still sticky after nearly two years, but he had no time to rinse it off. When they arrived, twenty minutes late, the Federation's president already in the middle of his opening remarks, most people finished with their salads, he saw that maybe a third of the men in the room weren't even wearing ties. Cynthia towed him through the center of the gym, ignoring his whispered objections. Her dress, green and sleek to her calves, managed to be at once elegant and casual, equally appropriate for a ballroom or a backyard barbecue.

"Sir, I can tell you're used to being the center of attention," the comedian said, giving him a conspiratorial smile, head cocked, as if they were in cahoots. "But please, this is my job." He stood at the edge of the stage closest to Paul, leaning forward far enough that his glasses slipped down his nose and revealed the eyebrows in their resting position, just as bushy and out of place under his high, creaseless forehead. "You're a pretty big deal around here, from the looks of it," he said. "Don't tell me: you're the one writing my check. Oh boy. Sorry kids, no Hanukkah this year. Daddy messed up big time, offended the Chairman of the Board." He waited a beat for Paul to respond, and when Paul didn't, tilted his head like a curious dog. "No? Jewish mafia? Am I going to wake up with a pot roast in my bed?"

The laughter had an edge of hysteria now, wicked-sounding, the accompaniment to a public beheading. The couple to his left was particularly stricken, both husband and wife unable to get themselves together even when the rest of the room began to settle down. Paul had met them before, at some other function Cynthia had dragged him to, but couldn't remember their names. The Meltzners? Freimauers? Because he and Cynthia had come in late, she hadn't had a chance to re-introduce them, though she'd made an exchange of little waves and mouthed greetings across Paul's lap when they'd sat down. Now the wife, a skeletal woman with a long neck and no lips, slapped her dessert plate—apple tart untouched—with bony fingers and sparkling rings. Her portly husband wheezed and sputtered, ears enflamed. They were the only other people at the table dressed for a black-tie event, and given how much the wife stood out in her sequins, how uncomfortably the husband, bald and bearded, was stuffed into his tux, Paul might have expected their sympathy. Didn't they see how easily they could have been in his place?

He managed to wiggle a finger between collar and neck, giving him just enough room to breathe. The comedian asked his name and held the microphone in his direction. He didn't want to answer, but neither did he think he had a choice. "So, seriously," the comedian said, not looking at all serious with his big phony smile and dancing eyebrows, "what is it you do, Paul?" When Paul answered, the comedian threw up his arms and made a horrified sound. "Worse than mafia! I'll wake up with a lawsuit in my bed!"

He wondered how long this would go on and even more, how he'd ever escape from it. The comedian kept asking questions, each of which provided a new opportunity for jokes at his expense. Where did he grow up? "Brooklyn! I got shot there once!" Was that his beautiful wife beside him? "How'd you propose? Let me guess. Handed her a subpoena?" Did he have any kids? "Just stepkids, huh? What's the matter, Paul, too lazy to make your own? Shooting blanks in your pistol? Maybe you're wearing that cummerbund too low."

Cynthia hooted. The comedian winked.

What else could he do but play along, laughing and nodding, acting as if he couldn't wait for more? The comedian had him stand and show off his tux. Called him Daddy Warbucks. Said all the donation envelopes should go to him. "What sort of law do you practice, Paul?" When he answered, there came another horrified sound, eyebrows bouncing into and out of view. "Insurance! For the love of HaShem! Did you read the Robin Hood story wrong when you were a kid? Think you were supposed to steal from the poor and give to the rich? It's the other way around, Paul!"

There were few moments in his life when he found himself at such a loss that his mind emptied of all thought but the simplest sort. He was conscious only of a single phrase ricocheting in his head: don't cough, don't cough, don't cough. His cheeks ached from smiling. He kept feeling for pockets to stick his hands in, but the tux jacket didn't have any, so finally he hooked his thumbs together behind his back. The comedian's mouth was still moving, but Paul didn't hear a word now. Nor did he take in the laughter as anything more than flickering static whose volume rose and fell unpredictably. Later he'd wonder if this was what a stroke might feel like, or a seizure, and he'd remember the odd bliss that overtook him as he swayed in front of two hundred and fifty patrons of the Jewish Federation of Morris County, the unexpected flood of camaraderie and goodwill. All these lovely people, he thought. All these kind, generous souls.

But then Cynthia was tugging at his pants, and his senses returned to him. For a moment it was too much: the comedian's voice booming through speakers, the laughter and clinking of glasses, the fluttering red curtains, the smell of smoke and wax from an extinguished candle. "Seriously, Paul, you can sit now," the comedian said. "Don't make me call 911 again."

The chair was lower than he expected, and he fell into it with a grunt. He was no longer sweating. In fact, he felt a touch of chill on his neck, a prickle on his scalp. To his left, the bald husband—was his name Lowengard? Allen Lowengard?—had trouble catching his breath. He heaved and gasped as his wife pounded her bony fingers and bulging rings against his back. Paul pulled the tuxedo jacket tight around his middle and re-buttoned it at the waist. The gravy stain sneered from his sleeve, and he stuffed it down in his lap.

By then the comedian had returned to center stage. "How about a round of applause for our friend, Paul?" he said. "He's a good sport. And you know what? He saved the show. I had only like fifteen minutes of jokes ready. The rest of the time I would have just stood up here talking about world events. Nothing funny at all."

The clapping was brief and perfunctory. Cynthia looked away. Whatever instinct—or momentary illness—had made Paul magnanimous had vanished. The chill had seeped beneath his skin, maybe into his blood, and he glanced around the room with cold scrutiny. Tacky women draped with oversized necklaces dwarfed by oversized bosoms. Men with toupées and sagging jowls, some wearing open butterfly collars ten years out of date. Who were they to laugh at him? He straightened his bow tie. Maybe it was for the best that he'd worn his tux. Maybe he'd never go anywhere without it.

"Speaking of world events," the comedian said, his strut across the stage full of triumph and swagger. His eyebrows were most likely hidden again, waiting to spring, but with his back turned Paul could see only how narrow his shoulders were under the silver jacket, how frayed the cuffs of his jeans. "Looks like the Berlin Wall's coming down any day now..."

Even rarer than moments when Paul's head emptied were those in which he felt in full possession of his thoughts, unclouded by caution and self-doubt. The urgency he'd felt earlier crystallized now, but not as panic or flight. Words formed clearly and firmly in his mind, and in the briefest instant he managed to consider them carefully, weighing each until he was satisfied. He brought his hands to his mouth, cupped them around it. He cleared his throat without making a sound. The whole thing felt leisurely, or at least seemed so in retrospect, though not a moment had passed. The comedian turned slightly to face the audience, microphone pressed to his lips. Whatever joke he'd planned about the Berlin Wall he hadn't yet begun.

"What do you care, Stalin?"

Paul was more aware of his breath moving through his hands, warming them as it passed, than of the sound of his voice. But the comedian's startled expression, eyebrows frozen high on his forehead, and then another eruption of laughter, confirmed that he'd actually let the words out. And just then he recalled the names of the couple to his left. Kestenbaum. Arnie and Beryl Kestenbaum. Cynthia had pointed them out during a high holidays service, when they were called up to the bimah, Arnie to lift the Torah out of the ark, Beryl to say the prayer before the first reading. Big donors, she'd told him. They'd paid for the new carpet in the sanctuary upstairs, as well as for the expansion of the parking lot out back. Cynthia, recently elected treasurer of the local Hadassah, was angling to hit them up for a gift to support the chapter's new lecture series. No wonder she'd insisted on taking a seat at their table, cutting through the middle of the gym while the Federation president was speaking. Paul remembered the smug look of beneficence on both their faces when she'd made him shake their hands after the service, the expectation that they'd be recognized and thanked for their deeds.

Now Arnie was wheezing again, Beryl once more pounding his back, and since they were no longer laughing at him, Paul reached for the water pitcher and filled Arnie's glass. When the noise died down, the comedian muttered, "Enough from you, Paul," and then continued with his joke, which received a few titters in response. He went on to the next one, and that, too, elicited only mild reaction. His forehead shone in competition with his silver jacket. His eyebrows stayed where they were, stuck above the rims of his glasses. Stillness deprived them of their surprise and menace. He moved haltingly across the stage, bracing, it seemed, for another outburst. Cynthia, too, expected more, giving Paul an uneasy glance followed quickly by a second one, as if she saw something in his face she didn't recognize. Or else she saw what she'd always seen, except she'd remembered it wrong, or until now hadn't looked closely enough.

For his part, Paul eased back in the chair, hands in his lap. He had no intention of cupping them around his mouth again, no intention of calling out. He listened politely to the rest of the comedian's act, chuckling once or twice, and clapped vigorously when he finished. He drank several more gulps of warm white wine. The comedian left through a door behind the stage. Soon after, the Federation's executive director took the microphone and made his pitch for support, describing various programs and benefits to the community. Donation envelopes appeared at each table, passing from hand to hand.

"I didn't know your husband was so funny," Beryl Kestenbaum said, speaking to Cynthia but giving Paul's shoulder a gentle shove. Her eyes, reflecting candlelight, were as bright as her rings. In her voice was a note of something like envy.

"A riot," Cynthia agreed, and then quickly changed the subject, describing the first lecture in her Hadassah chapter's new series. "I hope you can make it."

"Will you be there," Beryl asked, leaning back to take Paul in, "causing more trouble?"

Cynthia took Paul's hand and yanked it onto her lap. "I'll make sure he behaves himself next time."

Arnie Kestenbaum, breathing evenly now, took out a checkbook and propped a pair of reading glasses on his nose. He was once more smugly venerable, as if a few minutes earlier he hadn't been laughing so hard he'd drooled onto his lapel. Any kind of attention was just fine with him. He folded his check twice, tucked it in the envelope, and slid the flap along the tip of his tongue. Paul asked to borrow his pen, and Arnie handed it over with a closed-lip grin of approval. The gravy stain was in plain view, but Paul made no attempt to hide it. His own check he filled in as he usually did at charity events—$100—and then, after considering a moment, added another zero.

"A nice evening," he said to Cynthia as they made their way through the parking lot, newly blacktopped thanks to the Kestenbaums, white lines crisp between each car. She looked at him strangely again, seemed about to say something, and then stopped herself. He gave her his most innocent smile.

When they reached his car, he opened the passenger door, helped her in, and circled around slowly, pausing for a moment to catch his reflection in the back window. He could hear the words he'd shouted, but only as they'd sounded in his head, hardly more than a whisper. He lifted his eyebrows and let them drop. Big shot, he thought, trying to decide if the tux made him look like someone other than he was, or if he was still himself in spite of it.

# GROW OR SELL

# 1991

**WHEN KYLE ASKED FOR** help with a school project, Paul agreed without hesitation. He took the request as affirmation of his importance in Kyle's life, of the trust that had built between them over the past ten years. "Glad to," he said, not waiting to hear what the project entailed, and experienced such a flood of gratitude he nearly thanked Kyle for asking. Kyle, for his part, only nodded.

If Paul had thought about it for a moment first, wariness might have tempered his enthusiasm. Kyle was a senior in high school with a solid B average, which to Paul meant his teachers didn't take grades seriously. From time to time he'd glance at Kyle's papers and homework assignments, the best of which were full of spelling errors, meandering sentences, unfinished thoughts, and red ink. The worst were simply illegible. How he managed to pass any of his classes, much less to meet the requirements for graduation, Paul had no idea, except to believe that failing marks were reserved only for those students who didn't turn in any work at all.

To everyone's surprise, though, Kyle had actually studied for the SATs, and a few weeks earlier he'd received an acceptance letter from Rutgers, the only school to which he'd applied on time. Since the letter had arrived he'd hardly picked up a school book, instead heading out every evening in the car Paul and Cynthia had bought him for his seventeenth birthday, a used Volkswagen Rabbit, silver, with a black stripe the previous owner had hand-painted down the side. It's a chick car, Kyle had said when Paul first brought it home from the lot. Why can't I get a pickup truck? Soon enough, though, he began rolling it through the car wash every week, changing its oil after every five hundred miles, throwing a fit when Paul, clearing the driveway following a light snowfall, accidentally nicked its passenger door with the corner of his shovel.

Where he drove after dinner neither Cynthia nor Paul knew. He had a part-time job as a bagger at a supermarket but kept his hours to Saturday and Sunday afternoons. Did he have a girlfriend? they asked, and Kyle only shrugged and said, "I get some sometimes." Paul would have liked to probe further, but as long as he was home before his curfew—ten o'clock on weekdays, midnight on weekends—Cynthia insisted they allow him his privacy. He usually pulled into the driveway with forty-five seconds to spare.

"In five months he'll be gone, and we won't have any idea what he's up to," she said. "It's time to start getting used to it."

And if, in the meantime, he flunked his classes and didn't graduate? Paul asked.

"Then he'll learn something about independence. And the consequences of fucking around."

Unlike most teenagers Paul knew—and unlike himself at the same age—Kyle wasn't the sullen, angry type, but rather dopey and remote, always snickering at some private thought, or trying to make jokes out of things that weren't funny. Paul would sometimes forget to be careful after putting a fresh blade in his safety razor, and when he came downstairs with a red mark on his Adam's apple, Kyle would say, "Trying to off yourself again?" Or Paul would come home from a difficult day at work, one of his briefs having failed to stop a suit against his firm, and Kyle, catching his look of frustration, would smile sympathetically before asking, "Hemorrhoids acting up?"

When he returned from his evening excursions, Kyle would go straight for the refrigerator, tossing a few grapes into his mouth, unwrapping a block of cheddar and taking a nip from the corner, tipping the orange juice carton to his lips. If he noticed Paul watching, he didn't let on, which gave Paul the opportunity to assess his appearance. Was his hair messier than when he'd left? His clothes more rumpled? Paul tried to get a glimpse of his eyes and a whiff of his breath—if he was driving the Rabbit after drinking, surely Cynthia would have to ask questions then—but he never caught anything more than Kyle's ordinary look of glazed indifference and a smell somewhere between body odor and the fresh mud tracked in on his shoes.

"You'll burn out the motor if you keep the door open," he said.

"C'est la vie," Kyle said.

"A new fridge isn't cheap. Say goodbye to your paycheck for the next three months."

"Que sera sera," Kyle said.

"Have a nice time tonight? Anything interesting going on?"

"Murder and mayhem," Kyle said. "Mysteries and illuminations. Sex, drugs, and rock and roll."

"Appreciate it while you can," Paul said. But Kyle's head was back in the fridge, and Paul couldn't be sure he'd heard.


What Paul really wanted to know was whether or not Kyle was conscious of the approaching transition, if the thought of leaving home caused him any turmoil. He paid close attention to the way Kyle acted around his mother, looking for signs of clinginess, and when he saw none, tried to determine whether apathy might be a mask for unspoken fears. When Cynthia tweaked his ear on her way past, Kyle smacked her hand away. Was there more than irritation in the gesture? Could he be making up for the grief he felt, pushing away what would soon be lost?

Only with Paul's ailing cat did Kyle show any affection. Every morning he lifted Franklin from the living room ottoman on which he spent most of his time sleeping, draped him over a shoulder, and scratched his rump with one hand while shoveling cereal into his mouth with the other. Franklin was eighteen now, with thyroid problems and bad eyesight, and Paul didn't expect him to live out the year. To his surprise, though, he wasn't anguished by this expectation as much as resigned to it, as if Franklin's fate had been sealed long before he'd even come into the cat's life. In fact, the vet had already suggested more than once that they might consider putting Franklin to sleep, given how little he ate, how much weight he'd lost, how much pain it caused him to stand and stretch his paws. But Paul determined not take any action until Kyle was gone. Wasn't it hard enough that he had to say goodbye to everything he knew, to ready himself for a brand new life?

Yes, he was only going an hour away, and at least two dozen kids from his high school would accompany him. But unlike Joy, who, to Paul's astonishment, had transformed from girl to full-blown woman during high school, Kyle seemed hardly to have matured at all. True, after being undersized his entire childhood he'd shot up more than a foot over the past four years, giving him three inches on Paul, but his face was still a little boy's, round and hairless, cheeks always the slightest bit flushed. It didn't help that he had his hair buzz cut every month and wore almost nothing but sports jerseys or t-shirts with the logos of his favorite teams: the Jets in the fall, Knicks and Rangers through the winter, and as if to punish Paul for undetermined crimes, the Yankees all spring and summer.

Even if he managed to keep his grades up, he didn't look like a kid ready for college, and for this Paul suffered on his behalf. He remembered too well his own last months in Brooklyn, before heading upstate, the hours he'd spent looking out the windows of his parents' apartment, trying to memorize details of the streets below. For weeks stomach-aches tormented him, and in school flashes of panic made him gasp for air. To make things worse, his mother looked as stricken as he did the last few weeks before his departure, if not more so, retreating to bed for most of every day. One night, late, she woke him with loud sobs and a cry through the thin wall separating their bedrooms: "My baby!" The next morning she was up early, singing to herself, cutting bread for breakfast, frying eggs and onions. "I don't want you to forget where you came from," she said, placing a full plate in front of him. All month her meals had grown increasingly extravagant, which likely contributed to Paul's stomach troubles. Reggie, two years younger, asked if she'd also get eggs every morning before heading off to college.

"Aren't I your baby too?" she asked, with a smirk not so different, now that Paul thought about it, than the one Kyle turned on him from the refrigerator. His mother, red-eyed and exhausted, replied only, "You going away? I should be so lucky, I'd cook you an elephant."

His father took a different approach, trying to calm Paul's nerves by comparing his departure to one his grandfather, Itzik Haberman, had taken in 1905 from his town in White Russia after a pogrom left two uncles and a cousin dead. "What you're doing, it's nothing," Paul's father said. "You want to feel sorry for yourself, go to college in Bombay."

Now, in the kitchen, Paul gestured for Kyle to have a seat beside him. Instead Kyle stood across the counter, still holding the juice carton. His boyishness had one advantage. Unlike Joy, and Paul, too, he'd never struggled with acne. His face was as free of blemishes as it was of stubble. The buzz cut made him look less military than pre-pubescent, the border of dark hair slicing a perfect curve across his forehead. Today's Yankees shirt was at least two sizes too big, the shoulder seams falling halfway down his upper arm, the hem hanging to his thighs.

"Keeping up with your schoolwork?" Paul asked. "You know, just because you got into college doesn't mean you're finished here yet." Kyle took another gulp of juice. "If there's anything you want to talk about," Paul went on. "Maybe something you don't want to say to your mother—"

Kyle looked at him closely now, smirk blooming into full grin, and waited for him to go on. The words cost Paul significant effort, and at first he was proud of himself for making it. But sensing the mockery in Kyle's gaze, he found himself growing bitter. His own father had never offered him anything so straightforward and comforting. He hadn't even tried. "It's not easy," he went on, "getting ready to turn your whole life upside down, leave your home, your mom, your cat, and, and—"

Before he could name himself among those things the boy would miss when he left, Kyle laughed, loud. Then he tilted the juice carton all the way up, held it against his mouth for a good ten seconds, and tossed the empty carton into the sink. "This fucking place?" he said. "I been ready to blow out of here since I was fourteen."

"That belongs in the garbage," Paul said.

"Que sera la vie," Kyle answered, and sauntered first to the living room, where he scratched Franklin's rigid ear, and then to the stairs. Paul didn't want to believe Kyle really cared so little about the life he'd abandon at the end of summer. But he also remembered his own first drive to Ithaca, his mother resting her head against the passenger window, his father white-knuckled on every curve. The farther they got from the city, the higher they rose into the misty hills above the Finger Lakes, the deeper Paul descended into a mysterious trance, the sound of the radio growing distant, the trees outside the borrowed car closing in, his outer layers going still, it seemed, so whatever new version of him would emerge could make its way to the surface. By the time they arrived he was so eager to get his trunk unpacked, he nearly forgot to hug his parents goodbye. More than a week passed before he thought to call home.

Now he wondered if, after dropping him off, they'd ever hear from Kyle again.

It was only a few days after this conversation, however, that Kyle came to him about the project—a sign that he was having doubts, feeling the tug of nostalgia. Paul wanted to take advantage of the moment; he signed on before Kyle described what sort of help he needed.

The assignment, the culminating project of American History— not the Advanced Placement version Joy had taken, or even an honors section—tasked Kyle with researching family background, conducting interviews and combing archives, which would serve as the basis for an essay defining his roots. The title was supposed to be something like, "How I Became an American." The whole thing struck Paul as juvenile, appropriate for seventh grade, maybe. "Dad's away all month, so I can't write about the Demskys," Kyle said. "And I'm tried of listening to Grandpa Maizel's stories. So I guess I better do your family."

This was the closest Kyle had ever come to acknowledging that they might indeed consider themselves related even though they didn't share a genetic line. So Paul refrained from saying what he thought, which was that the idea didn't seem quite consistent with the spirit of the assignment. How, after all, could Kyle claim Paul's roots as his own? Instead he clapped his hands and took a seat on the couch, ready for an interrogation. But Kyle only looked at him, one eyebrow dipping. "It's not due for a month," he said, and then went out the back door. The Rabbit's little engine revved and puttered down the street.

It was another week before he asked Paul any questions, and though during the intervening time Paul had been preparing to answer, going over his father's stories in his mind, when the moment came he found he had less to say than he expected. The trouble was, he had *only* his father's stories, and nothing else. And because his father, dead three years, had forced them on him when he wasn't in the mood, he hadn't listened very closely. He didn't know the name of his grandfather's town in White Russia, nor the first names of his grandfather's parents or the uncles and cousin killed in the pogrom. He didn't know the name of the ship his grandfather had boarded in Hamburg. His grandfather had died before Paul turned eleven, and until then it was understood that he would never speak a word about the place he'd left behind. What Paul could remember of him was mostly a hoarse voice and persistent cough, and the dreamy smile he wore while crunching hard candies between half-rotted teeth. He wished Kyle were interested in things he knew—about his five paternal uncles, for example, who'd given his father such a hard time about missing their Thursday bowling night for his honeymoon that he stayed at the alley on the night of Paul's birth, which happened, he always claimed, at the exact moment he spared on a dime store split. Weren't those the roots that mattered?

"That's a good question," he said whenever Kyle asked one he couldn't answer. "We could see if my mother knows. Probably not a good idea, though. She hates being reminded of the past. Maybe Aunt Reggie." Kyle scratched his notebook with a pencil, not looking disappointed so much as acquiescent, as if he'd expected little and gotten even less. "Let's call Reggie now," Paul said. "I'm sure she'd love to talk to you." But of course no one picked up at Reggie's number. She might have been traveling with one of her boyfriends. Or she might just as likely have been in the apartment, ignoring him. Since getting her first answering machine she never went near a ringing phone. "It's important," he said after listening to Reggie's long recorded message. "Kyle needs your help." If he was lucky, she'd call back within the month.

"I got to go to the library," Kyle said, and off he and the Rabbit went.

Paul didn't hear any more about the project for five days, during which time he forced himself to keep from asking about it. Kyle was back to his routine of disappearing after dinner and returning seconds before curfew, and Paul worried he'd given up on the project altogether. And now if he flunked his history class and didn't graduate, Paul would be at least partly responsible. He wondered, briefly, whether there was a part of him that wanted it this way, to keep Kyle close while he could. But then, looking for a bedtime snack, he pulled out the block of cheddar with teeth marks in the corner. "The sooner he gets his own fridge the better," he said to Cynthia.

When Kyle finally brought up the project again, he did so casually, halfway through dinner. "I found out what Haberman means," he said through a mouthful of potatoes.

"Let me guess," Cynthia said. "Man of iron. No, no. Little man, big heart."

Paul wanted to tell her to be quiet so he could hear what the kid had to say. But Kyle was taking his time now, washing the potatoes down with a leisurely swig of water. "Well?" Paul asked, finally, when it seemed he wouldn't go on.

"One who grows or sells oats."

Cynthia laughed—mean-spiritedly, Paul thought. "That explains why you're so handy in the yard."

It had never occurred to Paul to wonder about the name, but now he wished it were more distinguished, something that suggested his family's unique qualities, though what those were he couldn't have said. He didn't even like oatmeal.

"So," Kyle said. "Do you grow or sell?"

This time Cynthia snorted and looked away. Kyle smirked. What was funny about oats? "Who, me?" Paul asked.

"Your, you know…your people. Ancestors."

"Good question," Paul said. "I'll have to look into it."

Kyle pulled a Yankees cap over his buzz cut, spent a few minutes petting the cat, and drifted out. And for some reason Paul had the feeling that this was the night he'd miss his curfew. Only by a few minutes. Then, tomorrow, a few minutes more. By the end of the week he'd be home only in time to raid the fridge for breakfast.

After he'd cleared the dishes, Cynthia, eyes flashing mischief, kissed him on the neck and pulled him toward the stairs. "Come on, Farmer Haberman. Time to sow some oats."


"Wasn't Hamburg," Kyle said two evenings later, without preamble, while cutting into a chicken breast. He pronounced the name like the sandwich, with the last syllable cut off. "Your grandfather. He left from Rotterdam, on a ship called *The Patricia*."

"You don't know what you're talking about," Paul said, harshly, with a sting of anger he didn't understand. Only afterward, catching a glance from Cynthia, did he check himself, force a smile, and add, "Where did you get that idea?"

"Ellis Island," Kyle said. "At the library. They hooked me up with the number for the archives."

"They must have made a mistake," Paul said. "Dad—your Papi— he always said Hamburg. Sounds like homburg—you know, the hat— only with an a."

"Rotterdam, Hamburg, what's the difference?" Cynthia asked.

"There must be another Itzik Haberman," Paul said.

Kyle chewed, swallowed, and began cutting a new bite before answering. Paul expected him to flaunt his usual smirk, the one that suggested everything and everyone was a joke to him, none of it worth his time. Go ahead, Paul thought, and I'll wipe it off with the back of my hand. The thought surprised him less than the accompanying feeling, a pleasantly righteous fury. But Kyle showed him a straight face, composed if not earnest, and said, "Not one who got here in 1906."

"Oh five," Paul said.

"He might have left in oh five, but he landed on January 14, oh six."

"Maybe," Paul said.

"Place of origin, Slutsk," Kyle said.

Once again Cynthia laughed a cruel laugh. "That explains Reggie."

But this time Kyle didn't join in. For a kid who'd spent more hours watching comedy acts on cable than doing homework the last four years, he was oddly serious now, grave even, giving Paul a hard stare, challenging him to argue. If he wasn't trying to make fun of him, what was he doing? Was this some form of bonding after all? "With a k," he said, and then repeated the name, enunciating the last letter. "Slutsk." Why did Paul have such a hard time staring back? Instead he glanced at his severed chicken breast, a few stray strings of meat looped in the juice of his green beans. If he could have stopped Kyle from going on, he would have. But he had no idea how. "A town of twenty-thousand at the turn of the century. Thirty miles south of Minsk."

"Sounds about right."

"Major center of Jewish life at the time."

"A great place, except for the pogroms."

"There weren't any pogroms in Slutsk. Not before World War Two," Kyle said.

"Are you calling my grandfather a liar?" Paul asked, but now there was little force behind the words. Anger he could remember distantly at best. Had he really imagined smacking Kyle's grinning face only moments ago?

Kyle shrugged. "There was one in Gomel. Another in Mogilev. But those were pretty far away."

"And his uncles? His cousin?"

Another shrug. "No records on them."

Paul had other questions, but he kept them to himself. Why else would his grandfather have left his family, gone off by himself across the ocean to a country where he didn't know anyone and didn't speak the language? Why in the world would you do that, unless you were afraid for your life?

Kyle went back to eating. Cynthia said, "That's impressive research, kiddo. Good preparation for next year."

"I want to see your sources," Paul said.

"It's a good thing he did leave," Kyle said, after wiping his mouth with a napkin and shoving his plate away. "Would have been screwed otherwise." Without another word, he pushed his chair back and stood. "I'm out," he said, and headed for the door.

Paul had eaten less than half his dinner, but when he brought his fork to his mouth, the chicken smelled gamey—undercooked, maybe?—and he set it down. "Wait a minute," he called. "Screwed how?"

Kyle stomped into his sneakers. "Slutsk Affair," he said. The door shut behind him.


On the weekend he could have looked it up. He had books to drop off at the library, and before searching for new ones, he could have stopped at the card catalogue. And if he didn't find what he needed at the township branch, he could have gone to the larger county one on Hanover Avenue and asked a librarian for help. But instead he did the crossword and watched golf on TV and took a walk with Cynthia, through their neighborhood and up to the new development under construction at the top of the ridge, where a few skeletal frames stood against yards of blasted granite and bare earth, new curbs white as bones, bulldozer and backhoe slumped like extinct creatures beside holes they'd dug to bury themselves.

Early the next week, coming home late from work, Paul spotted the Rabbit leaving the driveway. He didn't think at all before following, passing the house without touching the brake, as if he'd never intended to stop. It was dark enough that if Kyle glanced in his rearview mirror, he wouldn't have been able to make out Paul's car, only a pair of headlights half a block away. Kyle kept an easy pace, turning onto Lenape Road and then onto Skyline, heading around the side of the ridge in a direction Paul never drove. They passed the last of the new developments and then a muddy depression full of weeds that had once been a reservoir. And here the road changed names, from Skyline to Okenaki, fresh tar giving way to crumbling pavement. Ahead, dense woods, the last in the county, as far as Paul knew, crowded the south slope of Union Knoll. A spiny shadow rose over the tops of birch and oak, and it took him a moment to recognize it as an abandoned fire tower, left over from days when the entire ridge was a wilderness ready to ignite.

There were no streetlamps here, only the red of Kyle's rear lights. And now if Kyle glanced behind he'd surely realize Paul was following. But Paul had the feeling that Kyle knew already, that he was leading rather than being tailed. On the right an old wooden sign came into view, letters etched into two silvered boards, only a few flakes of varnish remaining.

## COMANCHE BOWMAN
## ARCHERY RANGE AND CAMPGROUND

It was at least fifty years old, hanging from rusted hooks, and beside it a gap opened in the trees that must have once been a driveway. The place was a relic from the time of Paul's childhood, though of course he'd never been anywhere near here then.

It was hard to believe the ridge had been occupied fifty years ago, the road so overgrown now it was nearly impassable. Who'd been here then? Fathers and sons shooting arrows? Teenagers wrestling each other out of clothes and steaming up canvas tents? Not far past the sign the pavement turned to gravel, and this, too, seemed decades old, so uneven Paul had to hold his mouth open to keep his teeth from clattering. And yet the Rabbit kept its steady pace, its taillights growing more distant as Paul slowed to maneuver around fallen branches and rocks the size of skulls.

Soon the road narrowed. Leaves and brush scraped against his passenger door, and huge tree roots rocked the car from side to side. The Rabbit disappeared around a curve. If there was a moon out, the canopy overhead blocked it. The only light came from the front of Paul's car, reflecting here and there on the dusty surface of week-old puddles. If he kept going he might get stuck in a bog, or else get lost.

When another branch crossed his path, he pulled to a stop.

Whatever was ahead of Kyle, Paul wouldn't see. It took him ten minutes, working the car back and forth across gravel and weeds, to turn around and make his way out.

He had no intention of bringing up the project again. As far as he was concerned, Kyle could keep his discoveries to himself. And for a week he did. But then one evening he lingered after dinner. He hovered in the kitchen with Franklin draped over his shoulder, waiting until Paul had finished loading the dishwasher before handing him a sheet of paper. "I know you think I'm an idiot," he said, and Paul was so surprised that he didn't answer right away, as he knew he was supposed to. The appropriate words came to mind quickly enough: *Of course I don't*, or, *Whatever gave you that impression?* But he couldn't manage to get them out. Instead he glanced at his cat, translucent eyelids and limp paws, and then at the paper, guessing it was an outline for the essay—a sketchy one at best—and before taking a close look, he reached for the pen in his shirt pocket, ready to make corrections.

But there were no Roman numerals, no titles or topics or subheadings. Nothing but a list, with three columns. Name, age, place. The first names varied, but all the last names were the same: Riva Haberman, 31, Slutsk; Aron Haberman, 42, Slutsk; Liza Haberman, 7, Slutsk; Sofia Haberman, 3, Slutsk.

He stood at the sink staring at the paper long enough for Cynthia to ask what was on it. But he didn't answer. "Totally fucked up," Kyle said. "One of the worst massacres of the war. Four thousand people in two days. Rounded them up and shot them in the street."

The page was full. Maybe thirty, thirty-five Habermans in all. Fanya, 19, Sonechka, 4, Nekhama, 28, Yessel, 65. His grandfather had never mentioned the fate of the family who'd stayed put. Neither had Paul's father, nor any of his uncles. They'd purposely cut all ties, leaving specific suffering to others. They'd contributed to funds for displaced persons, nodded with somber justice when Eichmann went to the gallows. They reserved tears for the day the Dodgers moved out of Brooklyn. And Paul had been perfectly happy to go on living without any thought of the past he'd had no part of. His roots were shallow, no more than a few inches into soil. No wonder the slightest tug made him tilt.

"I contacted Yad Vashem," Kyle said. "This is what they sent."

Paul handed the paper to Cynthia. She read it and covered her mouth with a hand. "Oh, Paul," she said, and her eyes watered before he could turn away.

Kyle stood at the edge of the kitchen, scratching Franklin just above the tail, eyeing him. What did he want? Did he think these names and numbers were supposed to mean something? Until a week ago, Paul had never heard of Slutsk. As far as he knew, it was an invented place, as unreal to him as Crown Heights must have been to Kyle. But Crown Heights was the place Paul had left, and there no one had been rounded up and shot in the street. Few had died of anything more violent than a heart attack or a slip from a tenth-floor fire escape. Why should Cynthia cry as she handed the paper back? Why should everyone look so serious, so full of pity? He read more names: Slava, 26, Grish, 82, Dora, 10. Who were these people to him? Who was Kyle, for that matter?

"It's better to know, right?" Kyle said, his expression different from any Paul had seen on his face before, no hint of amusement or ridicule. It made him look older somehow, his features brittle with doubt. Before he could go on, Paul waved a hand in the direction of the door.

"Don't you have somewhere to be?"

Franklin's tail flicked back and forth in sudden irritation, and Paul had the uncomfortable feeling that the cat had figured out what was in store for him when Kyle went away. Before Kyle made a move, Paul left the kitchen. He dropped into his chair in the living room, picked up the crossword and studied a pair of clues: 81 Across—Samantha's daughter; 83 Down—Cacao exporter. He listed off every South American country he could think of, but none fit. And Samantha? Was she a Biblical figure he'd forgotten from tedious Hebrew school afternoons? If he recalled correctly, Enoch had begat Methuselah. Whom had Samantha begat?

He glanced at the paper again. Taube, 39, Geshiel, 64, Baila, 13.

The question occupied his concentration for ten, fifteen, twenty minutes, only at the end of which did he realize he'd been chewing his pen. When he pulled it out of his mouth, the plastic was mangled and covered with blue spittle. Bitter ink washed back and forth across his tongue. He looked around for something to spit it into—a tissue, a flowerpot, the gaping fireplace, Franklin's fur-covered ottoman—and then swallowed.

At the end of the summer, a few days before the start of freshman orientation, business took Paul unexpectedly to London. Cynthia took Kyle to New Brunswick on her own and settled him into his dormitory. "He's ready," she reported when Paul returned. "Whether he knows it or not."

Together they cleaned up the mess Kyle had left in his bedroom, and among unreturned library books and magazines—some with Yankees players on their covers, some with nearly naked girls—Paul discovered a paper titled, "My Journey to Being American." It chronicled three branches of the Demsky family, from the Ukraine to the Bronx, citing interviews and records that were obviously made up. There was no mention of Paul or Slutsk or the people Itzik Haberman had deserted. The paper was full of spelling errors, meandering sentences, unfinished thoughts, and red ink. The teacher had given it a B+.

It went into the trash with everything else. A week later, Paul called the vet to make arrangements.

# AROUND THE CAPE OF GOOD HOPE

## 1993

It was late September and barely light, clouds squatting heavily on the horizon. If dawn had broken, Paul couldn't tell. Across the street from his house, an unfamiliar car idled, a compact Honda from the previous decade, and behind the wheel a hunched figure in a knit cap, too shadowed to reveal any features. He thought vaguely of burglars and the cash he kept hidden in the medicine cabinet, but a year before, after a rash of break-ins in the neighborhood, and despite Cynthia's objections, he'd had a security system installed. Any burglar would notice the warning stickers Cynthia found so ugly—"I'd rather have all the windows broken," she'd said—and stay away. Only after he made it to the end of the block did it occur to him to take down the license plate number, just in case of trouble, but by then he was anticipating the train ride and the rumbling hour he'd have to read the paper, and he couldn't be bothered to turn around.

He forgot about the car by the time he made it to work and didn't think about it again until three days later, when he spotted it through the family room window, just after dinner. This time it was on his side of the street, at the edge of the property line, facing the wrong direction, wheels turned to the curb. Again he could make out only the top of a knit cap over the edge of the driver's door, and what he thought was a finger occasionally tapping the steering wheel. The car was dusty, as if it had been speeding all night down desert roads.

The light caught a crack in the windshield, beginning in the lower left corner and branching, veiny, across the width of the glass. Paul thought again about the license plate, but to see it clearly would have meant going at least halfway across the front lawn, and in the dusk the car appeared menacing enough that he preferred to stay inside.

He thought, too, about calling the police, but he was sheepish where law enforcement was concerned, ever since, a year before, he'd mistakenly dialed 911 when he was trying to reach information. Instead he called to Cynthia, who'd just gone down to her basement sewing room. After the kids had left for college, she'd dragged her old sewing machine down from the attic, but instead of making clothes for future grandchildren or replacing missing buttons on Paul's shirts, she volunteered as a costume designer for a community theater group at the JCC. Over the summer she drove to thrift stores and garage sales all over the state, and now that rehearsals were on she was gone four nights a week, making sketches and discussing fabric choices with the director. The theater company's selections were predictable—mostly Neil Simon and Arthur Miller—and their productions were some of the worst Paul had ever seen. But he went faithfully to at least two showings of each, straining to compliment Cynthia without lying outright. The costumes made him feel as if he were really in Brighton Beach, he'd tell her; the Puritans' hats were so authentic he might have mistaken them for originals.

Now she was working on dresses for the opening scenes of *The Heidi Chronicles*, short, shapeless floral sacks like the ones she'd made for herself in the late sixties. When he stuck his head in the stairwell and said her name, she didn't answer. He heard only the hum and beat of the sewing machine, slowing down, speeding up, and slowing down again. It went silent when he called a second time, but still not a word from Cynthia. "It's important," he said, wishing he sounded more certain, especially when she let out a long breath and pushed her chair back, its wooden feet squawking on cement.

Of course, by the time she made it upstairs, the car was gone. He should have known it would be. To keep from having to face the look of weary frustration she was sure to turn on him—a pinching of lips that made her nostrils widen—he kept staring out the window, shading his eyes with the curtain. "He must have seen me," he said. "He's casing the place."

"At dinner time?" Cynthia asked.

"I didn't say he was any good at it."

"It was just a kid."

"He was up to something," Paul said, replacing the curtain. "He's been here twice. He was wearing a black knit cap."

"They all wear knit caps now, even in the middle of July. It's a fashion thing. He was probably listening to music or smoking grass. Or maybe he had a girl with him. Don't you know what kids do on quiet suburban streets? Was I the only one who ever smelled Kyle's clothes for four years?"

"There wasn't anyone else in the car," Paul said. "I would have seen her."

"You said he was hunched down. Maybe the girl was bent over. You know, looking for something in his lap."

Paul felt himself flush. He pushed the curtain aside once more. The street was still empty, a seedy little pool of water where the car had been.

"You should find a hobby," Cynthia said, heading for the basement stairs. "Something to keep you busy after work."

He didn't like the insinuation: that he was bored and lonely now that the kids were away, that he didn't know how to occupy himself without Cynthia's attention. Had she forgotten how many years he'd spent this way before they'd met, before he'd agreed to share her life with all its kid-noise and chaos? Those nights when Joy and Kyle shouted at each other down the hall, breaking whatever concentration he had to pay bills or do the taxes, he'd longed for the solitary evenings he'd given up, when he could stretch out an activity like reading the *Times* from six until midnight. And now that he had his concentration back, there were any number of things toward which he might direct it. For the past few months he'd been reading books about the great explorers from the Age of Discovery, and tonight he was in the middle of a detailed account of Vasco da Gama rounding the Cape of Good

Hope. Only for some reason he couldn't focus on the words. Even sunk down in his leather armchair—the one piece of furniture he'd brought from his apartment—with a cup of herbal tea on the table beside him, he couldn't keep his gaze from drifting to the window. He stood and peered out every few minutes, finding himself unreasonably disappointed each time there was nothing to see.

Eventually he turned on the TV, keeping the volume low enough that Cynthia wouldn't be able to hear it through the floor. And when, two hours later, her footsteps sounded on the stairs, he shut it off and pulled the book back onto his lap, blinking up at her as if he'd been so lost in the fifteenth century that he had a hard time finding his way back to the present. "Is it bedtime already?" he asked. "Seemed like you just went down there."

"Need some water," she said, turning the corner into the kitchen. "I've got to give it another hour."

The book was heavy on his legs. He turned a page, followed a sentence halfway across, lost it, and tried again. Out the window, the street was deserted, not a hint of life in either direction.


On Monday morning, the car was back, and Paul found himself strangely relieved to spot it at the end of the driveway. In daylight he didn't know what had seemed sinister about it before, a little maroon turtle with its head pulled in, caked with grime rather than dust, and now he had no qualms about approaching. Still, he did so under the pretense of hauling the garbage can to the curb, though it didn't need to be out for another day. There was the knit cap sticking up over the dashboard, and when he came close, Paul half-expected to see another head rise out of the driver's lap.

Or did he hope for it? On maybe a dozen occasions in Manhattan, he'd witnessed people engaged in sex acts—through open apartment windows, in a darkened doorway near Penn Station, once in the copy room down the hall from his office—but to see it on this placid street, where the children used to ride their bicycles, where months could pass without his hearing a car horn or a police siren or the sound of breaking glass: that would be outrageous, enthralling. Though he'd never imagined it before, now that the possibility had presented itself, it struck him as something he might have been wishing for all the years he'd lived here.

But as he dragged the garbage past, he was disappointed to see only a single head, its top covered in black wool, the lower half pale except for a few scattered patches of stubble. He caught a quick glimpse of the boy's face before it turned away—long jaw and pointed chin, a nose that sloped steeply between half-lidded eyes, thick brows that blended with the edge of the cap. The boy sank lower in the seat, as if that would keep Paul from noticing him, and his hands, small and ruddy, with blunt fingers, jammed between his knees. On his lap was a spiral notebook, palm-sized. Paul could make out a few marks but no words. Now he could examine the license plate, but it told him nothing except that the car wasn't from out of state. More interesting were the bumper stickers on the trunk: one from Drew University, another touting Jerry Brown for President, a third suggesting—or commanding—that he fight conformity.

Just as he settled the garbage can behind the car, the neighbor to his south—a black man about his own age—pulled out of his garage. Some years ago, when the man and his family had first moved in, Paul had unintentionally offended him. Cynthia had baked cookies as a welcome and asked Paul to deliver them, but when the neighbor answered the door, Paul mistook him for one of the movers—he was wearing faded dungarees and a frayed sweater—and asked to speak to the new owner. The man identified himself, crossing his arms over his chest, and Paul apologized but forgot to hand over the cookies. The neighbor hadn't spoken to him since.

He drove a dark green Corvette from the mid-seventies, impeccably maintained, washed and waxed every week, and no matter how many times Paul told himself there was nothing odd about a black man in a suit driving a Corvette, nothing at all out of the ordinary, when he was safely out of sight, he couldn't resist the impulse to stare as the neighbor rolled down the street. Now, though, in plain view, the last thing he wanted was to face him as he drove past, to have his polite nod and awkward smile ignored. He might have made a break across the front lawn, but unless the neighbor was fiddling with his radio, he was sure to catch sight of Paul running away. Instead, almost without thinking, he opened the Honda's passenger door and slipped inside.

As soon as he sat, the boy startled and turned to him, flipping his notebook closed. He wore a flannel shirt and black work boots, and if not for little metal hoops in both lobes, he might have been trying out for a part in a remake of *On the Waterfront*. Behind one ear was a cigarette, a pen behind the other. Paul wondered what the neighbor would make of a scruffy white boy in a filthy import, loitering at the curb. Would he think to take down the license plate number? If he slowed to look, Paul didn't know it; he hunched even lower than the boy as the Corvette thundered past, and stayed that way as the engine grumbled into the distance. The inside of the Honda smelled of ashes and wet moss. The grime on the windows dimmed the light. Now that the boy was looking at him, Paul thought he had a morose face, nothing at all threatening about it, his features seeming to slide downward toward the patchy stubble on his jaw. "Morning, Mr. Demsky," the boy said, his voice a croak, as if he'd been smoking for thirty years, though he couldn't have been older than twenty-two.

"Mr. Haberman," Paul said.

"Aren't you Joy Demsky's dad?"

"Stepdad."

"Right. I knew that. She told me about you. Paul."

"Mr. Haberman."

The boy pulled the pen from behind his ear and scribbled, holding the notebook close to his chest. "I don't mean to bother you or anything."

What would be noteworthy here? Paul wondered. How early he left the house in the morning? How long he ran the sprinklers? Mostly, though, he was curious to know what Joy had said about him. Had she told the boy he was paying her college tuition, because her real father, who owned a house on Budd Lake and another in Vermont, who last winter had vacationed in Thailand with his fourth wife, claimed his cash was tied up in investments and business inventory? Or had she mentioned instead that once, when she was ten, she'd caught him at the open refrigerator, with his finger in a tub of whipped cream? He had the urge to leaf through the boy's notebook and tear out anything incriminating. Though there was no one to see him now, he stayed low in the seat.

"Joy's not here," he said. "She's away at school."

"She told me about this place, but I could never really picture it. You know, with all the details. Those trees, and that big rock, and those ugly bushes. The smell of cut grass."

"Those are rhododendrons," Paul said.

"The way the paint's peeling up there on the eaves. The whole weird suburban nightmare."

"We're painting the trim next summer," Paul said.

"Not like my version of it's any different. Not the overall picture. But the details."

"She doesn't really live here anymore," Paul said. "She's not planning to come back after graduation."

"Don't you think I know that?" the boy said, and let out a scratchy laugh that turned into a brief cough. "Trust me, I know. My life would be a lot different if it wasn't true."

"I told her she should move into Manhattan. That's the place for young people. But she's thinking about grad school in Boston. Or else California."

The boy sat up and slapped the notebook against his knee. When he spoke again his voice wasn't raised as much as strained, as if it cost him terrible effort to push air out of his lungs. "I know she's not here. I'm trying to soak up the atmosphere."

Paul's vision for his later years had always included both kids living in Manhattan, Joy in a SoHo loft, maybe, Kyle in a hovel on the Lower East Side. Then he and Cynthia would join them when they retired—finding a place as close as possible, he thought, to his old apartment—and the four of them would go to shows together, and museums, and even lectures. They'd all ride the subway to visit his childhood neighborhood in Brooklyn. He'd let the kids choose restaurants, let them talk him into Ethiopian or Tibetan; he'd always snatch the bill before either of them could think about paying. But neither of the kids had ever expressed an interest in living in the city, or anywhere close. Nor had Cynthia, for that matter. Lately she'd been complaining about the cold and her circulation and suggesting they take vacations to the Caribbean. It wasn't impossible to imagine her wanting to spend winters in Florida, stretched out beside a pool.

"The neighbors won't like a strange car sitting in the street," he told the boy. "They like their atmosphere the way it is."

"I'm just collecting details," the boy said.

"You could collect details in Williamstown."

"It's research. For a class."

"On what? Landscape architecture?"

The boy looked away and muttered, "Poetry."

"This is at Drew?"

"County," he said, and when Paul turned toward the back of the car, as if he could double-check the bumper sticker from where he sat, the boy added, "My brother went there. Used to be his car."

How anyone could write a poem about the view from the curb looking up at his house, Paul had no idea. A teacher at Drew might have come up with a better assignment. But then, it had never occurred to Paul to write a poem about anything, and he didn't see why someone would. He didn't see why someone would make costumes for terrible plays, either, or embark on a treacherous journey around Africa, marauding villages along the way, or use up half of every Saturday washing and waxing an old Corvette.

"What's the poem about?"

The boy scratched the scruff on his chin and shrugged. "I'm supposed to describe the trees and bushes and peeling paint, and it's all supposed to be a metaphor for the way I feel. Except I don't feel like fucking trees and bushes."

The paint was indeed peeling on the eaves, but Paul hadn't noticed until the boy pointed it out. He hadn't noticed how big the rhododendrons had grown, or else he'd noticed but hadn't registered it. They'd come up only to his shins when he'd first moved in, when he didn't know what they were called, and now they were chest high, their branches gnarled, bent at knobby elbows where Cynthia had pruned them.

"She wants to know how I feel? I feel like an asshole." The boy snapped his notebook shut and leaned forward, head on the steering wheel. "We hang out all summer, like every night, and then she doesn't call once. Like I don't even fucking exist."

If the poem were Paul's, what would it say? Did he feel like the trees and bushes, surprised to find himself so deeply rooted, sagging after the long, humid summer? Or did he feel more like the peeling paint, flaking and fluttering in the breeze? Or was it possible to feel like all those things at the same time?

"I don't sleep with just anyone," the boy said. "I don't get those guys who'll pop any girl'll let him. Someone sees you naked and then you never talk to them again? It's too fucking intimate. It's got to mean something."

Paul didn't want to think about the boy naked, and especially not with his stepdaughter, but he couldn't help picturing Joy sitting right where he was, bare back exposed to anyone who might pass, head in the boy's lap, hair fanned across his legs. It was too warm in the car. On the dashboard were scuff marks from someone's heel. His fingers on the armrest touched something gluey. He rubbed them on the seat.

"I would have quit that job if it wasn't for her. Chef's on me all the time like I'm supposed to be able to scrub his grill and clean his goddamn pans at the same time. But she tells me to stick it out, I'm the only reason she comes to work every day, she doesn't know what she'd do in this wasteland all summer without me. You'd think it means something to her, too, right? I should have known better. She never brings me to hang out with her friends. She never brings me over here. I bet she never even mentioned my name."

"She calls her mother every week," Paul said. "But she never asks to talk to me."

"I feel like shit," the boy said. "That's my poem. Ode to a fucking toilet."

"Did she happen to tell you I'm paying her tuition?"

The boy opened the notebook again and scribbled. From this angle, even through a web of windshield cracks, the house against the backdrop of early autumn woods looked elegant, though it was built in 1976, when elegance was far from most builders' minds. The false shutters that didn't close, the concrete steps covered in moss, the rusting swing set just visible in the backyard, all of it as familiar to him now as the stone façade of his old apartment building, with its weathered awning and concrete planters the doormen used as ashtrays. And taking it in, he suffered an unspecified pang. Twelve years. He wanted to tell the boy he'd tried his hardest to be a real parent to the kids, or at least a real figure of authority and support, but he wasn't sure if that was true. He wanted to describe Joy as he'd known her over that time, the impossible transformations she'd undergone—from a precocious waif in muddy sandals, to an aspiring cheerleader with no rhythm, to a disgruntled punk rocker whose spiked bracelets left marks on the leather couch, to the sincere scholar in boots she'd become most recently. What had never changed was her way of looking at Paul with an odd sort of scrutiny, as if she didn't know where he'd come from or what he'd do next, as if, after twelve years, he was still just a stranger who'd showed up in the house one day and never left, his finger buried to the knuckle in whipped cream.

"Don't tell her I was here," the boy said.

"I'd like to see the poem when it's done," Paul said.

His train was due in twenty minutes, and his attaché case was still in the kitchen. If he didn't leave now he'd have to drive all the way into the city and pay for parking and tolls. The thought made him sit upright and rub his eyes, but looking out the cracked window, breathing in the smell of smoke and mildew, he couldn't quite shake the feeling of being half-asleep, unable to focus his vision. And just as he was opening the door, the shock of full morning light making him shade his eyes, Cynthia's car edged out of the driveway. His instinct was to duck down, as the boy did, but it was too late. Cynthia gave him a look similar to Joy's, one that said she still didn't understand him after all these years, that he still managed to surprise her. He gave a little wave and made his way back to the house.

•

That evening, Cynthia had already left for rehearsal by the time Paul made it home from work. He ate dinner, spent a few minutes trying to read, and then pulled out a pen and a pad of paper. He knew nothing about poetry. He'd read hardly any since high school, and aside from Robert Frost snippets he'd since seen on greeting cards, only one line stuck in his memory, by a poet whose name he couldn't recall: *I struck the board and cried, "No more."* He'd always liked the defiance of the words, though if he remembered correctly the poem ended in submission. The boy had talked about collecting details, but when Paul glanced around he saw nothing worth noting. A lamp, the TV, a stack of old magazines, his thick volume on da Gama, a bookmark less than eighty pages in.

When the doorbell rang, he set aside the pen and pad—still blank—with relief. He expected to find the boy in the knit cap standing on the front steps, asking to come in and absorb more atmosphere. And Paul would have let him, making coffee or offering a glass of bourbon, happy to fill even a small amount of the time left before Cynthia returned.

Instead, when he opened the door, there was a police officer, and behind him, the black neighbor, looking stern, arms crossed over a blue tie. "Sorry to bother you," the officer said, pulling on his chin. He was hardly older than the boy in the Honda, though his cheeks were freshly shaven, his voice clearly pitched, his face incapable, it seemed, of the kind of grief that made the boy lower his head onto the steering wheel. He was also far more polite than the last policeman who'd come to the house, after Paul had accidentally dialed 911 and then, realizing his mistake, hung up in a panic, without alerting the dispatcher. That one, closer to Paul's age, had delivered a long, severe lecture and just as Paul thought it was over, began writing out a ticket. "We've had reports," the officer said, turning his head just slightly in the direction of the neighbor, "of a strange car parked on the street in front of your house. And you know, with all the break-ins in the area, we want to make sure there's no trouble."

The neighbor stared hard at Paul, with a look either suspicious or skeptical. He had close-cropped hair, and his mustache was nearly as gray as Paul's. There was no reason he shouldn't have been a friend, or at least on speaking terms. Paul no longer liked the officer's smile, which now struck him as scoffing, as if the neighbor didn't have legitimate concerns. He wanted to take the opportunity to make things right, to repair past damages, to set his life—which, since he'd first spotted the Honda on the street, seemed misaligned, headed in the wrong direction—onto a proper course.

But just as he was ready to explain about the boy and his stepdaughter, about the poetry class at County, a thought came into his mind, a series of words so unexpected and mystifying that he took a deep breath and held it, turning the words over in his mind several times while he stood there, smiling stupidly at the neighbor and the officer, one hand on the door, already inching it closed. "Haven't noticed anything," he said. The officer thanked him and winked. The neighbor, stone-faced, turned away.

Paul hurried back to his chair, picked up the pen and pad, and with a burst of vitality he'd never felt before, or at least not for as long as he could remember, wrote feverishly:

*Around the Cape of Good Hope,*
*A black man in a green Corvette*

As soon as the words were down, the breath rushed from his lungs, and a woozy fatigue replaced his excitement. His fingers were already cramping around the pen. He set it down and yawned. He didn't know what to make of the lines, or what to add to them, and soon the letters blurred in his vision, his chin sinking to his chest.


He woke to find Cynthia standing in front of him, the pad in her hand. Her look was puzzled, or maybe concerned, eyes partially squinted, brows nearly touching. But she didn't ask him about what he'd written or why. She didn't ask him about the car on the street, either, or the boy with the knit cap. Instead, she told him about new troubles with the production at the JCC. The director had a cold. The actress playing Heidi had put on weight and no longer fit in the dresses Cynthia had made. "And the male lead just quit," she said. "We need a new Peter."

Paul was groggy, and embarrassed that she'd seen the pad, and also, as he roused himself, overtaken by intolerable sadness. How many nights would he spend like this, alone in the house, dozing in his chair, with nothing to occupy him but books he didn't want to read and TV he didn't want to watch and words that now, imagining them through Cynthia's eyes, he recognized as nonsense?

He struggled to follow what Cynthia was saying, and when he finally caught up, she was pacing in front of him, waving the pad. "I know you think it's crazy," she said. "But I talked it over with Riva, and she agrees. You're the right size and body shape. You'd fit into all the costumes. And just because you've never acted doesn't mean anything. You couldn't be any worse than Bob." Then she stopped next to his chair and laid a hand on his shoulder. "And it wouldn't hurt you to have something to focus on other than work. I hate to see you drifting like this. I always knew it would be hard when the kids went away, but I've been preparing for it since they were toddlers. For you, it's probably a total shock."

She set the pad on the table beside him, face down. He had an urge to pick it up and read the lines he'd written, to make sure there wasn't any hidden insight in them, some secret to living just out of reach. But of course he knew them by heart. Before he could make a move, Cynthia eased herself onto his lap. "It would give us a chance to spend more time together, too," she said. "Now that it's just the two of us, we can try new things. We've got to keep life interesting."

Her arms were around his neck, her face an inch from his. The lips he knew so well, the cheeks that had rounded out over the past twelve years, marked now by a few liver spots, the dark, mischievous eyes that hadn't changed since he'd first seen them, gazing at him across a seder plate. These were things he hadn't paid enough attention to, that he should have stared at, made notes on, every day. It had never really occurred to him that life ought to be interesting, that this was a privilege he deserved, or that he could choose to make it so. It *had* been, despite his lack of effort. And he supposed it would continue to be, whether he intended to work at it or not.

Cynthia kissed him and leaned away. Her smile was shy but unguarded, her expression full of expectation, of tentative hope. Was it his job to surprise her, tonight and for the rest of his life? "What do you say? Give it a shot?"

He tried to picture himself on stage, lights shining in his face, an invisible audience cringing every time he opened his mouth. He thought of the heartbroken boy in the knit cap, making notes about peeling paint, of da Gama shooting cannons at bewildered villagers in the name of Portuguese power, of his co-workers making love on a copy machine. So few things people did made any sense. But they had to do something with the time they had.

"What do I get to wear?" he asked.

# NOCTURNE FOR LEFT HAND

*HE'S BEEN WORKING ON the letter for almost a week, spending an hour or so after dinner jotting down his thoughts. If he were to compile all his efforts so far, the letter would be more than twenty pages long, carefully handwritten, starting in cursive and switching halfway through to print. But each evening he starts over from the beginning and as yet has nothing close to complete. "Dear Kyle," he writes again tonight, at the little desk that folds out of the bureau in his office—a piece of furniture he's had every place he's lived since college—where he does bills once a month and taxes once a year. "First, let me just say how proud I am. Of what you've done, of the person you've become. A stepfather's pride is different from a father's, I think. I don't have the same stake in your accomplishments. They aren't a product of my genes. I can't take any, or much, credit for your success. So it's just pride by association. I'm proud to have been around to watch this happen."*

*He has written these sentiments, in almost exactly the same way, the last three nights in a row, and he is reasonably happy with them now. They capture, closely enough, the feeling that struck him last week, when Kyle reported to Cynthia that he'd been accepted to medical school at Hopkins. At the time, once the astonishment passed, the intense disbelief, Paul was overtaken by such a swelling of emotion that he grabbed Cynthia and lifted her, with effort, off the ground. "I'll write to him right now," he said, without having been conscious of planning to do so, and without much notion of what the letter might say. All he knew was that he had to say it before the feeling passed.*

*"You could just give him a call," Cynthia said, but by then he was already hurrying to his office and deciding which color pen was most appropriate. Black would be too formal, he thought, too severe, but after a number of false starts, he concluded that blue was too whimsical. Tonight he has returned to black.*

*The opening paragraph has always been the easiest, and after finishing it again he leans back in his chair and gazes out the window at the cone of orange light cast by the streetlamp, the dark road on either side, the slick, tender leaves just unfurling from buds on the neighbor's oak. Then he continues. "I know we've had some rocky moments over the past few years," he writes, and debates once more whether or not to refer directly to the check bouncing incident of Kyle's freshman year, or the DUI incident sophomore year, both of which cost Paul less in money than in sleepless nights and heartburn. He wants to bring them up only to show that his feelings are complex and deeply felt, not sentimentalized by selective amnesia. It would be easier to pretend that Kyle has been a model child, studious and attentive from the start, but to do so would be to negate his remarkable turnaround, from a kid descending into criminality, or at least mediocrity, to one who's made the Dean's List in each of his last four semesters.*

*"But I always knew you could live up to your abilities," Paul goes on, deciding that "rocky moments" are as much reference to past troubles as he needs. "I always believed you could do whatever you set your mind to," he writes, and then stops. He can imagine Kyle reaching this point and laughing a derisive laugh, or worse, crumpling the letter in anger and tossing it into the wastebasket. In either case, there's no chance he'll buy this line, Paul knows. He wants to buy it himself, but the longer he stares at the words the less plausible they seem, the more delusional. The truth is, he didn't think Kyle could hack pre-med when he first declared his major, not even after that initial semester with near-perfect grades. Wouldn't he be better off with something less ambitious? he asked Cynthia at the time. Psychology, maybe, or nursing? Cynthia only shrugged and said, "If he fails he fails. There are worse things a person can do."*

*A year and a half later Paul thought Kyle was aiming too high when he heard which medical schools he was applying to, including several of the country's most prestigious, and wondered whether he should consider choosing a back-up or two. Had he looked at any of the second-tier state schools? And what about programs in Latin America? Paul had once gone to a gastroenterologist who'd gotten his degree in Bogotá. Again he said these things only to Cynthia, and he doubted she passed them on to Kyle. Between applications going out and responses coming in, Paul suffered a fresh bout of insomnia. What trouble would follow rejection? More bounced checks? Another DUI? Or something worse, something he couldn't yet imagine?*

*No, Paul didn't believe in Kyle, he never had, and now he thinks he's never believed in anyone's abilities, not his stepchildren's, not his wife's, not his own. He expects everyone to fail and cringes at the mildest risk. He tears up the letter and starts again. "Dear Kyle, First, let me just say how proud I am..." This time when he reaches the second paragraph he forces himself to be honest. "I should have believed in you," he writes, "but I was afraid of being disappointed, afraid to see you disappoint yourself. It was easier to think nothing would come of your hard work than to put my hopes in something that might not pan out. It's always been easier to expect the worst and be pleasantly surprised when the worst doesn't happen."*

*He feels sick as he writes these things, disgusted with himself and ashamed. But he can also sense the relief that comes with confession, the absolution to follow, shame and disgust already beginning to disperse as soon as the words are down. He wonders if he would have been more pious had he been raised Catholic, with the promise of dispensation and release every week. Jewish uncertainty has never suited him. This time he doesn't refer at all to Kyle's past transgressions, only to his own. He apologizes. He begs forgiveness. He imagines Kyle reading the letter on the frayed couch of the filthy apartment he shares with two other boys, neither of whom has much future, as far as Paul can tell, one an education major, the other doubling in Spanish and American Studies. He pictures Kyle's face as he gets to the letter's second page, where Paul promises to think only optimistic thoughts from now on, the skeptical lines of his stepson's mouth easing, eyes blinking and going red.*

*And before he finishes Paul is wiping his own eyes. Pride has returned, now in equal measure for himself as for Kyle. It's a brave thing to have written this letter, he knows it, and coming to the end he feels that he can now be brave in other things, too, he can live with hope and anticipation as he's never allowed himself before. He signs off confidently, "Love, Paul," and recaps the pen. His only regret is that he didn't use blue ink, which itself might have been a hopeful act, more open and vulnerable. He considers calling Cynthia and showing her the letter but then decides it's braver not to seek her approval, not to have her tell him how proud she is of his growth. The letter means more if it stays between him and Kyle.*

*He reads it through, from beginning to end. There are a handful of spelling errors he would like to correct, a few places where the wording could be more concise or elegant. But overall he is satisfied. Moderately so. Except that now he wonders if it might not be brave after all to burden Kyle with his feelings, to ask for understanding he may or may not deserve. Wouldn't the most courageous thing be to keep all this to himself and wrestle with his shortcomings on his own? If so, then the letter, he begins to suspect, is just as selfish and cowardly as his past behavior. Only more insidious, because of its façade of humility. Yes, he is now sure of it. How could he have fooled himself into believing otherwise? He folds it in thirds, tucks it beneath a stack of papers at the back of his desk, and rips a smaller sheet from a pocket notepad.*

*"Big congrats, pal," he scrawls with his blue pen. "Well done. Knew you could do it. Yours, P." Then he makes out a check for two hundred and fifty dollars. On the memo line he writes, "For celebration or moving expenses." He tucks the note and check together in an envelope, addresses it, stamps it, and closes his desk. Outside, a breeze rustles the young oak leaves. He is reasonably content.*

# WHA' HAPPENED

## 1995

PAUL COULD HARDLY BELIEVE he was sitting in the middle of Bryant Park eating lunch. Three years after the park re-opened, following a massive renovation and much public celebration, he still considered it forbidden territory, off-limits to him and everyone he knew. In his mind it remained the place he'd walked past as quickly as possible, twice a month through much of the seventies, on his way to the library. Back then the park was set higher off the street, with tall hedges blocking most of the view. He'd occasionally catch a glimpse of bodies curled on the pavement—sleeping, he supposed, or worse; who knew?—or a barrel of burning trash, or a prostitute in a sequined skirt beckoning with sultry eyes. He read news stories about drug pushers taking refuge among the old London plane trees, about ineffectual policing and outraged citizens.

Those were the city's darkest days, of course, when most of his colleagues fled to the suburbs—those, that is, who hadn't done so a decade earlier. But until he met Cynthia, Paul had never considered leaving. Even with the crime and the filth and the blackouts, he couldn't have imagined spending his days or nights anywhere else. As far as he had been concerned, Manhattan was the heart of the universe and always would be. Maybe its pulse beat with an uneven rhythm, and the blood pumping through wasn't always pristine, but from it life flowed outward.

But like most people who weren't degenerates, he didn't miss the crime and the filth, and he didn't mind seeing Midtown reborn. He wasn't sad to see the peep shows and porn theaters closed down, the men in sleeping bags cleared from Penn Station and Port Authority. Still, he thought of Bryant Park as a necessary void, a holding pen for seediness and vice and unspeakable acts. Where would those things go once you lowered the entrances and took out the hedges and exposed the benches to open air?

He was taken aback when his firm moved its offices from a building just south of Columbus Circle to one on West 39th, a block and a half from the park. It was one thing to pass by, to sneak a quizzical peek, but another to spend eight to ten hours of every day a few hundred yards downwind. For several months after the move Paul stayed away, taking the long route around Grand Central if he wanted to head uptown for lunch. His co-workers talked about the surprisingly good food at the grill abutting the library's west façade, about sitting at umbrella-shaded tables around the fountain. But still he kept his distance. He hadn't used the city library since getting married, and though he recalled the grandeur of the reading room, with its enormous chandeliers and soaring ceiling, he was satisfied to check out books from the branch in Morris Plains and return them on his way home from the train station.

Why, then, on the first warm day in April, did he find himself walking due north on Fifth Avenue? Was it curiosity that spurred him? Or nostalgia for the guilty little thrill with which he'd glance to the side as he passed the hedges? As soon as he turned onto 40th, the odd mixture of fear and wonder returned to him, and he recalled how often he'd had to fight the impulse to climb the steps, to follow the tilt of a hooker's head, to duck under a gate and disappear down one of the twisting paths. What he'd understood at the time was how easy it would be to lose himself, to give in to the draw of those unimaginable spaces where even armed policemen wouldn't set foot. Back then, when he had no significant attachments, nothing but will or dignity or simple restraint to keep him from abandoning himself to whatever ugly desires lurked inside, the park served as a reminder that his life could take a very different shape if he chose. A caution or a taunt or a beacon, depending on his mood.

Of course he knew it would be different now. He'd read and heard enough to be prepared for the open view across the central lawn, which was dotted with half-naked college students and foreign backpackers exposing pale limbs and flat bellies to the bright sky. He wasn't surprised by the office workers munching salads under umbrellas and dribbling dressing onto their suits. But the details he couldn't have imagined, and the effect of the whole was dizzying. Garden beds tossing up color between concrete paths. A statue of hunched, bosomy Gertrude Stein, looking disappointed, it seemed, to find herself in New York rather than Paris. Another of Goethe, jowly and stern, staring at children squealing on the carousel. Pigeons fluttered from the library's roof onto William Cullen Bryant's bald, bronzed head. All around, new office towers rose like cliffs, Sixth Avenue cutting through like a canyon, and in the distance a crane swung so gently he thought for a moment it was being moved by the breeze.

In his office he'd left behind a banana and sandwich—lean turkey and light mayonnaise—thinking he couldn't possibly stay here long enough to eat. But now, though there were plenty of healthier options, he lined up at a hot dog stand. He shook his head no to each of the vendor's offers of extra toppings—onions, sauerkraut, chili—but the vendor didn't see or didn't understand, and he came away with a bun so loaded he had to ask for a second paper sleeve. The whole thing, along with Ruffles and a Dr. Brown's Black Cherry he'd first told himself he shouldn't buy and then told himself he should drink only half of, cost over ten bucks.

He tried to find a spot near the chess tables and was disappointed when none were open. But when he crossed to the opposite promenade he was glad not to have settled in too soon. Of all the things he could never have imagined, this ranked highest: ping-pong tables just a few yards from 42nd Street. He took a seat in view of them, under the shade of a London plane. At the far end of a green table, a wiry guy in his thirties danced from one foot to the other. A red headband like the one John McEnroe wore in the seventies cut across his forehead, though his hair stuck up less than an inch from his scalp. Baubles of sweat hung from his earlobes, and his shirt stuck to his chest. He held his paddle like a cleaver and crouched low, and when the ball came his way he heaved forward to bat it back as soon as it ricocheted off the surface. Or else he dove to catch it on the corners, grunting or crying out, sometimes rolling on the ground and springing up just in time for the next volley.

The player nearer to Paul looked about sixteen, except that he wore charcoal suit pants and a white button-down, his jacket and tie folded against the trunk of a nearby tree. He was Asian, no taller than five-foot-four, so of course Paul automatically rooted for him. In big cities, small men thrive, his father had always said. Skyscrapers had a leveling effect. Beneath sixty, eighty, a hundred stories of swaying glass and steel, what did a few inches in one direction or another matter? At five-four you could stride down Broadway with as much pride as a seven-foot giant, and on the subway you were far better off: no stooping beneath handrails, no shuffling oversized feet to keep them from getting trampled. From your office window you could look down a hundred feet onto the sidewalk and feel no humbler than any of the tiny figures scrambling below.

But Paul also liked the Asian player's style. He held his paddle with a thumb on one side, four fingers on the other, the handle against his wrist, and he stood a good three feet back from the table, hardly moving anything other than his arm when the ball came streaking toward him. He didn't smile or grimace or make any noise. His only eye contact was with the ball. He'd unbuttoned just a single button of his shirt and hadn't rolled up his sleeves, and yet there were no signs of sweat on his forehead or under his arm. Even in the middle of a long volley, he breathed evenly, while his opponent wheezed and gasped. Paul dubbed him Takuro, after a shrewd business associate in Tokyo, always polite, never smiling, ruthless in negotiations.

The crowd clearly favored the wiry guy, an easy hero, with his courageous tumbles and melodramatic sighs, and every time he took a point cheers went up all around. But Paul knew what Takuro was up to when he let a few tough shots go without making much effort to return them. He was pacing himself, letting his opponent wear down, overextend, make mistakes. He was calm, unruffled, icy—adjectives Paul wished he could use to describe himself, instead of those he knew were more accurate: anxious, sensitive, equivocating. Go Takuro, he thought, leaning forward in his seat, so focused on the back and forth that he gobbled half his chili dog before remembering to open the chips. His can of Dr. Brown's was already two-thirds empty.

Only when the score reached five-all, Takuro serving, did he notice the child. Maybe two years old, barefoot, wearing a little white dress with a pattern of red cherries and green stems. From the flower bed separating the tables from the crowd, she watched the game as intently as Paul did. Because her hair and skin were dark, he guessed she was Takuro's daughter, here to support her dad, and she was just as silent and impassive, eyes fixed on the ball, skinny arms linked behind her back. The only movement she made was to lift a foot and scratch a toe against the calf of the opposite leg. When Takuro served, and the wiry guy—he had height, so why should he get a name?—made a breathless backhand, the ball skittering at an angle seemingly impossible for Takuro to reach, she didn't show any sign of distress, any emotion whatsoever. And when, against the laws of physics, Paul thought, Takuro did manage to reach it, legs moving so fast Paul couldn't be sure he'd seen them, and sent a shot with so much forespin it skimmed the net and bounced twice for a point, she didn't clap or cheer or raise her hands, didn't do anything but continue to stare. Not like the fans of the wiry guy, who groaned and held their heads, nor like Paul, who jumped out of his chair, spilling the last swallow of Dr. Brown's onto the concrete pavers, and cried, "Yes! Beautiful!"

His cry did catch the child's attention, and she half turned to him without shifting her feet, which were planted squarely in a geranium, exuberant pink blossoms rising up to her shins. She was a lovely child, he thought, though he never found kids younger than seven anything but terrifying, and in general had never taken much interest in other people's children. But he felt a swell of affection for her, and for Takuro, too, who took his daughter to the park during his lunch hour, when most men would have happily left theirs in daycare.

The score was now seven to five, and Takuro was in control. The wiry guy was out of breath, drenched, struggling despite the headband to keep sweat out of his eyes. On Takuro's next serve he blew an easy return, sending it straight into the net. Paul sat down with satisfaction, happy to let the tension of the moment ease, to give up suspense in favor of inevitability. The child was still looking at him, turned fully to face him now, the geranium's blooms trampled under her heels. She had two fingers in her mouth, but not the ones you'd expect: the middle and pinky, with the ring finger tucked down against her chin. He gave her a little wave and when she didn't react, a wink. She stared and sucked her fingers. Her features weren't quite what he expected, either, not distinctly Asian like Takuro's but a mix of genes from at least two continents. If Takuro were married to the beautiful slim woman in short skirt and designer heels sitting a few feet away, the two of them might have produced such offspring, and for this, too, Paul envied him—all his youth's potential, all the unfilled years ahead.

But the slim woman wasn't the child's mother, nor Takuro's wife. Before the game was close to being finished, she tucked her salad tub under an arm and walked away. The actual mother, he could see now, stood a few yards down the promenade, talking to a woman wearing a baseball cap over badly dyed red hair. What he could see of her was a lumpy backside in capri pants and an ankle covered with either a birthmark or a blotchy tattoo. From her hand dangled a pair of tiny sandals. She paid no attention to the child, who was drooling onto her fingers, nor to the ping-pong table, though she blocked the view of at least three people sitting behind the shrubs. Shouldn't she at least cast an occasional glance to make sure the child was safe? This was still Midtown after all, not the pit it had been fifteen years earlier, but no place to let a kid run free. And why not put on her sandals if she was going to stand in the dirt?

Of course it was none of his business, and even more, not his responsibility. He shouldn't have waved or winked at a strange child. If the mother had caught him at it, she would have taken him for a creep. The last bite of chili dog clung in his throat, and he had no more soda to wash it down.

Game point. The wiry guy had no fight left in him. An angry scrape ran from forearm to elbow. The color had drained from his face. Paul worried he might pass out before finishing. But he managed to get into his crouch, bobbing from one foot to the other. His spirit was admirable if not entirely dignified. Paul wanted Takuro to give his opponent one quick glance, a little nod of recognition, but he only straightened his sleeve, adjusted fingers on the back of his paddle. Go easy on him, Paul thought, feeling the chili dog, the onions and sauerkraut, sitting heavily in his stomach, his mouth dry from the salty Ruffles. He was ready to head back to the office now, though he had another hour before his next meeting and had planned to visit the library. But he was no longer in the mood for soaring ceilings and grand chandeliers. Takuro raised the ball to serve.

It ended quickly. Two volleys and a hard forehand right down the center line, where it short-hopped against the wiry guy's paddle. Then the ball sailed straight up, a high arc above the net. Everyone watched it, waiting, holding breath—everyone that is, except for the child's mother, still talking to her friend in the cap: "I never said I would. I said I *might*." The wiry guy hadn't quite given up. He was still in his crouch, holding the paddle in front of his chest with both hands, a pose of humility, of prayer. Takuro stood aside, gazing up with his usual indifference, as if it were all the same to him where the ball landed. Paul's tongue stuck to the roof of his mouth, and he would have given anything for another sip of Dr. Brown's. The drops he'd spilled pooled next to his chair. He was standing again, though he didn't remember having pulled himself up. He wanted the game to be over, but he also wanted the ball to stay in the air for as long as possible, lost against a backdrop of sunlit leaves.

It missed the table by two inches and landed with hardly a sound in the gravel by Takuro's feet. The wiry guy lowered his head. Takuro laid aside his paddle and adjusted his sleeves. Paul was no longer sure he'd rooted for the right person. Weren't there other considerations than height? He was pleased, in any case, that Takuro was the first to round the table, hand raised. The wiry guy grasped it firmly, and for the first time their eyes met, one head tilted back, the other angled down. A gentler end to the David and Goliath story, Paul's favorite as a child. Maybe he missed the violence, the upsurge of triumph that could come only with a giant laid out dead on the ground. But this version was more appropriate to the new, civilized Bryant Park: Goliath accepting David's superior skill and leaving him in peace.

Already a new pair of players had picked up the paddles and taken their place at either end of the table. Fresh arrivals from nearby office towers replaced those who'd moved on. Paul reached down for the empty hot dog sleeves and Ruffles bag, and only then realized he'd stepped into the puddle of Dr. Brown's, which had splashed onto his toe. And it was while trying to wipe it that he saw the child moving farther away from her mother, deeper into the park. If the mother noticed she gave no sign. She was still talking to her friend, gesturing with both arms, the little sandals flopping against her wrist.

Not my problem, Paul thought.

In his adult life, how many times had those words crossed his mind?

The child glanced at him again, peeking around the trunk of a London plane, and this time she pulled her fingers from her mouth and gave what looked like a smile, sly and secretive, though he was too far away to be sure. More certain was the gesture she made with her wet hand, a scooping motion, its meaning definite. Come with me.

There were times in Paul's life when he felt as if he were being watched by the cold eye of an impatient audience, waiting for him to provide amusement. And as much as he resented it, he felt oddly obligated to do his best. When the child slipped behind the tree again, what he wanted to do was throw away his trash and head straight back to his office, taking the shortest route possible through the center of the park, stepping over the stripped bodies of students and backpackers, cutting between the carousel and ticket booth, leaving the place behind for good.

What he knew he should do was approach the mother, politely

mention that her child was running away and likely to be snatched by a child pornographer who still haunted this section of Midtown, and prepare to get told off. But he didn't like the look of her now that he could see her face: jowly and aggressive, facing her friend with a hard, skeptical squint, her wide-hipped stance making her belly—hugely pregnant, he realized—stick out as a challenge. And if he stopped to speak to her, he'd lose sight of the child, whose legs he now saw poking out from behind another tree, several yards down the row. How had she gotten so far? Then there was the flash of her white dress, red cherries streaking across the path and out of view. He left his trash where it was and hurried after her.

As soon as he stepped out of the shade, the sunlight struck him a blow. He had to stop in the middle of the path, blinking and cupping hands around his eyes. For a moment he saw nothing but squared patches of green and white—the central lawn stretching in front of him until it met the library's marble steps. Then people came into focus, lying down, sitting, walking, obscuring his view like fog. Over the grass, white bowling pins turned end over end, spinning between a pair of bare-chested jugglers. The sound of an accordion drifted from somewhere out of sight, playing a tune that was almost but not quite familiar. A huge belch welled up in his chest, but he let it out quietly, in three or four installments. He'd regret the chili dog for the rest of the day and probably all night. Though the hum of traffic sounded distant, all he could smell was exhaust.

And the child? He couldn't spot her anywhere. He should have been troubled by this, frantic maybe. He'd seen the look on the faces of parents who'd lost a kid in a crowd, a terror unlike any he could imagine, and then the shaken expression when they snatched the little hand again, the gradual onset of relief warring with imagined scenes of despair. But he felt the relief already and guessed relief was all he'd feel. He'd experience no guilt walking away. He wouldn't tell anyone in his office about the child, nor mention her to Cynthia when he made it home in the evening. With luck, he'd forget her by the end of the week.

But then: a tug on his trouser leg, and there she was, standing at his feet, looking up at him not with a smile but the same open stare with which she'd watched the ping-pong match—maybe full of wonder, maybe of the empty thoughts of a dimwit. The hand fixed to his pants was wet, though it hadn't been the one in her mouth. A convex film of yellow snot bubbled from each nostril. Up close her hair was wispier than it looked from a distance, and through it he could see patches of scaly scalp. "Where's your mother?" he said, more sternly than he meant to, and to make up for it, asked what her name was. Of course if her parents had taught her anything, she wouldn't tell him. He bent down and tried again. "Should we go find your mother?" Then, feeling unreasonably silly, added, "Your mommy?"

"Uh-oh," the child said, as he attempted to pry tiny fingers from bunched cloth. But their grip was surprisingly strong, or else they were stickier than he'd realized. Her head was angled back as Takuro's had been when looking up at the wiry guy, and this, Paul decided, was what made him so uncomfortable around children. Having imagined himself David all his life, he hated stepping into Goliath's shoes, waiting for rocks to smack him between the eyes.

He pointed in the direction of the ping-pong tables. "I think your mother's over there."

"Uh-oh," the child said again. "Wha' happened?"

What else could he do but lift her up and carry her to the woman who, neglectful or not, was the mother she was stuck with? But when he reached for her, she let go of his pants and bolted away with a little squeal, a sound of delight, he guessed, though it could just as easily have been one of fear. He didn't know which for sure until she stopped a few feet away and gave him a look over her shoulder. This time the smile was distinct. Yes, she was playing with him. Did he look like someone in the mood for games? At lunchtime, on a weekday? Did he seem like someone who had the temperament for them?

In half a dozen years, when Kyle was in Little League, Paul had played catch with him ten times at most, because Kyle always turned what Paul thought of as important practice into a series of ridiculous challenges: how high he could throw the ball, how hard he could make a grounder skip off the lumpy lawn, how far he could make Paul run for an errant toss. At ten or eleven, Joy would sometimes get him to wear bedsheets and act out a royal melodrama she improvised on the spot. But she usually ended up scolding him for giving in too easily to the princess's demands, for not keeping up his English accent, and after a while she stopped asking him to participate, replacing him instead with a huge stuffed elephant her father had given her for Valentine's Day, having missed Hanukkah by almost two months.

The child waited until he'd nearly reached her before sprinting ahead. If he'd really tried, he could have caught her, of course—his legs were twice as long as hers—but he couldn't help imagining how foolish he'd look diving after a dirty, barefoot toddler, and even more, how people would stare at him if she screamed in earnest. So instead he followed her in this halting manner across the lawn, until they reached the fountain, where she clambered onto the cement lip and ran precariously around the edge of the pool. Above her a stone chalice squirted a stream of water ten feet into the air, and its spray drifted onto her shoulders. She was now on a level with his eyes, and straight on he could see how disproportionately big her head was compared to the rest of her, how unbalanced, and thought it was only a matter of moments before it tipped her into the water. Already he wondered if he'd have time to pull off shoes and socks before stepping in to fish her out. It depended, he supposed, on whether she landed face up or down.

But instead of falling, she raised up on her toes and stuck out her tongue, catching mist. Then she sat, splashing her feet through the water in an uneven rhythm, two kicks from the right foot followed by one from the left. If he could have trusted her to stay where she was he would have run for the mother then, but the odds were low that she'd be here when he returned. He would have called Cynthia to ask for advice if there were a payphone in sight. What he saw instead were the two ping-pong players, the wiry guy and Takuro, side by side, walking toward him like a pair of warriors striding away from battle. Both carried hot dogs in paper sleeves. Unlike Paul, they deserved all the chili and onions they wanted. They'd worked for it. But when they were close enough he could see the wiry guy's dog was spread only with pickle relish, Takuro's nothing but mustard. He wanted to ask for their help. Would they watch the kid while he looked for the mother? But when they came even with him, he only managed to call, "Nice game."

Takuro gave him a glassy look and would have kept walking if the wiry guy didn't stop and smile. His headband was gone, but a line of dried sweat marked its place across his forehead. He took a bite of hot dog and tipped one ear toward Takuro. "Never seen him lose," he said while he chewed. "Two years running."

"Does he play professionally?" Paul asked.

"Nah. Portfolio manager."

"Makes sense. Nerves of steel."

"Closest I ever came is eleven-eight. Saw another guy take him to game point."

"Did he break a sweat then?"

"One slice, then two serves to his backhand. Done."

Up close Takuro's boyishness bordered on petulance, as he worked his jaws and scowled, staring off toward Sixth Avenue. His tie hung loosely around his neck, his suit jacket draped over a shoulder. A pinprick of mustard dotted his shirt. Paul was working himself up to mention the child. Weren't they already a part of it, since he'd seen her while watching them play? Weren't they as responsible for her as he was, or as any stranger in the park? But when he glanced behind, she was no longer kicking her feet in the pool. In fact, she was no longer sitting on the fountain at all, and he bent over the edge, expecting to find her floating, or submerged.

"That your kid?" The voice was deeper than the wiry guy's, huskier, perfectly calm. Takuro's. Only this wasn't the voice of a Takuro. It had neither the accent Paul had been imagining, nor the whispery deference that made Paul's Japanese business associate tolerable. More likely his name was Tommy, though Paul couldn't quite adjust to the change.

"What the hell," the wiry guy said. Paul followed the line of Takuro or Tommy's jutting chin, and then he saw: in the right lane of Sixth Avenue, there was the child, tiny as a doll against the open stretch of pavement and the line-up of cars waiting for the light at 41st.

"She doesn't look anything like me," Paul said, weakly. What glitch of evolution made morons most likely to reproduce? He'd let his own genetic material go to waste, and now in another hundred years only brutes would inhabit the planet, articulate as apes and less well groomed.

The dress printed with cherries stirred in the breeze. One bare foot reached up to scratch the opposite calf. Beside him, neither the wiry guy nor Takuro or Tommy made a move. The light changed to green.


Afterward, he didn't remember running to the child, nor making the decision to do so. Did he skirt the food kiosks and tables around the fountain or charge between them, upsetting people's drinks? Did he take the stairs one at a time or stumble down all three in a stride? All he knew was that he'd scooped her up around the waist with his right arm—his weak one—while his left waved at cars barreling toward them, in big arcs, like a flagger's at an airport. There may have been time to turn and run back to the curb, but his momentum had him moving in the opposite direction, and it took all his effort to keep from pitching into the next lane. Please see me, he thought, with a measure of self-pity, believing no one ever had.

At least some of the drivers must have seen him, because horns sounded as soon as he pulled upright. But the car in his lane didn't slow at all. In fact, it accelerated, its grill pointed solidly at his waist. He was still waving, but if the driver noticed he or she gave no indication. In his mouth, the taste of chili powder mixed with acid. He managed to tuck the child around his side and stick his left hand straight in front of him, fingers spread, and for some reason he thought, sadly still, my ping-pong hand, though he'd never picked up a paddle.

Only at the last minute did the car swerve. It was an old Buick Regal or Chrysler LeBaron, a boxy thing from the mid-eighties, with a high dashboard the driver could hardly see over, and a square trunk that fishtailed as it heaved into the next lane, cutting off a cab. It missed Paul's leg by inches. The wind blew him back on his heels, but he was able to keep his eyes fixed on the driver, hunched down so low he couldn't tell if it was a young man in a hooded sweatshirt or an old woman with a handkerchief tied tightly as a helmet over her hair. And before the Regal or LeBaron was all the way past, the wind stirred something in him—not rage, exactly, or hatred, but flames of a different, wilder sort, and he ran after, at least a dozen steps, his left fist raised and shaking. "Go fuck yourself!" he shouted, as its engine coughed and then revved, blowing through a yellow light at 42nd and speeding uptown. "Go fuck yourself!"

These were words that had crossed his mind often enough in the forty-five years since he'd first heard them, shouted by the proprietor of a bakery on Utica Avenue, after a patron complained that his bread wasn't fresh. But before now Paul had never spoken them aloud, at least not in public. They may have crossed his lips from time to time while he was safely enclosed in his car, with the windows rolled up and heat pouring out of the dash and the radio playing, after he'd jammed on the brakes to let a puttering station wagon merge in front of him on I-80. More often he heard the phrase in the silent voice that was deeper and louder and pushier than the one that left his throat, that talked a blue streak between his ears from the time he woke up until he was back in bed. Last week in the supermarket, for example, when the customer ahead of him blathered on to the cashier for a good five minutes about the difficulty of finding effective arthritis medication. *Go fuck yourself!* he thought when the cashier suggested four Excedrin with a shot of vodka, and again when the customer couldn't find her checkbook and emptied her purse onto the conveyor belt. *Go fuck yourself!*

Or, earlier this month, when he called in a roofer to replace a few shingles that had blown off the back porch during an early spring storm, and the roofer told him the entire thing needed replacing—not just the shingles but the plywood underneath. He brought Paul out of the house to tell him this, pointing to a spot where the pitch of the roof sagged. "Like a ninety-year-old tit," he said. It was drizzling, and Paul was in slippers and socks. He knew the roof needed replacing; the entire porch needed replacing, because to build it Cynthia had hired an unlicensed contractor who'd cut every corner he could. It was all she could afford at the time, a year before she and Paul met, and though they could have easily replaced it now, they hardly ever sat out there since the kids had moved away. They were debating whether to fix it or get rid of it altogether, to give Cynthia more room for garden beds. Of course it was sagging. Did the roofer think Paul was blind?

Paul cried silently, *Go fuck yourself! Go fuck yourself!* as the roofer drew up a bill for the missing shingles, along with a bid to replace the roof, a bid so outrageously high Paul knew he would shred it the moment he walked inside.

The phrase was so much more descriptive than "Fuck you," a slur Kyle, while in high school, had liked to hurl around indiscriminately, saying it to his sister, to Cynthia, to the TV, with a smirk and a little shrug, as if his insincerity took all the force out of the words. Paul had no doubt the baker on Utica Avenue had been sincere, had even meant the phrase literally, as he grabbed a rye loaf and gave an underhanded jab at the customer who doubted his integrity. Yes, Paul wanted the roofer to go off somewhere and fuck himself, brutally, with an instrument that would cause him pain. When he did get around to tearing up the bid, after stripping off his wet socks, he thought, *Go fuck yourself with a two-by-six!*

And now, standing three feet into the right-hand lane of Sixth Avenue, with a grubby child in his arms, and traffic backed up behind him, he actually let the words out. They felt so good passing his teeth he shouted them a third time, with a flourish, after the Regal or LeBaron cleared the 42nd Street light. "Go fuck yourself with an exhaust pipe!" For the first time, he actually believed his father's line about small men and big cities, which he'd secretly thought was nonsense. After nearly fifty-five years of living in it and working in it, only now did he feel fully a part of the city—not just an observer of its madness and energy but a participant, alive and writhing, fist raised over his head. He wished he'd been shouting all along.

It was wanting to hang onto the feeling for as long as possible that kept him from hurrying back to the sidewalk. But as soon as he began to enjoy it he knew it had begun to fade. What replaced it of course was a furious flood of hot embarrassment as cars started to ease around him, and he caught several gawking, horrified faces behind passenger windows. He knew what they were thinking: you could clean up Midtown all you wanted, get rid of the pimps and hookers and junkies, put cafés and ping-pong tables in the park, but you'd still have the same unhinged place, teeming with lunatics.

With draining adrenaline came a rush of sound, horns honking for three solid blocks. "Get your fucking kid out of the street," someone called, and only then did he feel the weight of the child in his arm, the fabric of her dusty dress, one bare foot against his back, the other pressing into his belly. Only then did he smell her bittersweet breath and oily hair and what was unmistakably a soiled diaper. Only then did he realize she had one of her filthy fingers in his ear and two others working at his mouth. "Uh-oh," she said when he pulled her hand away. "Wha' happened?"

Back on the sidewalk, he hesitated before putting her down. He had a flash of the car charging at him, and then a flash of what might have happened if it hadn't swerved: his body flinging through the air, flopping on the pavement, the child squashed beneath him. Or, if he'd stayed on the sidewalk, and only the child's body went flying. What would he have done then? Rushed into the street or scuttled away?

The sidewalk was bustling, people hurrying past in either direction. The ping-pong players had disappeared. No one else was coming up to congratulate him.

Hadn't anyone seen what he'd done?

The child stuck her fingers in his mouth again, and again he tasted stomach acid. He set her on her feet, and once more she bolted away. He prepared to follow, but this time she ran straight to her mother, who stood beside the fountain now, her back to them, her enormous taut belly catching sunlight. The child raised her hand, and the mother took it without any sign of surprise, without any hint that she'd been looking for her or realized she'd been gone. She expected nothing else but the little fingers slipping into hers. Linked now as if they'd never been apart, the two walked downtown. Not once did the child glance back at Paul.

So that was it. No one but he would know what had happened. He could tell people in the office, if he wanted, and Cynthia, but even in his imagination the words sounded too ordinary. They didn't capture the blast of car horns, the whoosh of air against his knees. They had no way of bringing back the softness of the child's legs against his arm, the fruity sour smell of her breath. On his way back to work he passed the carousel again, and only now did he take notice of the horses beneath the bobbing children, their faces frozen in expressions of excruciating pain, as if the golden poles keeping them in place had been driven down through their saddles and straight into their backs.

# A COMPLETE UNKNOWN

## 1997

JUST BEFORE HIS OFFICE phone rang, Paul had been debating whether or not to leave work early and enjoy the last stretch of fading daylight. It was mid-September, cloudless, just enough breeze to occasionally lift a flag on a nearby rooftop, rippling it for a moment before letting it drop. His receptionist had already gone. His hand hovered over the receiver for four full rings. Leave it, he thought, before picking up to hear a young woman's urgent voice. Without announcing who was speaking, she told him she was pregnant, her boyfriend was moving to Miami, she was sorry, she was leaving tomorrow. For a moment Paul thought it was Joy, and he couldn't decide if he was supposed to congratulate her; she was twenty-five, living in San Diego, and last Paul had heard she was on her third boyfriend in as many months.

Only when the woman said, "I know I'm supposed to give two weeks notice, and if you don't want to pay me, I guess that's your right," did he realize it was the nurse's aide he'd recently contracted to care for his mother, who last spring had broken a hip and begun what Paul suspected would be an excruciating decline. His sister Reggie had encouraged him to move her to an assisted living facility, had even given him the name of one she'd heard good things about, but he wasn't ready. He'd interviewed more than a dozen people for in-home care and hired this one not only because she was the most attractive but because she'd promised to stay at least a year. But now she said, "I'll leave breakfast out for her, but you'll probably want to get here before noon. She gets cranky if her lunch isn't ready on time."

Paul didn't take betrayal lightly. Or at least he didn't want to. He'd always liked to think of himself as a person who stood his ground, who wouldn't let anyone cross him without consequences. When the Dodgers moved from Brooklyn to Los Angeles, he'd sworn not only to give up allegiance to the team he'd devoted himself to since he was old enough to walk from his parents' house on Crown Street to Ebbets Field but quit following baseball altogether. Basketball, too, for good measure. Football he'd never cared for. From then on, he decided, he'd watch only tennis and golf, automatically rooting for the underdog.

The problem was, he couldn't just abandon Gil Hodges like that, or Newcombe, or Duke and Pee Wee, or that new kid Koufax, who hadn't yet lived up to his promise. So he snuck glances at box scores and caught a few games on the radio, and when Gil hit his 300th home run, he secretly cheered. A few years later, when the league expanded and a new team came to Queens of all places, he went straight out and bought tickets for opening day. He was doubly proud when Koufax threw his first no-hitter against Paul's very own hapless Mets. It was a good day for the Long Island boroughs, for Jews, for people with split or shaky loyalties.

By then he was in college, and what interested him even more than baseball was folk music. Because he didn't yet know how to drive, he spent a whole day on buses and trains to get from Cornell to Newport in order to hear Pete Seeger singing with Sonny Terry. That was the first and only time he slept on a beach. The only time he skipped class was when Dave Van Ronk played a coffee house in Ithaca. And when Dylan went electric, he was as outraged as any of his folkie friends. He gave away his 45s of Peter, Paul, and Mary singing "Blowin' in the Wind" and "Don't Think Twice, It's All Right." He stopped listening to Joan Baez, too, for not having done more to prevent the travesty. Eventually he sold his record player and shaved off the uneven start of a beard. He quit drinking coffee. Not even half a decade later he voted for Nixon and then lied about it to his mother, who wouldn't have forgiven him.

But lately, while driving the Imperial to the station for his morning commute, or to theater rehearsals at the JCC—he'd recently played Sergeant Toomey in *Biloxi Blues*—he'd turn the dial of his radio, and catching a few beats of a tune he found compelling, would pause and listen, only to realize he was hearing Dylan's nasal honk, backed by drums and organ and electric guitar. And instead of snapping it off, he'd let the song play through, sheepishly drumming his thumbs on the steering wheel, enjoying, despite himself, the twang of guitar and the pulse of rhythm. After hearing it a second time, he'd hum along, and though he found the lyrics too complex to sing—far more so than the songs he'd memorized in college—later, at work, he'd find a few phrases playing over in his mind.

For the past seventeen years he'd lived less than a mile from Greystone Park, the state mental hospital where Dylan had made his famous visits to a dying Woody Guthrie. Until recently, it had never occurred to him to wonder about the nature of their conversations, to imagine what wisdom might have passed between them. But now, whenever he rolled slowly through the shadows cast by the original asylum buildings, stately and neglected, the site of well-documented scandals and unknown atrocities, he couldn't help picturing the two of them in a cold bare cell, strumming guitars, discussing old ballads. He'd always driven these roads slowly—there were crosswalks every block, the occasional bewildered patient shuffling over the pavement, and speed traps at either end of the hospital grounds—but now he'd pass at a crawl, glancing up at the high barred windows in the stone façade.

Did Dylan describe his strangest dream? Did Woody tell stories of life on the road? "Follow your own path," Paul imagined him saying. "They'll call you Judas, but you'll get over it."

Though she'd left after twenty-eight days, Paul sent the nurse's aide her full month's pay. He scrambled to find a replacement, this time calling a service since he had no time to place an ad or conduct interviews. But when the agent said it would be at least two weeks before they could send someone, he called half the assisted living facilities in the city. The only one with an open apartment was the one Reggie had suggested, which wasn't his first choice. The last thing he wanted was for his mother to think he'd chosen the cheapest place he could find, especially since he had to pay an enormous fee to book the apartment on such short notice.

He begged Reggie to help with the move, but she already had other commitments, she said, she couldn't just drop everything and put her life on hold every time her mother needed her, and besides, she went on, hardly taking a breath, Paul was the favorite child, the one her mother had always coddled, and why should she spend her day listening to the complaints of a woman who'd never respected her, never took the time to understand her interests, never did anything but criticize her clothing, her hairstyles, her cooking, her romantic attachments. "Good luck," she finished. "Tell her I'm out of town. Up on the Cape or something. Tell her I don't have a phone there."

His mother had been shrinking for years, the bones in her back compressing and bending her forward, and since her fall she stood crookedly, leaning on a cane. The top of her head reached no higher than the base of Paul's neck, but still he pictured her as he'd known her fifty years before, towering over him, feet spread apart, hands on hips, head wagging. His whole life she'd worn her hair up in a tight bun, giving her another two inches on his father, who'd stood five-three in shoes. In the hospital, though, while her hip was healing, the bun had collapsed, and her hair had tangled. To Paul's astonishment, she'd agreed to let the nurses cut it into a short curly bob that ended just beneath her chin. The rest they saved and braided into a rope, and when Paul came to visit on the weekend his mother showed it to him with pride, first holding it up and then swinging it down hard on her blanket, where her knee must have been. He couldn't believe how long it was, longer than his forearm and hand combined, fingers extended. How had so much hair fit together in a ball not much bigger than his fist? The bun must have been so tight his mother would have felt her scalp stretch whenever she moved her jaw.

Without it, her face did seem looser, eyes hooded and dreamy, brows arched expressively, a little smirk on one side of her mouth, white ringlets resting on either cheek. Paul might have believed she was laughing at him—because he'd put on a few pounds, maybe? because he'd made the mistake of wearing a blazer in the car and had sweat rings under his arms?—if he didn't see the same smirk an hour later, when she was sleeping. He supposed it was the morphine that gave her such a placid look, but he couldn't help wondering if the haircut had something to do with it, too, releasing her from a long confinement.

On the day of the move she still wore the smirk, though she'd been off morphine for more than a month and was now, if she remembered to take any pills without the nurse's aide to dole them out, down to two Percocet a day. And she did seem amused as he made her breakfast, sticking a frozen biscuit sandwich in the microwave and then squirting cheese onto his sweater when he cut it into small triangles she could fork into her mouth. He'd worn casual clothes for the occasion—khaki chinos, old brown loafers—and had even brought a pair of Cynthia's garden gloves to carry boxes, but the sweater was merino wool, and now he'd have to bring it to the dry cleaners. She didn't laugh or make a remark as he scrubbed the greasy spot with her sponge, just looked up at him from the awkward angle caused by her hunched back, blinking and smirking. He hoped the expression meant something—that she was enjoying her new station in life, maybe, that she found humor and lightness in it after a bitter decade since Paul's father had died. But when he put the plate in front of her she wrinkled her nose and said with familiar resentment, "About time."

"You're welcome," Paul said.

She brought a forkful to her mouth, studied it, and set it back down. "It's plain."

"What do you mean, plain? It's got eggs and cheese."

"I like the, what's it called. The pink stuff. Salty."

"Bacon?"

"No, the other one. Softer."

"Ham? Since when did you start eating pork?" He opened the freezer, but there were no other biscuits, nothing but orange juice concentrate and a bag of corn kernels covered with ice crystals. "You'll have to settle for egg and cheese."

"The girl ate them all."

"What girl?"

"The colored one."

"Demond? The cleaning lady?"

"The other one. The brown one."

"I don't know any brown girls," Paul said.

"Spanish," his mother said. "Porturican. Whatever it's called. Hardly wears any clothes."

"Jessica. The nurse you scared away. She's Cuban."

"Every time she bends over you see all the way to her belly button."

"You don't have to worry about seeing it anymore. And I'm sure she didn't eat your biscuits." All around were things he needed to pack into boxes before the movers arrived in the late afternoon: dishes and glasses, massive photo albums with scuffed covers, his mother's collection of porcelain dolls. Most of it, along with the furniture, would go into his basement until his stepkids were ready to fight over who would take what. Reggie had claimed the dolls and expected Paul to double-park outside her building on West Fourth and run them upstairs. He had no time to argue about ham. "Please. Just eat what you've got."

She made no move to pick up the fork, just watched as he began to load a box with the few things she'd take to her new home. New and last, he couldn't help thinking. Her eyes tracked him from the kitchen to the hutch in the dining room, where he wrapped a decorative china bowl she'd never once used, as far as Paul knew, in three sheets of newsprint. It unnerved him to have her staring, saying nothing. He'd made sure to remind her of the move every day for the last week, but he didn't know what she retained. Most of his life he'd known far too much of what she thought. She'd never kept a thing to herself, especially not a thing to do with her displeasure. He'd heard weekly that he didn't visit often enough, that his wife was haughty, that his stepchildren would never love him as a father. For the past ten years he'd heard over and over how disappointing her marriage had been: how his father had never taken her anywhere; how he'd never, in fifty years, bought her a present she liked; how he'd never learned to dance though he knew dancing made her happier than anything.

Now Paul wished she'd tell him she didn't want to go. She might have shouted at him: why don't you just put me straight in the grave. He wished she'd at least acknowledge that she knew what was happening. He wished she'd take a bite of the damn biscuit. Most of all he wished she'd stop smirking at him.

"It's a while before lunch," he said. "You'll be hungry. And you can't take your pills on an empty stomach." No answer, no movement but blinking eyelids. "You're going to like it there," he said for at least the tenth time in the past few days. He'd said it to himself at least a hundred times more, which still wasn't nearly enough to make him believe it. "You won't be alone so much. It'll be nice to eat with other people, don't you think? And they've got a card room, and exercise classes, and guest speakers. It'll be like living at the old club on Utica Avenue. Only there's no pool."

Into the box he placed things she probably had no room for in the new place, less than half the size of this apartment. Crystal candlesticks. A brass ashtray she'd never allowed his father to use. A dozen photographs in musty frames: one of her and her teenage friends—"the girls," she still called them, though all but two had died and those left were in their mid-eighties—wearing slinky dresses and flapper hats; one of his father; another of Paul and Reggie; several of Joy and Kyle, whom she'd never treated as real grandchildren, though they were the only ones she'd ever have. "It'll be easier for me to visit there," he said. "I can take a cab up at lunchtime. When I can get away, that is. Maybe once a month or so. We can take a walk to the park when your hip's better."

The next time he passed through the dining room he stopped at the table, lifted the fork to her mouth, wiggled it back and forth. But she wouldn't open. The ringlets on her cheeks were girlish, and Paul had a vision of what she'd been like as a child: stubborn, selectively mute, inscrutable. At times he'd regretted never having had the experience of raising an infant, longing for the hardships he'd heard new parents complain about with such false, dreamy frustration. But he suspected now—or rather admitted to himself what he'd known all along—that he would have been lousy at feeding and changing diapers and shaking rattles. He had no patience for it. He dropped the fork, harder than he meant to, and it bounced off her plate onto the table. The triangle of biscuit slipped off the tines and leaked oily cheese onto the wood. He wiped it up, cleaned off the crumbs, replaced the fork. His mother sat and blinked.

"You're a grown-up," he said. "If you want to be hungry, that's your business."

In the bedroom, he tried to breathe easier, but his lungs felt as if they'd been cinched with wire, halfway up. He transferred clothes from her dresser into two suitcases. A decade after he was gone, the room still held the memory of his father's cigars. The smoke was in the wallpaper, he supposed, in the carpet and curtains, in his father's old leather armchair, the seat upholstery cracked and split in the middle, with a bit of cotton stuffing poking out. Paul had already decided to take the chair to his office, though he hardly had any room for it. He refused to imagine it in Kyle's apartment, or cradling the backside of one of Joy's California boyfriends.

He shouldn't have felt sentimental about this apartment. His parents had moved in only a few years before his father's health began to fail, and the time they'd spent here had been mostly miserable. He didn't associate it with his childhood, a borough away. He felt no connection to Forest Hills, though it was only one subway stop from Shea Stadium, and over the past decade he'd taken in a few dozen Mets games after stopping in to see his mother. It had been a place of loneliness for her, a place Paul associated with guilt and obligation, a place to which he always dreaded returning. He should have been happy to see it go.

"Just memories."

He gave a start, in part because he hadn't heard his mother approach, and in part because he was afraid she'd read his mind. She was standing in the doorway, leaning on her cane, her new ringlets lit up from behind by the hallway light. He was tempted to add that some memories are worth forgetting. Instead he piled more clothes into the suitcase, hastily now. One of her blouses bunched up, but he didn't bother to smooth it before laying a pair of slacks on top. "Lot more memories to come," he said.

She waved a hand in front of her face as if to bat away his words. "Like a dream," she said.

When he finished with the clothes, finished with a long struggle to zip the second suitcase, he wasn't quite ready to leave the room. "You've probably got space for a painting," he said. "Want to take any of these?" He hadn't looked at the paintings for years. Or maybe he'd never looked at them. They hadn't been in his parents' bedroom in Crown Heights, and he didn't know when they'd appeared. A landscape with mountains and trees. A portrait of a dreamy young woman looking off to one side. A Paris street scene, with sidewalk cafés, iron balconies, people and dogs similarly groomed and morose. Paris, a place his mother had always wanted to go, where his father never took her.

Only then did he notice what was hanging above the bed. "Where the hell did that come from?"

His mother was silent again. Maybe she shrugged, maybe she didn't. He slipped off his shoes and climbed up. The mattress squeaked, a sound he found nauseating.

"How long has this been here?"

Polished brown wood, four inches tall. A mournful bearded figure, arms spread, eyes closed, wearing nothing but a cloth around his waist, braided twigs on his head, and little nails through his palms.

"Did Jessica put this here?" he asked, pulling it from the wall, and when his mother didn't answer, added, "The brown girl?"

Why did he trust anyone? He'd given her a job, he'd offered her a dollar more an hour than he'd promised in his ad, he'd said she could take a paid vacation after working for a year. One gesture of good faith after another, and all she'd done was stomp on his generosity. He hopped down from the bed and headed for the trash can in the kitchen. Only when he came close did his mother grab his arm and pull it up so she could see what was in his hand. "Him?" she said. "He doesn't bother me." She pried the crucifix from his fingers with surprising strength and set it on the dresser. Then she gestured at the paintings on the walls, or maybe it was the furniture she was pointing to, or the walls themselves, the whole room, the memories it contained. "It can all stay." She turned and hobbled into the hallway. "Let's go already."

The Waterview Terrace was on 81st between Riverside Drive and West End Avenue, just a block and a half north of the apartment where Paul had spent the whole of his fourth decade. Along with traffic sounds through the open window came a pleasant breeze, the smell of diesel and fish, the eager cry of a seagull. As he hung his mother's clothes in her new closet, a wave of nostalgia struck, not for childhood but for days that were once open and waiting to be filled—sometimes lonely, yes, but ripe with potential. The sound of car horns, the restless air stirring the drapes, brought a suggestion of youth and vigor that made Paul wish he could spend the rest of his Saturday roaming the city, breathing in its smells and listening to its cacophonous music without the intrusion of his mother's groan as she lowered herself into a chair, and of the TV, turned up too loud, as she pressed buttons on the remote control.

"You're going to like it here," he said again, more doubtful now than ever as he took in the kitchenette's aluminum sink, the cheap pressboard cabinets, the institutional paint job, the sad attempt to make the place look homey with ugly lace curtains and doilies under table lamps and coffee maker. The box of his mother's knick-knacks didn't help. The china bowl took up too much space on the counter, and the framed photos didn't all fit on the dresser. The one porcelain doll he'd kept for her he had nowhere to put except on the shelf at the top of the closet, where his mother couldn't reach it, or even see it. One of its eyelids had stuck shut, its wink less coy than distraught or diseased.

On a side table next to the armchair, he set a snapshot of Joy and Kyle from three years ago, when they'd come home for Passover. "Joy decided to stay out West. Says she's addicted to sunshine. Cyn and I are planning to visit in November."

"Regina lived in California," his mother said.

"I don't know if you can call it 'lived,'" he said. "She wasn't even there six months."

"She went to school."

"Of a sort, I suppose. The Haight-Asbury School of Mind-Expanding Debauchery."

"Your father never took me anywhere."

"So I've heard. Good thing he made up for it by being such a kind and easy-going person."

"I'm the only one of the girls who never went to Paris."

"And half the girls died of lung cancer because they smoked like French hookers."

"I was the best dancer out of all of us."

"I remember," Paul said. "You did the Charleston at my wedding."

She clicked off the TV, waved her hand as if to shoo him, and said, "Like a dream."

He'd planned to stay for lunch, to get her settled, to make sure she wasn't disoriented by the new surroundings, the new routines. But by the time he shepherded her into the elevator, he was already thinking about leaving. He'd take her as far as the dining room, maybe, or pass her off on one of the aides in the lobby. He'd hurry back out to Queens, finish the packing, and with luck he'd still have an hour to catch dinner before the start of the Mets game. Even this late, there was sure to be space available in the upper deck. Or maybe he'd find a scalper in the parking lot and treat himself to the best seat he could bargain down to under a hundred bucks. He'd call Cynthia and let her know he was coming home late. Reggie could get the dolls another day.

With them in the elevator was an elegant Indian woman in a wheelchair. White hair, red sari, perfect posture. British accent when she said good morning. Paul introduced his mother, who managed to slide behind him, so the woman had to lean back in the chair to see her. "She just moved in," Paul said. "She's a little nervous."

"Welcome," the woman said. "I'm sure you'll be very happy here."

"That's what I told her," Paul said, with gratitude.

"The people are very kind. And there's much to keep one occupied."

"I told her about the exercise classes. And the card room."

"The Thursday lectures are very informative," the woman said. "Sometimes my son joins me. He quite enjoys them."

"Oh," Paul said. "Isn't that nice."

"He works downtown, but he comes all the way up on the subway at least once a week for lunch. He's very attentive."

"I wish I had that kind of time," Paul said.

"He's coming today, in fact." Paul smiled but didn't respond. He hoped if he stopped talking she wouldn't go on. They still had seven floors left. But it was clear she had plenty more to say. "I'm meeting him in the lobby, and we're going out to a restaurant. The food here does get tedious after a while. As does the company. It's really quite essential to have regular visits from family. One could become very depressed otherwise."

Paul coughed and cleared his throat, hoping to shut her up. But it was his mother who rescued him. "Smells funny in here," she said. The woman's smile disappeared. She sat straighter in her chair. They descended the last three floors in silence.

When the elevator doors opened, the woman charged into the lobby with startling speed, head tilted forward, hands pumping rubber wheels. But before Paul had to face the enthusiastic greeting of her attentive son, he and his mother were met not by an aide but by an old man in a blue cardigan, one pair of glasses on his nose, another on a cord around his neck. His body was a big round ball, no distinction between belly and chest, but his legs were surprisingly thin, swimming in baggy trousers, and he had a strange prancing gait, lifting up on his toes with every step. Paul wondered if he worked for the Terrace. Some kind of manager, maybe, here to welcome new residents. Except on his feet he wore leather slippers, deeply creased across the toes and backless, heels bare and yellow. "Mitzi," he said, and took Paul's mother by the elbow. "I've got a seat for you at my table. Good people there. No yackers."

No one had called his mother Mitzi since the last of the girls moved to Florida, twenty years ago. To his father she'd always been Mimi or Mother. Among her mahjong partners, whom she wanted to impress and intimidate, she'd gone by Miriam. To her face, shopkeepers had called her Mrs. H., though when she was out of earshot, even if Paul lingered nearby, she was The Mayor of Utica Avenue. "The Mayor wasn't happy with the grapes today. Had to eat half a pound to be sure they weren't ripe."

But the old nickname didn't surprise her. Or at least she showed no sign of being surprised, though she showed no sign, either, of being pleased by it, or offended, or even having heard the word. She disengaged from Paul and started hobbling away with this stranger prancing beside her. "Excuse me," Paul said, and only then did the old man turn to him, raising the second pair of glasses and holding them up over the first.

"Sorry, Paulie-pal," he said. "I've only got one seat saved."

Paulie-pal. Mitzi. Half-formed memories arrived like puffs of smoke, dispersing as he tried to grasp them. The apartment on Crown Street. The swim club on Utica. His father's cigar in an ashtray. Ice cubes rattling in a small glass. His mother's laughter. "Mr. Fatts?"

"Hey, who you calling fat?" The old man slapped his belly. It was the same line he'd used when Paul was a boy, though it had been funnier when he was a hundred and fifty pounds, his belt buckled on its tightest notch. "You're a big boy now. You can call me Herman."

"I can't believe it," Paul said. "It must be forty-five years."

"Believe it, boy-o. We all get here eventually. It'll be you, before you know it."

"You were in California. I didn't know you'd come back."

"History lessons some other time. We've got to get in there before all the rolls are gone. Come on, Mitzi."

His mother didn't glance back at Paul as she walked away. She transferred her weight from her cane onto the old man's arm, and her steps seemed to grow stronger, more balanced, as the two of them disappeared into the dining room, from which Paul heard a joyous clinking of plates and silverware, a rumble of excited talk. He should have been pleased to hand his mother off into such spirited company, but astonishment made him lightheaded, and once again he found himself forgetting to breathe. Herman Fatts. How was it possible? Of all the places in the world, how could he be here? He no longer wanted to finish packing his mother's apartment. He didn't want to wander the city, either, or watch a Mets game. He just wanted to go home to

Cynthia, to a quiet dinner and a TV movie, to a predictable life that didn't throw him into confusion at every turn.

But when he tried to leave, a small crowd blocked the revolving door out of the lobby. There was the dignified Indian woman in her wheelchair, and in front of her two aides in forest green uniforms, with the Terrace's logo—a river passing under a bridge—embroidered on their chests. "I'm sorry, Mrs. Randawaha," said one of the aides, heavy, black, hair dyed orange and straightened stiff to her shoulders. "We'd like you to stay inside."

"But I've told you. My son's expecting me."

"If he comes, he can meet you in here," the aide said.

"He isn't planning to park," Mrs. Randawaha said. "He'll be alarmed when he pulls up and doesn't see me."

"I thought you said he was coming by subway," the aide said.

"Excuse me," Paul said, and when no one moved out of his way, asked, "Can I help here?"

The other aide, a skinny young man with pitted cheeks and wet-looking hair, gave an extravagant sigh. "We go through this every day."

"What's the problem?"

"We can't let her out."

"This isn't a prison," Paul said, short of breath. "She's not an inmate."

"Last time we got a call from the cops. They found her in the middle of Columbus Circle, blocking two lanes."

"Your son wants you to stay inside," the first aide said, bending down close to Mrs. Randawaha's face. "He doesn't want you to get lost again."

"I spoke to him this morning," Mrs. Randawaha said. Her posture was no longer quite erect. In fact, it looked as if she were in the midst of collapsing, the upper portion of her body tilting to one side. Her voice, too, had lost its force and now came out as hardly more than a whisper. "He told me to be outside. Promptly at noon. He's taking me to, to…"

"Well, I talked to him just half an hour ago," the aide said. "And he told me he might get held up at work. He said you should stay inside, and if he doesn't show up by twelve-thirty, you should go on and have lunch here without him."

"Why didn't he call to let me know?"

"He tried, but you must have already left your room."

The other aide said to Paul, without bothering to lower his voice, "He hasn't been here in two years."

"Excuse me," Paul said again, and this time he edged around the wheelchair and ducked between the two aides until he could reach the nearest wing of the revolving door. But before he could push it, a hand snatched his wrist. Brown, bony, with deeply grooved nails. "Please," Mrs. Randawaha said. "Please, get me out of here. I can't eat another meal…"

It took both aides to extract his wrist, and when they did, a red mark appeared all the way around. Unlike his mother, Mrs. Randawaha kept her eyes on him until he turned away, swinging through the door and hurrying as fast as he could out of sight.

"Herman Fatts," he said, setting the box of porcelain dolls in front of Reggie, who lay back in a recliner, eyes closed, fingertips pressed to both temples. "After all these years. Can you believe it?"

"On a day like this," Reggie said, moving only her feet, "I believe anything." She wore leather slippers not much different from Herman Fatts's, only hers were brand new, with a fluffy wool lining, and her heels were pristine, skin pale and smooth, no calluses or corns, though she was on her feet all day. "You could tell me John Lennon was there, holding hands with Janis Joplin, and it wouldn't surprise me at all."

Reggie was only two years younger than Paul, but the more time passed, the more they seemed to separate in age. She was slim and fashionable, with hair dyed so carefully you could mistake it for natural, and people often guessed she was in her early forties. Unlike Cynthia, born a month earlier, she hadn't yet gone soft in the backside and thighs, didn't have burst capillaries under her eyes or wrinkles around her mouth. When she was younger, Paul had attributed her looks to lack of stress, and her weight to cigarettes. But she'd quit smoking more than fifteen years ago, and if you believed her, stress was the only thing she experienced from the moment she woke up until she went back to sleep.

For years she hadn't worked at all, instead living on an inheritance from a childless uncle, which paid for her apartment, her clothes, her series of vaguely artistic and penniless boyfriends, her one brief and disastrous marriage. Paul had received the same inheritance, and along with fifteen percent of each month's paycheck and half his yearly bonus, it had gone into mutual funds whose dividends he immediately reinvested. According to his financial advisor, if he didn't start spending more money, he'd have enough to retire for three hundred years. "Take a trip," he said whenever Paul called to ask if he should move more funds from securities to bonds. "Buy yourself a boat or something." Paul was thinking about replacing the Imperial.

Reggie's investments hadn't been so prudent. To celebrate her fiftieth birthday, she'd opened a designer boutique in SoHo with a friend she'd known for less than three weeks. "It's always been my dream," she'd told Paul at the time, though that was the first he'd known of it; before that he'd thought her dream had been to live in Japan, which she'd never visited because she didn't eat fish, or care for its smell. For a year the store had done wonderfully, with a write-up in the style section of a neighborhood paper Paul had never heard of, with two customers who'd played small roles in independent films, with account books running only mildly in the red. And then things got rocky, when Reggie turned out to be a lousy bookkeeper, when the friend turned out to be a thief, when designers asked to be paid. Within three years, the remainder of the uncle's money was gone, and the store closed.

Afterward, following a long period of depression and recovery during which Paul covered her rent and sent a check for food and necessities, Reggie took a job—her first since high school, as far as Paul knew—at Macy's. For a while she stood behind the watch counter, and now she was in intimates. "Do you know how mortifying it is to look at women in their underwear all day?" she said, finally opening her eyes and noticing the box of dolls at her feet. She leaned forward, picked one up, turned it over a couple of times, raised and lowered its arms. "The really fat ones I can handle. It's the ones who think they're smaller than they are. Today, my god, you wouldn't believe it. I had this one, easily a 42D, who insists I put her in a 38C. She can't close the clasp of course, so I've got to yank it all out of shape to get it around her. And then she stands there admiring herself in the mirror, bulging out everywhere, the lace is about to rip, I don't even know how she can breathe, and you know what she says? Let's try a size smaller."

Paul had stopped paying her rent, but he still sent a check once a month to supplement her wages. He'd go on doing so until she retired, he suspected, and then he'd have to triple the amount. If she was going to thank him, it would probably be after he dropped dead.

"I wouldn't have recognized him in a million years," he said. What he couldn't explain was how uneasy he was made by the sight of the tubby old man with two pairs of glasses, and even more by the weird suspicion that he wasn't really Herman Fatts, or rather that Herman Fatts had transformed into someone entirely different, not over forty-five years but overnight. To distract himself he examined a few snapshots propped on a bookshelf, none of them in frames, all of them showing Reggie in stylish clothing, set off against natural scenery: waves on a beach, a waterfall surrounded by ferns, a field of young corn. Implied was the eye of the photographer—sappy, deluded, doomed. Paul hadn't met the new boyfriend yet, or even heard about him, but he had enough money, it seemed, to own at least a camera and a car. Paul gave him six months at most. "If I saw him on the street, I would have passed right by. Isn't that strange? Someone who was such a big part of our lives?"

"He wasn't a big part of *my* life," Reggie said. She was sitting up now, pulling each of the dolls out of the box in turn, examining it carefully from several angles, tipping it forward to make sure its eyes closed properly. "I hardly remember him."

"He was in our house every Friday night for at least five years. We saw him at the swim club every day in summer. We went to that hotel in the Catskills to watch him perform."

"He never paid any attention to me," Reggie said. "You were the one he always wanted to talk to. And mom, of course."

What Paul remembered was this: a thin, handsome neighbor, not much younger than his parents but unmarried, living with his widowed mother in an apartment building at the corner of Crown and Troy. No one seemed to know how he entered their lives. Maybe he'd filled a prescription for his mother or bought a fountain drink at Paul's father's drugstore. Maybe he'd joined Uncle Al's card game at the swim club. Maybe Paul's mother had heard him singing to himself in the vegetable market and invited him to dinner. However it happened, by the time Paul was seven or eight years old, Herman Fatts was a fixture at their table, in their living room, around their chairs beside the pool.

He worked in a furniture warehouse in Red Hook, but really he was an actor, waiting for his career to take off. After dinner he sang Bing Crosby tunes and delivered monologues from plays no one had ever heard of and then pretended to be Gene Autry in *The Last Round-Up*. He put on records and danced with Paul's mother around the coffee table. He spun stories of fighting Germans in France, though Paul's father said later, with an edge of spite out of character for him, that the closest Herman got to France was an outdoor café in Flatbush; he spent the war right there in Brooklyn, working in the same warehouse, which then stored uniforms and blankets.

But the stories mattered less to Paul than the way Herman would kneel and look him in the eye, the surprise of those dark brows and shadowed jaw coming down to his level. Herman didn't ask silly questions about what he wanted to be when he grew up or who he thought would win the pennant—the distracted, obligatory questions he was used to adults posing—but instead brought up serious matters he'd read about in the paper. What did Paul think about sending the boys to Korea? Was he scared of the Russians getting the bomb? Did he think flying saucers were real? Paul had few opinions about these things, but he'd try to answer anyway, muttering a few words about *War of the Worlds*, which he'd just read for the third time. And in the process he'd find himself growing confused, feeling even younger than he was, and smaller. The apartment, too, the building, the city, all of it so much smaller than he wanted it to be, the world so vast and indecipherable he felt dizzy trying to imagine it whole. His mother would laugh at his answers, but Herman would listen as if nothing he'd ever heard had been as interesting, encouraging him with occasional nods, and when Paul finally sputtered to a halt, would teach him a card trick. "You're a smart kid," he'd say when he left for the night. "A whole lot smarter than a forklift jockey like me."

And then, in 1953, Herman decided to make his break in the pictures. He packed up his belongings and bought train fare to Hollywood. Paul was twelve, a month away from his bar mitzvah, at which Herman had promised to sing. "Sorry, Paulie-pal," he said, with no more than a chuck on Paul's chin. "Duty calls. I'm tired of the small-time." And like that, he was gone. When the Dodgers left five years later, Paul had the feeling that California was swallowing everything and everyone he'd ever loved. In his mind it wasn't a state but a vortex, and he swore he'd never set foot within five hundred miles. For several weeks after Herman left he stayed away from the swim club. For a year he refused to go to the movies, to which his father had taken him every Sunday. But when he passed the local theater he couldn't help glancing at the posters and looking for Herman Fatts's face.

"I always thought he'd make it big. For a long time I expected to see his name in the papers."

"If he made it big you wouldn't have seen his name," Reggie said. "He would have changed it to something less ridiculous."

He went to the window to check on his car and was satisfied to see it sticking out into a lane of traffic, a significant presence, hazard lights blinking, other drivers easing around it. "What I don't understand is how he seemed to know Mom would be there. It's like he was waiting for her."

With a groan, Reggie raised the recliner, stood, carried the box to the bookshelf. "She doesn't know I have these, does she? I hope you didn't tell her you were giving them to me."

"I wonder if they kept in touch all this time," Paul said.

"If she asks for them, I'm not giving them back. They're mine now." She began arranging them in the same order in which his mother had had them arranged in the apartment in Forest Hills, which he guessed was exactly how they'd been arranged in the apartment in

Crown Heights. He knew their horrible faces better than he wanted to, the round, red cheeks, the pursed lips, the stiffly parted hair, and he couldn't imagine why Reggie would want to look at them every day. He was glad he'd no longer have to see them when he visited his mother.

"If so, why wouldn't she have mentioned him?"

Reggie glanced at him over her shoulder, with a sad little smile not so different from his mother's smirk, and it brought back again, now that he was primed for it, the feeling of shrinking in a universe ever expanding. "Oh, Paul," she said, with sympathy as surprising as a slap. "You could trade glasses for binoculars and still not see a thing. I envy you."

"I don't wear glasses," he said.

She turned her attention back to the box, set the last of the dolls on the shelf. Then she took a step away and studied them, hands on hips. "There's one missing."

"What don't I see?"

She faced him again, but now the sympathetic expression was gone, replaced by a ferocious one, face all pale angles under dark spiky hair. Even now, though, to Paul's disappointment, she looked a dozen years his junior. "What did you do with it? Did you keep it for yourself?"


His mother and Herman Fatts. He couldn't believe it. Or rather, he didn't want to believe it and tried his best not to before giving in. Believing, in any case, was better than picturing, which was what he did while driving uptown, fast, the Imperial keeping pace with the cabs on Eighth Avenue, charging through yellow lights, weaving around pedestrians, passing the entrance to the Lincoln Tunnel, which should have led him home.

Beside him on the passenger seat lay the rope of his mother's hair, white clumps braided around each other, the occasional black strand twisting through. He'd found it on his last sweep of the apartment before the movers arrived and couldn't decide whether or not his mother would want to hold onto it, or if it would be a painful reminder of healthier, stronger days. On the same sweep he'd come across the crucifix again, indignant once more at the thought of the nurse's aide—the lovely Jessica, who'd worn a tank-top to the interview, and a skirt so short he had to look away when she crossed her legs, who'd smiled at him with wide, pink, glossy lips—and again determined to throw it away. But when he reached the kitchen he had second thoughts and instead set it on the stove, leaving its fate to the new tenants. Now he wished he'd tossed it out the window, and the braided hair, too. The latter he balled in his fist when he got stuck at the intersection of Broadway and Amsterdam, and to his surprise it disappeared entirely in his grip. He smacked the steering wheel, and when he opened his hand, the braid sprang out, impossibly long, and settled across his lap.

Afternoons in the Crown Heights apartment, once idyllic in memory, now became sordid. There was Herman Fatts, several hours before heading to his swing shift at the warehouse, showing Paul the headshots he'd sent off to talent agents and theater companies, reading from scripts, while Paul's mother lounged on the sofa, shoes off, the hem of her dress at her knees. "Why don't you go out already," she'd eventually say. "It's too nice to be inside all the time." And without a thought about leaving Herman and his mother alone, Paul joined the punchball game in the neighborhood's vacant lot, his father behind the pharmacy counter two blocks away. Never once did he question Herman's abrupt departure, nor did he wonder about his father's brief, unexplained bitterness. That his mother stopped laughing he'd noticed only vaguely, thinking it had to do with the headaches his father tried to ease with a generous selection of pills. He'd paid so little attention to the world around him it was no wonder he never realized how little of it he could trust.

Dinner was over by the time he arrived at the Waterview Terrace, and the lobby was quiet. A few residents sat reading or snoring under lamps scattered around its edge, including Mrs. Randawaha, slumped in her chair, a book on the floor beside one of its wheels. He expected the aides behind the reception desk to stop him and ask where he was going before he reached the elevator, but they didn't even look up when he passed. Anger rose in step with his ascent, and by the time he made it to his mother's floor he was shaking with outrage, slapping the braid against his thigh, ready, finally, to say enough was enough, to cut all ambiguous ties. The Dodgers who'd abandoned him; Dylan who'd confused him; Jessica who'd tacked a crucifix over his mother's bed and quit after less than a month; Reggie who'd known Herman Fatts had been back in New York since the early eighties, who'd known he and their mother had reconnected a decade before their father died, who'd suggested the Waterview Terrace because she knew he lived there—all of them could go to hell. He'd never think a generous thought about anyone again.

He knocked hard enough to hurt his knuckles. It usually took his mother a few minutes to haul herself out of her chair and hobble across the apartment, longer if she had to find her cane, and he worried the wait would dampen his fury. But this time the door opened right away. And there was Herman Fatts, holding a finger to his lips. "Quiet, Paulie-pal," he whispered. "She's sleeping. Big day for her."

Now Paul could see in his face what he hadn't seen earlier: the handsome features slightly distorted by weight and gravity, the eyes that fixed on his with strict attentiveness, eyes Paul could still imagine gazing out from a movie screen. Given a moment he *might* have recognized Herman on the street, Herman wearing a puffy mask and a white wig. He thought he should imagine himself, as a boy, punching that handsome face, defending his father's honor, but mostly he saw it backlit by curtained windows, reciting lines from *Hedda Gabler*.

Herman reached out for the braid, and Paul relinquished it, with relief, before following him inside. There'd been changes in the apartment since this afternoon. Flowers in a glass vase on the coffee table, fruit in the china bowl on the counter, a woven blanket draped over the armchair into which Herman eased himself, dropping the last few inches. The bedroom door was open partway, and though it was dark, Paul could see a hump on one side of the bed, the rest empty and waiting. Herman was out of breath, his mouth open, huge belly heaving, and after a moment he started to cough. Let him choke, Paul thought, but half-heartedly, and immediately felt ridiculous. Herman was still wearing his cardigan and slippers, at least, and not, as Paul had been picturing with horror on the drive uptown, a bathrobe and nothing underneath. "Do you want some water?" he asked, but Herman waved the braid and gestured for him to sit.

What was happening to his anger? As usual, the moment he became aware of its power it began to slip away, to morph into the bewilderment that came to him more naturally, that made anger seem pointless. By the time he hit the couch cushions he felt drained and thirsty. He should have gotten water for them both. What good would shouting do? What purpose would condemnation serve? The questions that had seemed so important a few hours ago—about what had happened to Herman in Hollywood, about whether he'd ever made it into the pictures, about why he hadn't let Paul know he was back— meant nothing in this cramped space, with its undersized furniture and oversized TV: hardly more than a dressed-up hospital room, where his mother would wither and fade, and after her someone else, and someone again after that.

"Mitzi tells me," Herman said, hoarsely, and then cleared his throat. "She said you've been doing some acting."

"A little," he said. "At the Center. Nothing very good. Not like you."

"It's all relative," Herman said. "That's the only thing I learned in California. No matter how good you are, there's always someone better." He draped the braid over his knee and stroked it with a thumb. After a moment he leaned forward and lifted his second pair of glasses, giving Paul the serious look he'd so often turned on him as a boy. "Tell me, though. Does anything feel better than taking a bow and listening to applause?"

In five years Paul had been in as many productions, but he'd hardly mentioned them to his mother, and he'd never thought to invite her to one of his shows. He'd played a gay doctor, a witch hunter, a disgraced lawyer, and in the most baffling two months of his life, a mute slave named Lucky. As Sergeant Toomey, unstable and anti-Semitic, he'd spent the previous spring bullying Eugene, the play's hero, in a southern drawl Cynthia said wasn't the worst she'd ever heard. He'd had no training, hardly any direction, and he'd forgotten lines in at least three performances, once going utterly blank, staring at the female lead without moving or even blinking for so long that she rushed over to him, thinking he'd had a stroke. He once walked into a chair that had been set off its mark, knocking the wind out of him, but that time he carried on, delivering his lines doubled-over and croaking.

At first he told himself he did it to spend more time with Cynthia. But two years ago she'd had a falling-out with the company's director, and when she quit as costume designer Paul kept on. What he'd never imagined was how much he could enjoy being a man others feared, even for two hours at a time. He couldn't have known how energized he'd feel ordering a seventeen-year-old boy—the director's son—to stand at attention or drop to his chest and do push-ups in the rain. Those nights he came home with a jaw sore from working Toomey's Mississippi accent around his resistant mouth were some of the most satisfying he'd ever had.

And this is what he found himself explaining to Herman Fatts, who prompted him with questions that made him talk without restraint, without wondering how much he should say, how little sense any of it made. With his words came another feeling he'd forgotten, the torpor that follows release, his eyes pleasantly itchy, the couch cushions growing softer beneath him. "I'm not sadistic like Toomey," he said. "Or at least I don't think I am. But I understand why he goes crazy. Suddenly the world's so different. He's surrounded by these people who're nothing like the ones he's used to, the way they talk and act…It would make anyone a little nuts." He looked to Herman for confirmation and received it only in the form of steady eye-contact, the thumb still running over the braid. "No matter who I play," he went on, "I always seem to find something of myself in him. Who knew I had so many people inside me?"

Herman didn't answer, but he continued to give Paul that look of focused attention, of openness and generosity, that as a boy had made him wish, on multiple occasions, that Herman were his father, and not the man who stood behind a pharmacy counter all day and asked distracted questions about what Paul wanted to be when he grew up. Only now did it occur to him that he'd betrayed his father each time he'd wished it, and was betraying him again tonight. His father, short and mild-mannered, with a weak chin and wiry brows over eyes that blinked in puzzlement at the complicated world around him. His father who was capable of serious conversation only about baseball, who never took his mother abroad, who never brought her flowers or spoke a word of affection without undercutting it with a joke: *your mother's the most beautiful woman in the city,* he'd once said as the four of them— his mother carrying Reggie, Paul holding his father's hand—walked down a crowded street in the middle of summer, bare-shouldered girls passing on all sides, and then added, *too bad your father's farsighted.*

In the bedroom his mother stirred, and Herman, with effort, pulled himself up from the chair and crossed the room, his odd prancing steps, wide torso wobbling on too-thin legs, the braid flung over a shoulder. At the door he turned back and said, "Thanks for...you know. Not everyone would be so understanding." Before Paul could correct him, he went on. "I've missed you, Paulie-pal. I'm glad we'll be seeing more of each other."


The indolent feeling didn't leave him as he drove home, listening to a station that played rock songs from the sixties and seventies, songs he'd blindly dismissed at the time, scorning them without hearing a note. No Dylan songs came on, but he heard echoes of Dylan in plenty of others, simple drumbeats punctuated by attempts at poetry. He should have been hungry—all he'd eaten were the last egg and cheese biscuits in his mother's freezer—but he felt strangely engorged, as if he'd been stuffing his mouth non-stop since morning. The freeway was relatively empty, and he sailed west without having to brake, the Imperial, shocks recently replaced, floating as smoothly as it had twenty years ago when he brought it home from the lot.

By the time he left Waterview Terrace he found that he had forgiven his mother and Herman, without having intended to do so. Why begrudge them any moments of happiness now, when they had so few left? And because it was easy, he also forgave Reggie for lying, Jessica for leaving, himself for having failed to stand up for his father. After all, a forgiving nature was one of the things his father had passed along to him, as well as his weak chin. Within days of the Dodgers leaving for L.A., while Paul was still grief-stricken and outraged, his father was talking about Duke Snider's suntan and the odds that Koufax would marry a movie star. Aside from his one spiteful comment about Herman's war stories, he never said another word against the man, nor against his unfaithful wife, whom he'd loved and cared for in his limited fashion for the rest of his days.

And Paul had learned other things from his father, too. For one: don't take anything for granted. On his way out of the city he stopped at a florist's shop and bought Cynthia a bouquet. By the time he made it to his exit he was thinking less about Herman Fatts and his mother than about Cynthia's reaction when he handed her the flowers, though most likely she was already asleep. He was thinking, too, about booking them a trip to France.

When he turned onto the road that skirted Greystone, he forgot to slow down, and that was a mistake. Before he'd passed the first building—a newer one, still in use—red lights twirled in his rearview mirror. The Imperial made a little choking sound when he cut the ignition. The officer took his time getting out of the cruiser. While he waited, Paul stared up at the lit windows of the asylum—no: hospital, he thought; just a hospital like any other—in hope that someone might look out.

# NOCTURNE FOR LEFT HAND

ON EITHER SIDE OF *him, rapt attention. Maybe even rapture. The orchestra charges into the allegro of the final movement, and he can feel the kids—no longer children but always "the kids" in his mind—bracing themselves, leaning forward in their seats, Kyle's elbows on his knees, Joy's hands pressed between crossed thighs.*

*They are listening to Mahler's Fifth Symphony, in the second tier of Avery Fisher Hall, and even from this distance he can see sweat shining on the bald spot of the guest conductor, a short, round Argentinean bristling with dark hair on cheeks, chin, and neck, everywhere but a clear circle on his crown. All evening his movements have been jerky and frenetic, pained even, as if his joints are stiffening as the concert proceeds. Whenever the music grows softer, his grunts are audible over the hum of oboe or the whistle of flute, and between movements he appears on the verge of collapse. Now, when he jabs his baton at the brass section, and then lifts, lifts, lifts, Kyle makes a move as if to stand, and Joy claps a hand over her open mouth.*

*This night is everything Paul has hoped it might be, everything he has imagined, not just in the hours leading up, but for years prior. It's just luck that both kids are visiting at the same time, luck that they have an evening free from seeing old friends on the same night Cynthia has a school function she can't skip, luck that he's been able to get tickets at the last minute. When, that morning, he casually suggested the three of them go into the city, catch an early dinner and a concert, they didn't deflect, didn't make excuses or roll* eyes or exchange skeptical glances. "Sounds lovely," Joy said, and Kyle agreed. "Man, I miss New York," he said. "Baltimore just doesn't cut it."

In their mid-twenties, they have become urbane, sophisticated, cultured. They travel regularly. They dress well, Kyle in slacks and wingtips, Joy in a sleeveless black dress, too short, maybe, but otherwise elegant. On the drive in they talked about other concerts they've seen in the last year—a Cuban jazz trio in a Los Angeles club, the Czech National String Quartet playing Dvořák and Smetana in a Prague chapel. At dinner they ordered the most unusual items on the menu, pappardelle in rabbit ragu, trout poached with sage and blueberries. They have seen interesting movies, have read interesting books. They tell stories about interesting friends. They seem to enjoy Paul's company. And now they are moved by Mahler's heroic composition, by the conductor's maniacal energy, by the orchestra's delicate skill and rousing spirit. What else can he ask for?

And yet, sitting in seat 13, row CC, second tier of Avery Fisher Hall, he is terribly bored. Bored! He has never been so bored in his life. The exhilaration of the music bores him. The precision of all those violins moving in synch bores him. Even the conductor's hysterics, the wild flinging of his baton, the sweat matting hair around his bald spot, all of it strikes Paul as flaccid and predictable, not an original gesture in his entire repertoire, every moment studied and rehearsed, calculated to bring Paul's stepson to his feet, to make his stepdaughter cover her mouth with a lovely slender hand. You're so boring! he wants to shout at the conductor when he slices the baton through the air for the finale, at the musicians when they hit the last note and freeze, at the audience members when they jump to their feet and cheer. Boring, boring, boring!

He even wants to say it to his stepchildren, these beautiful young people just embarking on adult life, armed already with sophisticated tastes and admirable habits for which he has never allowed himself to take credit but now gives himself all the blame. What sort of people might they be if he hadn't interfered? Don't do it, he wants to tell them. Don't wear slacks and elegant dresses and listen to boring old Mahler. Don't read interesting books and talk about them with your interesting friends. Stop now while you have the chance. Do something wild and reckless and unexpected. Track wildebeest migration in the Serengeti. Prospect for precious metals atop *secluded Alaskan mountains. Knock over liquor stores to support a gambling addiction. Anything. Just, for God's sake, don't be like me.*

*Because yes, of course, his real boredom is with himself. He has felt it nagging, with increasing urgency, all evening. In the car, when he struggled to find something meaningful to add to the kids' lively conversation and then, failing, fell silent. In the restaurant, where he ordered the same scallops with asparagus he'd ordered a month earlier, before going to the ballet with Cynthia. And now, edging down the aisle, creeping along with the buzzing crowd, nodding in agreement that this was the best performance of Mahler's Fifth he has ever heard. He wishes he could say something shocking and original. He wishes he could provide the kids stories to tell their friends. Their real father, at least, has been inconsistent enough to keep them wondering about him all these years. What thought have they ever given Paul when he's stepped out of sight?*

*Joy takes his arm when they reach the stairs and holds onto him as they descend to the lobby. "That was delightful," she says, and he has the feeling that she has been thinking the phrase over for some time, maybe planning to say it since before the concert started. Even her smile seems practiced. "We should do this every time I'm home."*

*Kyle adds, as they push through glass doors into the courtyard, the fountain lit up and burbling high over their heads, "I'll never hear that fourth movement the same way again. The CD doesn't do it justice."*

*The night is warm and clear, a few stars visible despite the city's glare, and it seems to Paul that he is glimpsing the depths between them, far into that dark empty place. On and on it goes. One dull life leading to another. What crimes he has committed.*

*When they reach the parking garage, however, the kids hesitate. Joy takes her hand from his arm. Kyle, he notices, has unbuttoned the second button on his shirt and rolled his sleeves. Their expressions are no longer placid and satisfied but oddly expectant, maybe uneasy. "Thanks for this, Paul," Kyle says. "It's been great, really. But—"*

*"We're heading downtown," Joy says, and takes a step backward. Something in her voice has changed. There's impatience in it, defensiveness, and he guesses that this is the first honest thing she's said to him all day. "Some friends are meeting us."*

*"But the car," he says, and gestures at the garage. Wearing the short black dress, he realizes now, had nothing to do with the symphony, or with him. All evening her thoughts have been elsewhere. He knows nothing of their lives, not really, except that they are nothing like his own. "I mean, I drove you—"*

*"We'll take the train home," she says. "Don't worry about us."*

*"Downtown?" he asks. He knows he shouldn't hope for them to invite him along. If they did, he couldn't promise to be as interesting as the most tedious of their friends, though he might order a drink he's never had before. He shouldn't, but he can't help it. He has never wanted anything more.*

*But already their backs are turned. They are walking away from him. As soon as they reach Broadway, they'll slip into the crowd and disappear, claimed by the city he has taught them to love, by the interesting lives he has wished upon them. "Enjoy yourselves," he calls after them. "I'll leave the back door unlocked." Kyle gives a thumbs-up without glancing around. Joy peeks at her watch. Paul hands the parking attendant his claim ticket and, picturing all the roads that lead away from here, tries to plot a new route home.*

# BETWEEN YOU AND ME

## 1999

PAUL WAS TIRED OF changes, but changes kept coming. His firm merged with a larger one for the third time in a decade, and once again the legal team was split between semi-autonomous departments with competing agendas and poor communication. Paul found himself working on contracts with an attorney half his age, a girl hardly out of law school, who pestered him constantly to start filing reports on his computer and sending them to her electronically. He still wrote out contracts by hand and had a secretary type them. He didn't see the point of sending an email to someone who was three steps down the hall, and who was in his office all the time anyway, hopping onto the corner of his desk, laughing at the dust on his computer's keyboard, asking if he knew how to turn it on. When he complained, subtly, to the chief administrative officer, a man he'd known for twenty years and considered an ally, musing over lunch that he found it strange when two people were given equal authority though one had far more experience, the only response he received was a long, reproachful silence.

The whole situation depressed him, and on weekends he sulked visibly enough for Cynthia to suggest he start seeing a counselor. Instead, he went to talk to Mike Molinoff, a recent acquaintance— no, friend; he could call him a friend—who also happened to be assistant rabbi at Temple Neveh Shalom. Rabbi Mike's office was in the synagogue's basement, whose asbestos ceiling had been ripped out a decade ago and never replaced. Wires dangled from a grid of exposed beams and pipes overhead, and the air below smelled of mildew. The office was cramped, hardly enough room for a desk and two folding chairs, a metal bookshelf stuffed mostly with bulging manila folders, the only adornment on the walls a framed degree from the Jewish Theological Seminary.

While he was peeking in, and thinking about retracing his steps to the parking lot, a hand clapped his back, hard, right between the shoulder blades. The mint he'd been sucking blew out of his lips onto the floor.

"What a nice surprise," Rabbi Mike said. "Playing hooky? You must've known how badly I needed an excuse to reschedule my morning."

"If you're too busy—"

"Forget it," Rabbi Mike said. "Hospital visits. Worst way to start the week. You saved my Monday." He nudged Paul out of the doorway and cleared one of the folding chairs, also stacked with folders. "Welcome to my humble—what? Den? Trust me, it's even worse than it looks. When the heat's on, those pipes rattle like crazy." On his way around the desk he crunched Paul's mint, which stuck to the bottom of his shoe. "What the hell? I swear, no one ever vacuums this place." He scraped his sole on the edge of a garbage can, then threw himself into his chair, clapped his hands. "Paul Haberman. In the shul. What a surprise. Like I said."

"I know I should come to services more often—"

"Forget it," Rabbi Mike said again. "Some people need the structure. You know, predictability. Good for those of us without imagination. But there are other ways of getting in touch with the Almighty."

Sensible. That's how Paul had come to think of Rabbi Mike. Not brilliant or mystical, just equipped with an uncanny ability to say exactly what needed to be said. He was in his late thirties, round-faced and clean-shaven, with black curls that covered his ears and touched the top of his collar, a pair of tortoiseshell glasses less rabbinic than beatnik. In the five months Paul had known him he'd been talking about going on a diet, losing fifteen pounds, but if anything he'd put on another ten. Paul wondered if congregants took him less seriously because his belly strained his shirt buttons, but Rabbi Mike had a way of tilting his head when he looked at you, a finger of each hand pressed to his lips, that made it seem as if his eyes were focused not on the surface of your skin but an inch or two beyond, somewhere inside your skull.

"So I take it this isn't a social call."

"I guess not," Paul said. "I'm here for your..." He couldn't bring himself to use the word "counseling," so instead finished, "professional expertise."

Rabbi Mike cracked his knuckles and sat up straight. What did he expect Paul to divulge? Marital trouble? Sexual problems? Kid with a drug addiction? Go ahead, his look seemed to say. I've heard it all.

"Nothing too exciting. Just some difficulty at work. I could use advice. Perspective."

The change in Rabbi Mike's expression was almost imperceptible, but Paul caught it all the same: shoulders sinking, smile flickering downward at the corners. Disappointment? Annoyance? Would he rather be making rounds at the hospital, offering words of comfort to the sick and dying? "All right, then," he said. "This is why I get paid the big bucks. Fire away."

Paul had gotten to know Rabbi Mike at the gym of the Whippany JCC. Three Sunday afternoons in a row they'd ended up on adjacent treadmills, Paul lasting half an hour on a mild incline, Rabbi Mike ten minutes on flat ground. While Paul finished, Rabbi Mike mopped his face with a handkerchief and chatted. "This is my wife's idea," he said. "Thinks I'm headed for a heart attack at forty. I try to tell her not to worry. My people have always been round. My grandfather? Five-two and two hundred pounds, and he lived to ninety-four." He reminded Paul of men he'd grown up around in Crown Heights. For one, his accent was pure Brooklyn. But even more, he spoke with an easy familiarity, as if he took it for granted that you'd known each other since one or the other of you was a few days old. "If anything's going to give me a heart attack," Rabbi Mike said, still breathing hard, "it's walking on this death machine."

One afternoon, Paul was still in the parking lot, looking for his car, when Rabbi Mike came outside, hair wet, enormous gym bag slung over his shoulder. Paul had been up and down every aisle but couldn't spot his Imperial among all the squat, sloping Toyotas and Hondas, Acuras and Lexuses, which were distinguishable only by the college logos stuck to their back windows: this one's daughter went to Penn; this one's son, a dolt, went to Montclair State. And only when he saw one with stickers from Williams and Rutgers did he remember he'd driven Cynthia's Accord. His own car, now twenty years old, was in the shop with transmission problems. The Baron had finally retired, and his new mechanic was young, humorless, and never remembered Paul's name. Along with the transmission, the car also needed a new alternator, he said, and quoted a ridiculous price before suggesting Paul consider trading it in. Paul spent an afternoon looking at *Consumer Reports*, which recommended a variety of squat, sloping Japanese models, and then called the mechanic and told him to go ahead and make the repairs.

Rabbi Mike hailed him from two aisles away. "You in a hurry?" The big bag pulled him sideways. What did he have in there, a spare Torah? He couldn't have needed much gear for his ten minute stroll. "Feel like grabbing a bite on the way home?" It wasn't quite four-thirty. When Paul hesitated, he added, "All she's going to feed me is rice and steamed broccoli. I'm dying for a burger."

He ate steak fries, too, and a big salad with French dressing, from which he scraped off the bacon bits, plus two bottles of Heineken. Whenever the waiter came near, he'd call to him for something he'd forgotten—ketchup, salt, extra dressing—and then needle him about how long the food took to arrive. Paul guessed this was his way of joking around, though his demands had an edge of impatience to them. "Got to keep them on their toes," Rabbi Mike said, when the waiter stepped out of view. Paul kept up with him bite for bite, and afterward spent an hour groaning on the toilet. When his heartburn passed, guilt replaced it. The next week he spent a full hour on the treadmill.

But from then on he and Rabbi Mike stopped at the steakhouse on Route 10 every Sunday afternoon, though Paul limited himself to a few onion rings and a sour pickle. At first Rabbi Mike did most of the talking, which set Paul at ease—even more so when Rabbi Mike started complaining about his job. Neveh Shalom had never had an assistant rabbi before. The congregation had doubled in size over the past decade, and the long-time rabbi, David Aronson, was already past retirement age. "But Aronson doesn't want to give up anything," Rabbi Mike said. "He wants to do all the services, all the bar mitzvahs, all the funerals. All I do is give speeches to the Men's Club and discipline fifth graders who misbehave in Hebrew school."

As it happened, Cynthia had served on the committee that had hired Rabbi Mike—she was president of Hadassah now, and a member of the synagogue's board of directors—and Paul had heard more about the process than he first let on. He knew, for example, that Rabbi Mike hadn't been the committee's top choice—in fact, he was third out of three finalists—but he was the only one willing to accept the salary. The only one, that is, who didn't negotiate at all. According to Cynthia, they had no doubt he was knowledgeable and intelligent, a dynamic speaker and an accomplished scholar, but his manner was brusque. The congregation was used to Aronson's paternal generosity, his patient smile, his sagely stooped posture. The committee members weren't convinced Rabbi Mike would be effective at the human side of the job. They made no commitment to promote him when Aronson finally retired.

"If I have to listen to his greeting every week for the next two years, I swear," Rabbi Mike said through a mouthful of burger. "'Good evening, my friends,'" he went on, his impression sounding less like Aronson's sober, resonant voice than that of a mediocre Elvis impersonator, "'and thank you for being with us during these beautiful and troubled times.' Puke." Aronson was as inspiring as gelatin, Rabbi Mike said, and as ambiguously kosher. He delivered sermons as if they were news reports, and he handled the Torah like a piece of luggage, wrestling it into place and jabbing it with the silver pointer. "You know how he's always got his eyes closed when the cantor's singing? That's not rapture. The guy's figured out how to sleep standing up."

Though Cynthia went to services every Friday night and most Saturday mornings, Paul joined her only when she pleaded or threatened—"If I keep showing up alone, all the widowers are going to start hitting on me"—and even then he did so reluctantly. Just stepping into the sanctuary filled him with impatience, recalling long mornings in uncomfortable clothes, when his mother would pinch his leg if he started to squirm. He'd never minded the solemn opening prayers that prepared him to daydream for the following two hours or the rousing Adon Olam with which all the congregants leapt out of their seats and headed for the brownies and grape juice in the ballroom next door. If he could have snoozed or read a book through the middle part—the endless succession of Torah readings, the silent Amidah during which people showed off their piety by standing and swaying far longer than necessary—he might have come more often. As it was, he spent most Friday nights at home, watching old movies.

He did happen to be present, though, on one of the Fridays when Aronson relinquished the bimah to Rabbi Mike, whose bulk made it look diminutive, flimsy as cardboard in front of the sprawl of his suit. Aronson looked just as insubstantial, thin as a stick on a high chair beside the Ark's rippled velvet curtain, his face almost as pale as his white beard. Paul's ordinary tendency would have been to appreciate his dignified lack of distinction, but he had Rabbi Mike's words in his head—*as inspiring as gelatin*—which made him look at the old rabbi with mild disparagement. He also enjoyed the sly power of having a secret over him: "This is just between you and me," Rabbi Mike said at the steakhouse every Sunday afternoon. "As far as he knows, I lick the ground he walks on."

In any case, he preferred Rabbi Mike's way of leading the service, not bothering with the responsive readings of English translations Aronson indulged at length, cutting off the silent Amidah when a dozen people were still standing and swaying. He snapped his fingers when he announced the page numbers for the next prayer, and when the cantor's singing veered from melody to unnecessary flourish, he stared straight ahead and drummed his thumb on his thigh. His brusqueness was more asset than liability, as far as Paul was concerned, though when it came time for the sermon he slowed his pace, approaching the bimah with a new kind of concentration, taking off his glasses and wiping them on his multicolored tallis while glancing from one side of the sanctuary to the other. Ten seconds went by, twenty. He set his elbows on the bimah, adjusted the microphone. People shifted in their seats, rustled the pages of their siddurs, coughed. Only when it seemed he wouldn't say a word did he finally replace his glasses and begin in a voice not much more than a whisper, making people lean forward in their seats and adjust their hearing aids.

Paul enjoyed the sermon, despite its being pitched at the young people in the room. Rabbi Mike began with a description of the comic book characters he loved as a boy: "Not just any superhero, mind you. I wasn't into the Flash or the Green Lantern. How excited could you get about a guy with a light bulb on his finger? I'm talking Marvel Comics. Spiderman. The Fantastic Four. The Incredible Hulk. Couldn't wait to get my hands on the next installment." What he loved about these characters, he said, was that they were just ordinary people who'd been touched by something special, who were called to action by a world in need, who took on fighting for justice reluctantly but with great sacrifice, who kept their power secret from even those closest to them.

And here he made an impressive turn, reminding Paul why, despite his weight and his shaggy hair, he was at the front of the room. "Ordinary people tasked with impossible challenges, their powers as much an affliction as a gift. These are the superheroes we know, the ones we need in our lives, and their stories are what give us a glimpse of God's presence in the world. Just think about Moses in today's Torah portion, with his speech impediment, his reluctance to believe in his abilities, his sudden outbursts of anger..."

What Paul admired most was the performance. He'd become sensitive in his acting years to the nuances of playing a role. He took note, for example, of the way Rabbi Mike stood increasingly straighter as he went on and how his voice gradually rose, accentuating the rhythm of his words, until he was nearly shouting at the end: "Each of you is Moses. Each of you knows what is being asked of you—by your families, by your communities, by your planet, by your God—and each of you can heed the call if you choose."

It was a rousing finish, and a few people forgot themselves and clapped before the cantor started the next prayer. Cynthia whispered, "I knew we hired him for a reason." Rabbi Mike, looking drained, went back to drumming his thigh. At the kiddush, congregants crowded around him by the food table, where he stood stiffly, arms crossed over his chest, answering questions with a dismissive shrug, occasionally reaching out for a cookie. Paul felt his own waistband pressing into his middle, and when Cynthia offered him a brownie, he turned it down. Eventually he caught Rabbi Mike's eye and gave him a thumb's-up. Rabbi Mike winked. In a corner of the ballroom, old Rabbi Aronson sat alone, nibbling cheese.

Soon after, Paul told Rabbi Mike what he knew about his prospects for landing the head rabbi position, about the board's concern that he couldn't handle the human side of the job. He encouraged him to make personal connections in the congregation, to smile more often, to kiss a few babies. "You know, put on a show," he said. He may have been betraying Cynthia's confidence, but friendship deserved honesty, he thought, and anyway, if the information improved Rabbi Mike's image, it would benefit everyone. Still, he added afterward, "Just don't let on that it came from me."

"If they wanted some kind of teddy bear they should have hired one," Rabbi Mike grumbled, biting a steak fry in half and then calling out to the waiter that his burger was undercooked. "You call this medium? It's still squirming." Still, he thanked Paul and told him he owed him. "I'll put in a good word with the big guy," he said, and pointed up.

To help bolster his standing in the community, Paul convinced Rabbi Mike to audition for a part in the JCC's spring theater production, an adaptation of *Cat on a Hot Tin Roof*, set not on a plantation in the deep south but in Frankfurt in 1934. He didn't see the point of re-imagining Big Daddy as a wealthy Jewish merchant whose fortune is threatened by the rise of Hitler, but the director, Riva Edelstein, insisted she understood what their audience wanted. She also insisted on playing Maggie opposite Paul's Brick, and it was torment to see her spilling out of a chemise for six evening performances and two matinees, to have her meaty hands spread on his chest and her hot breath in his ear, shouting what was supposed to be a sultry whisper: *You've got a nice smell about you*, or, *I know something that'll make you feel cool and fresh.*

"She's the spitting image of Elizabeth Taylor," Rabbi Mike huffed, out of breath, on the treadmill the Sunday after a rehearsal. "Only in the wrong movie. She got it mixed up with *Who's Afraid of Virginia Woolf?*"

"Maybe that should be the fall production," Paul said. "We'll set it in Spain during the Inquisition."

"I was thinking *Oedipus Rex*. In Jerusalem, 1948."

"You'd make a good father-murdering, mother-loving king."

"You can have it. I'll take over lead when you retire."

Riva cast Rabbi Mike as Gooper, Brick's conniving brother, who schemes to turn Big Daddy's money over to the Nazis. "Perfect for me," he said. "It's preparation. Just wait till my sister tries to get ahold of our old man's will." Together he and Paul convinced Riva to drop her awful German accent and lie with her knees flat so she didn't flash the first row. After rehearsal, too, they often stopped for a meal, and though Rabbi Mike had a natural presence on stage, knew how to project his voice, he still asked Paul for tips—how best to memorize his lines, how to get into character—which flattered Paul enough to make him forget he'd never had any formal training. They'd discuss their characters' motivations and psychology and analyze the play's themes and moral complexities, and during these talks Paul would occasionally be reminded that Rabbi Mike was indeed a rabbi, that despite his youth and his size he had insight into the workings of mind and heart that made Paul feel like a child. "I know what I know," he said when they were puzzling over what made the play so powerful, what had kept it on stage for more than forty years. "That's knowledge.

I *feel* what I know. That's wisdom."

And then Paul would wonder what he was doing with a rabbi in a steakhouse on Route 10, what he could possibly offer him. Rabbis needed friends like anyone else, he supposed, but he wished he had some response other than a stupefied nod. A minute later Rabbi Mike was talking about Riva Edelstein's mottled thighs—"I don't know how you'll stand to look at those things up close. I'd rather stick a fork in my eye"—and Paul abandoned his doubts.

On stage Rabbi Mike's presence had a way of making him simultaneously confident and humble, and even with Riva's awkward revisions the play was the company's best yet. At the cast party, Rabbi Mike toasted Paul and called him the star of the show, and though his voice was hoarse, his armpit sore from hobbling around on Brick's crutch all evening, he stayed until Riva started turning out the lights and shooing everyone toward the door. The following Friday, Rabbi Mike led services again and referenced the play in his sermon, describing what he found universal about Brick's suffering: that in trying to bury uncomfortable feelings, to shun painful truths, he only intensifies them. His drinking, his difficulty connecting with his family, his avoidance of intimacy with his wife, are simply symptoms of his inner strife. "We've all got secrets, and thoughts we're ashamed of, and aspects of our character we'd rather not face. But only if we can be honest with ourselves—and with God—will we be free of those burdens and fully present to the people we love."

The truth was, Paul didn't actually hear the sermon. Around that time he'd been renting classic horror films from the thirties and forties, which he'd been afraid to watch as a boy, and that night, as soon as Cynthia's car pulled out of the driveway, he put on *Jekyll and Hyde*—the 1941 version, starring Spencer Tracy—and settled on the couch with a bowl of microwave popcorn, which at first he only salted and then, after a few bites, covered with more butter than it needed. Though the film didn't frighten him—if anything, he found it dull and plodding— he couldn't help recoiling every time Jekyll's eyebrows began to bush out, his mouth opening into a lecherous sneer. What bothered him was how much Hyde resembled the uncle who'd left Paul and his sister his inheritance. Jekyll didn't transform from a good man into an evil one; he changed from an uptown goy into a Lower East Side Jew. It was an insult—just because a person was ugly meant he was a killer?—and Paul found himself growing angry each time Hyde appeared. Before the film was two-thirds through, he pulled out the tape and switched on the news.

Cynthia came home an hour later, flushed and smiling, the straps of her dress digging into the soft flesh of her shoulders. "My husband, praised from the bimah," she said, kicking off her shoes and dropping onto the couch. He rubbed her feet as she described the sermon. "What shameful thoughts do *you* have?" she asked, stretching her arms over her head and letting her knees fall apart. He thanked Rabbi Mike silently, pushed away the image that sprang to mind—of Riva Edelstein beckoning in her white chemise—and leaned in his wife's direction.


It was a little more than two weeks later that Paul visited Rabbi Mike in his office. "I'm not sure what I expect you to tell me," he said, perched on the folding chair in front of the desk. "I guess it would be nice to know I'm not crazy. That it's reasonable to be so bothered by it all. And maybe if there's a way I can learn to manage…I don't know. I should probably just come listen to your sermons."

Already he regretted having started. To speak his troubles out loud made them sound petty and childish, something he might have brought to a grade-school principal. This morning he'd called in to work, claiming to have an unexpected doctor's appointment, and his fellow contracts attorney—her name was Katherine Harrow but she insisted he call her Kat—had been perfectly pleasant and considerate, saying she hoped it was nothing serious, that he should stay home if he needed rest. But the thought of her in the office on her own for hours, taking all their calls and answering questions he might have fielded agitated him enough that he felt his weight shifting forward toward his feet, the impulse to run to the train station nearly making him stand. What was he doing here, wasting the morning, when he should have been at work, protecting his livelihood?

By contrast, Rabbi Mike had settled into a posture of infinite patience, eyes locked on Paul, forehead lined just enough to give a sense of concentration—so different from the frustrated drumming of his thumb while the cantor sang his meandering tunes. Was this the real Rabbi Mike, or another performance? If he was bored, Paul couldn't tell. It was what made him so convincing during his sermons, so natural on stage: in moments like these, whatever he projected on the surface was all you could see.

"I've been doing the job since she was in pigtails," he went on, staring up at the criss-crossing pipes overhead, the rusty joints, the tangled wires—the innards of the building not meant for his eyes. "How can someone half my age think she knows more about the industry than me? No offense to young people," he added quickly, but Rabbi Mike showed no sign of being offended. "She says I haven't kept up with the times, that I don't understand all the changes. I *have* kept up. I just don't think all the changes are necessary."

"I know what I know," Rabbi Mike said. "I *feel* what I—"

"I told her as much," Paul said, suddenly irritated. Was this his only line? "But she doesn't listen."

And then Rabbi Mike was standing, holding out a hand as if to usher Paul away. In an instant, shame, that ubiquitous fish, swallowed the worm of his anger whole. Why couldn't he have more profound problems to discuss? Why couldn't he have kept his mouth shut? "What do you say to taking a walk?" Rabbi Mike asked. "I could use a coffee. They've got some in the front office, but it's sludge by now. There's a diner down the street. Not much better, but, you know, nice to get out of my—what?" He gestured at the walls, the gutted ceiling, the folding chairs. "My palace."

When they were on the sidewalk, Rabbi Mike stroked his chin, gave Paul a quick glance, and said, "Tell me. This new co-worker of yours—she's attractive?"

"For a toddler," Paul said.

The rabbi's laughter was forced and brief. "Seriously. She's not a bad-looking woman."

"Sure," Paul said. "But that doesn't have anything to do—"

"She's got a pretty face?"

"It's not terrible."

"What's nice about it? Big round eyes? Firm lips?"

"The lips are good. And the cheekbones, I suppose."

Without warning, Rabbi Mike put out an arm that Paul walked into, and only then did he realize they were at an intersection, cars rushing at them. "What about the body?" Rabbi Mike asked.

The light changed, and Paul stepped gingerly off the curb. "I've never noticed."

This time Rabbi Mike gave a genuine laugh. "Just like I never noticed the new doors on the ark are plastic. Or that my salary's half what they pay Aronson, or my office is a quarter the size of his. She's got a nice body, yes?"

"Better than the face," Paul said. They'd reached the diner, and Rabbi Mike held the door for him. He wanted to head straight for the bathroom. It hadn't been terribly hot outside, but his face was sweating, and he would have liked to wipe it off or douse it in cold water. But Rabbi Mike had him by the elbow, leading him to a booth in back. He'd noticed the rabbi's wedding ring on plenty of occasions, but only now did it occur to him to wonder why he'd never heard more than a few words about his wife and kids. Did he talk so little about Cynthia?

"So she's got a chest worth looking at," Rabbi Mike said, squeezing, with difficulty, into the vinyl seat, sucking in his belly to keep it from scraping against the table.

"Not huge or anything. Well proportioned."

"Then it's the legs. That's what gets you."

"The legs," Paul repeated, as if hypnotized. "She likes to show them off."

"And you can't help staring at them."

A waitress came to the table, as old as Paul and missing a tooth on her lower jaw, her bottom lip dipping into the empty space. They ordered coffee, and as she started to walk away, Rabbi Mike called her back. "Did I say I was finished?" She blinked at him. He scanned the menu and said to Paul, "I'm going to be good today. You'll be proud of me." And to the waitress, sharply, "Yogurt and fruit. No honeydew. I'm allergic. Anything for you?"

Paul declined.

"I hope it won't take all day this time." When she left them, he smiled sheepishly and adjusted his glasses. "Last week it took forty-five minutes to get a bagel. Anyway. Where were we?"

"I forget," Paul said. He was used to the way Rabbi Mike spoke to servers by now, but he didn't think he'd ever be able to hear the impatient, barking commands without cringing and looking down at his silverware.

"Your co-worker's legs," Rabbi Mike said. "Shapely? Slim ankles, long calves, nice toned thighs?"

"She runs at lunchtime," Paul said.

"So you spend a lot of time looking at them. And I'm guessing you spend some time thinking about them. In your office. When you come home. These legs are in your mind a good part of every day."

Paul shrugged. The window beside him was grimy, smeared with fingerprints. A few dark men loitered outside the store across the street, a little market that had recently begun selling shawarma and hummus along with beer and cigarettes. The road itself had been called Randall Avenue when he'd first moved in with Cynthia, but several years ago it had been renamed Martin Luther King, Jr., Boulevard. The changes were too many to list. Among them, that all the hair on his belly had turned white; that he had to take pills for cholesterol and blood pressure, plus melatonin to sleep; that he'd awoken one day to find himself approaching sixty years old.

"You don't have to be embarrassed about it," Rabbi Mike said. "It's perfectly natural. Here you've got this lovely young woman, half your age, and she comes into your office, what, three times a day, and maybe she even sits on your desk, so those legs she's so proud of are right in front of you, a foot from your face, almost like she's tempting you to reach out and stroke them."

"More like five times a day," Paul said.

The waitress came back with their coffee and Rabbi Mike's food. The rabbi made her wait while he pushed the fruit around the bowl, a couple of sliced strawberries, shriveled red grapes, hunks of pineapple.

"You didn't sneak any honeydew in here, did you? It'll make my throat close right up." Then a little smile. "I shouldn't have told you that. Now you can get back at me for lousy tips."

When he was satisfied that nothing in the bowl would kill him, he forked several bites into his mouth and for a minute was so absorbed in chewing that Paul thought he might be able to nudge him away from the thrust of their conversation, divert it toward loftier topics. "That sermon you gave a while back," he said. "The one about Spiderman and Moses." Rabbi Mike kept chewing, and when he finished the fruit, he spooned half the bowl of yogurt into his mouth, then washed it down with a colossal gulp of coffee. "You said something about the power each of us has—"

"Forget Spiderman," Rabbi Mike snapped. His vexed look was softened only by the flecks of yogurt on his chin. "That's kid's stuff. I'm trying to talk to you like a grown-up." Paul raised his coffee to his lips and kept it there. But he couldn't swallow any and instead let it flow into his mouth and back into the cup. "This is what I'm hearing. Five times a day these gorgeous legs, toned by running, are right in front of you, and you can't help imagining what it might be like to reach out and touch them, or maybe even to spread them apart and see what's in between—"

"I don't think—"

"There's nothing to be ashamed of," Rabbi Mike said. "Anybody in your situation would feel the same way. You've been doing your job for twenty-five years, and suddenly this woman comes along with skills you don't have, flaunting her perfect legs and her youth and her power. She'll be around long after you're gone, and in her eyes you're as up-to-date as an abacus and as virile as an office chair, and you don't know whether you want to slap her or shtup her—"

"I don't want—"

"Because probably you want to do both at the same time. I'm sure I would."

"I never thought about it," Paul said.

"The best thing you can do is be honest. Take control of your emotions. Otherwise you'll just stay mad at yourself."

"Who says I'm mad at myself?"

"You're depressed, right? Same difference."

Why did he care what the name of the road had become, or who'd bought the shop across the street? Why should it suddenly bother him that a synagogue he hardly ever attended might one day be taken over by this fat young rabbi with yogurt on his chin?

"Okay," he said.

"Okay what?"

"So maybe it's true."

"What is?"

"What you said."

"I need to hear you say it."

"Jesus."

Rabbi Mike laughed heartily now, the kind of laughter they'd shared in the Route 10 steakhouse after working out in the gym or rehearsing their play. But Paul had a feeling this was the last time he'd hear it. "He's a whole separate matter. For another day, maybe. Just get it out."

"I want to shtup her and slap her," Paul said, louder than he meant to.

Rabbi Mike leaned back in the booth and smiled, but his smile was a patronizing one, no longer chummy and familiar, no longer suggesting they shared similar thoughts. Had that been the performance all along? Paul felt oddly sleepy, though it was only ten in the morning. It had been foolish of him to imagine they were equals, a man of God and Torah and a contracts lawyer who played the lead role in amateur productions at the JCC.

"But here's the thing, Paul," Rabbi Mike said. "You can't do either. No matter how much you might want to. What you *can* do is show her you're competent, that you work hard, that you know your business, and know how to respect your peers without taking crap from them. And if you can just focus on those things, then you won't feel angry, or ashamed, or depressed. You'll just understand that the world puts challenges in front of you, gives you burdens to carry, and you deal with them the best you can. And if people don't appreciate what you've got to offer, that's their problem, not yours."

Exhaustion was creeping up on him, along with a desire to give in to it. His saliva had turned syrupy in his mouth and throat. He covered a yawn. "I'm afraid they'll push me into early retirement," he said. "I don't know what I'll do with myself."

"You and Aronson and everyone else," Rabbi Mike said, with a sharp flick of his hand. His patient expression was gone. He finally wiped his face with his napkin, glanced at his watch and then at the door. When the waitress brought the bill, he jerked his chin in Paul's direction. "He's buying." She gave Paul a look—of disgust, maybe? Sympathy? With the missing tooth and sunken lip it was hard to tell. Either way, he didn't doubt she'd heard every word he'd said. Nor did he care. He handed over a twenty-dollar bill with relief. He wouldn't wait for change. "I'm heading back," Rabbi Mike said. He shimmied out of the booth and stood, breathing hard from the effort. "I hate using the john in these places."

"All this," Paul said. "It stays between us, right?"

"Just make sure to tell your wife I'm not so shabby at the human side of things after all."

Before Paul could follow, the rabbi was out the jingling door. In the synagogue parking lot the old Imperial waited, patched-up and running, but creakier and less efficient than ever.


"Look at you," Kat Harrow said that afternoon, when she came back from lunch to find him in his office, computer humming. He'd managed to make it past the login screen but had yet to figure out how to open his mail. For the past twenty minutes he'd been pushing the mouse back and forth on his desk, watching the little pointer appear and disappear on his screen. He'd opened a dozen windows but didn't know what to do with any of them. He felt his uselessness expanding without bounds.

"I can adapt," he said. "Just takes a little prodding."

"That's my specialty," Kat said. "Or so my ex used to tell me. Let me help with this."

Instead of hopping onto his desk, she stood next to him, close, leaning over his chair to see the screen, those full lips and round cheekbones set off against its glowing layers, window upon window upon window. Her skirt ended two inches above the knee, and below it the skin was tan and taut and glazed with a post-run lotion rub. The fabric of her blouse was half an inch from his nose.

One thing hadn't changed: the way proximity to a woman's body stirred him, the enduring surprise of it, as if he'd been given a gift he'd never expected, hadn't even allowed himself to wish for. He still experienced it with Cynthia after all these years, on those rare occasions when her arms slipped around him. Even with Riva Edelstein, when her breath heaved in his ear. What was the feeling, exactly? Less hunger or lust than amazement at what life had to offer. He supposed this, too, would one day fade.

Kat clicked his mouse several times until all the windows closed. Then a new one appeared, with a long list of unopened messages. "Like magic, right?" she said.

"I know what I know," Paul said. "That's knowledge. I *feel* what I know. That's wisdom."

Around a slender, flexed arm, Kat looked at him with fresh attention. He breathed in the smell of her.

# ANYTHING QUITE LIKE IT

## 2001

To HIS SURPRISE, ONCE he retired, Paul didn't miss the morning train ride to Penn Station, the crowded subway, the walk down traffic-choked streets smelling of garbage. He didn't miss the view from his seventeenth floor office or the chatter of secretaries outside his door. He found himself perfectly content to spend all week in New Jersey, not even crossing from Morris to Essex County for a month at a time.

If Paul was surprised, Cynthia was flabbergasted, though she did her best to hide it. Only after he'd been home half a year did she confess to having been so worried when he was forced to accept the early retirement package—a generous one—and even more when he didn't subsequently try to find consulting work, that she surveyed all her friends and acquaintances about their legal needs. Maybe they wanted to draw up a new will? Sue a neighbor over a property line dispute? She'd expected him to sink immediately into despondency, moping around the house, demanding her attention, quickly growing old. But now she could only marvel at how relaxed he looked, how unexpectedly serene. "Your color's improved, too," she said. "All those years under fluorescent lights, your face was starting to turn gray."

It was true: he felt better than he had in years. He had more energy, he slept more soundly. His appetite increased, but he ate with moderation and wasn't tempted by sweets. Indigestion that had plagued him for longer than he could remember gradually vanished. "You look as good as when I first met you," Cynthia said, stroking his hair, which was now white everywhere except for a small, stubborn dark patch on his crown. With gusto that made her gasp, he grabbed her hips and pulled her to him. "Maybe I should retire, too," she said later, under rumpled sheets.

The only trouble was, he experienced a painful twinge in his groin while they were making love, and again several days later, when he was loading the recycling into the back of his car. My brand new car, he thought every time he saw it, though it was now nine months old. After two decades he'd finally traded in his Imperial, turning over the keys with as heavy a lump in his throat as when he'd had to put his cat down ten years before. He test drove a dozen smaller models before settling on a big black Jeep with tinted back windows and a chrome muffler. He enjoyed being higher up than people in compacts on either side and right away found himself far more comfortable than he'd ever been in the Imperial. As soon as he brought the new car home he realized he'd been driving hunched over since he'd first gotten his license, believing the cramping in his arms and back to be necessary consequences of navigating overcrowded freeways. For the first time, he took pleasure in cruising east on I-80, and last winter, when a sudden storm overtook him fifteen miles from home, he didn't panic as he might have before; even with a few inches of snow on the ground, the Jeep barreled up the steep curve of Crescent Ridge without slipping or fishtailing once.

Today, though, he wished the Jeep had a lower trunk, so he didn't have to lift the bags stuffed with newspapers and bottles so high. He held onto the bumper until the pain subsided and when it did, found a sheen of sweat covered his forehead and dampened his shirt. A pulled muscle, he guessed. He was no longer young, and Cynthia wasn't light. Next time he'd have to be more careful when he rolled her on top of him. He was careful now, bending at the knees and easing the bags into the car, and then again when he made it to the dump, gently sliding the newspaper into its bin, emptying the bottles all at once rather than tossing them one by one as he liked to, listening to their pop and the musical plinking of shards.

After years of stalling, the township had finally begun collecting recycling at curbside, but Paul still preferred to make the twenty-minute drive down Union Knoll and across Route 46. The dump had always fascinated him. He never tired of observing what other people brought, their secret lives partially illuminated by detritus. Last week a woman his age unloaded six bags heaped with empty Southern Comfort bottles. A few months earlier, a man and his teenage son emptied from their trunk a dozen porcelain toilet seats. Somewhere in between, a young couple tossed several mysteriously wrapped packages, the size of small children, lumpy and covered in what looked like gauze, before hurrying to their pickup and peeling away. Illicit behavior, Paul guessed, and considered investigating. He liked the idea of calling the police and helping them track down criminals. He'd even made note of the pickup's license plate. But worse than finding something horrifying would have been finding something mundane and soiling his clothes for no reason. So instead he went on with his day, which meant heading to the library, where he spent half an hour choosing books for Cynthia—suspense novels and gardening advice—another half hour perusing the legal journals he couldn't bring himself to carry away from the stacks, and then the rest of the morning reading the *Times* beside a window that looked out on a weedy lot easing down to a shallow creek.

Simple routines were what he liked most about being retired, following them and also breaking them whenever the mood struck: continuing to sit on the patio listening to Brahms, for example, when he normally went to the gym, or going shopping for new tennis shoes on the day he'd set aside to pick up his dry cleaning. Today's interruption, however, wasn't his choosing. After only an hour at the library, he drove into downtown Denville and pulled up in front of the bakery. Cynthia had charged him with picking up the cake for Joy's wedding, which was set for the following evening, ceremony and reception at a hotel in Morristown. It wasn't a job he relished—he had too many flashes of collapsed tiers and smeared icing to feel relaxed as he approached the counter—but he'd quickly agreed to do it, putting on a brave face Cynthia had seen through instantly.

"If you don't want to take it out of the car yourself, wait till I get home," she said. "Just make sure you park in the shade."

•

What troubled him more than the thought of carrying the cake, though, was imagining Joy cutting it and feeding a bite to her new husband. After years of burning through boyfriends a month or two at a time, she'd announced last fall, at twenty-eight, that she was engaged to someone she'd known most of her life, the son of one of her father's business associates. "It's the most romantic thing I've ever heard," Cynthia said after Joy called and told her the news. "They met when she was three."

He should have been pleased. He'd no longer have to see different men on Joy's arm each time she visited, never again encounter a stranger walking out of the shower with a towel around his waist, smiling slyly, as if they shared a secret or a private joke, before joining her in the guest bedroom. Last year it had been a muscled boy, bald prematurely, his shining scalp seeming somehow lewd. Paul kept wishing he'd put on a cap. At dinner he talked nonstop—about surfing (a subject in which Paul had little interest), about Zen meditation (even less), and about politics (though they agreed on many things, Paul couldn't stand his self-congratulatory tone)—and never took his hand from Joy's thigh, rubbing it just at the spot where the hem of her skirt met skin. Paul, sitting on her other side, could do nothing but watch, biting his lip every time the muscled boy's fingers slipped into the seam between her legs.

A husband, he'd always assumed, would have been far easier to take. Sure, at first he'd have his hands all over her, too. But the longer they were together, the more space would appear between them. As the years went by, as they had kids and grew bags under their eyes and worked their way toward middle age, they'd hardly even touch. If they managed to stay together, sooner or later they'd seem as intimate as business partners who'd shared an office too long.

But now that the time had come, he wasn't sure he preferred this new version of Joy's future: one man, with whom she'd share everything—not just her morning coffee and her unpaid parking tickets, but her most private thoughts and her deepest fears, her body and her bed. Even worse, one man connected to Russell Demsky, who, as usual, had found an excuse not to act like a parent. Paul was paying for the wedding, as he'd always known he would. Russell's cash was once again tied up in investments that were complicated to liquidate, though judging by the recent remodel of his house on Budd Lake, his business had been booming. He'd pay Paul back as soon as he could loosen some strings, he said over the phone, and then added, with preemptive indignation, as if Paul had made outrageous accusations, "If you want, I'll pay interest."

"How does four percent sound?" Paul asked, and for a moment there was silence on the line. Then Russell laughed, too loud. Before he hung up, Paul added, "Accrued annually, of course."

Yet it was Russell Joy would dance with after cutting the cake, Russell who would make the toast, while Paul sat on the sidelines and sipped the champagne he'd bought, surrounded by the groom's extended family, half of whom wouldn't speak English. Here was another thing he hadn't imagined: that Joy's husband would have such dark hair and skin, that he'd have a name like Aziz.

"An Arab?" Reggie said when he called to pass on news of the engagement. He'd waited a few days after they'd heard from Joy, in the event that she'd made the announcement impulsively and would soon change her mind. By then the initial shock had begun to ebb, giving way to an uneasiness he couldn't name. "What's she thinking?"

"He's not Arab," Paul said. "He's Persian."

"Like the Ayatollah," Reggie said.

"It's an ancient culture. As old as the Greeks."

"Does he bow down to Zeus five times a day? Are they going to be married by a priestess of Athena?"

In fact, they were going to be married by a friend who'd sent away for a minister's license in the mail and who was going to read one poem in English, one in Hebrew, and one in Farsi. But Paul didn't mention any of this. Instead, he reminded her that Aziz had started spending summers in New York the year he was born and had been living in the States full-time since he was eight. But Reggie didn't seem to hear a word. If Joy liked Middle Eastern men, she said, why not at least try out an Israeli first?

"He's practically family," Paul said. "And Cynthia thinks he's gorgeous. Of course he is, I told her. Joy's got taste, just like her mother."

To this, Cynthia hadn't responded, and neither did Reggie. Nor did he go on to say what he really thought: that he agreed with her, a Persian man couldn't possibly be right for Joy. Nor could an Arab, an Indian, a Spaniard, a Swede. Not even a Jew, unless he was on the short side, without the hairy arms and aggressive demeanor and lazy ethics of Russell Demsky. What she deserved was someone made stupid by her affection, who'd throw himself off a bridge if she asked him to—one who'd adore her, in other words, as much as Paul adored Cynthia. Most men, regardless of race or creed, were too arrogant for such humility. The young and good-looking ones especially so.

This was something Reggie might have understood. She'd recently fallen for a retired accountant and moved with him to a golf course in Cary, North Carolina, of all places. Though she hadn't known him until a year ago, he'd grown up a few blocks from them in Crown Heights, and their families went to the same shul. But more important, he was pudgy, soft-spoken, with a bad knee and a hip that needed replacing. She was happy for the first time in her life.

Weren't Persian husbands, particularly gorgeous ones, known for beheading their wives?

Over the years he'd met Aziz on several occasions, and true, before he'd become Joy's fiancé, Paul had found the boy reasonably charming. He had a strong handshake and a bright smile, and even as a ten-year-old, he approached adults without hesitation, as if he couldn't distinguish between those of his parents' generation and his own. At a big summer picnic at Russell Demsky's lake house—to which Paul went reluctantly, at Cynthia's urging—Aziz came up to him with a bucket and asked, "Have you ever seen anything quite like it?"

Paul sat by himself on a lumpy rock, looking out at the flat water, waiting for a breeze to ripple the surface. Joy and Kyle had finished swimming and were now stuffing themselves with watermelon, and Cynthia was talking to old friends he didn't know. Russell's house always agitated him. Even before the remodel, with its extensive addition, it had a meandering quality, narrow hallways leading to small rooms packed with too much furniture, all the floors spread with rugs whose competing geometric patterns made him slightly nauseous. Russell hosted these picnics mostly as a way to do business and show off his stock, and the place was full of customers, dealers, wholesalers— ruggers, Joy and Kyle called them—talking about fabric and dye and the quality of knots. Among them was Aziz's father, who'd been Russell's main supplier in Tehran before clearing out after the fall of the Shah.

At the time Paul didn't know who the dark-haired boy belonged to, only that he was grateful to him and his bucket for interrupting what had started as a moment of contemplation and had since lapsed into one of boredom. He liked the boy's faintly British accent, which seemed to have less to do with geography than with class and good manners. From the bucket came an unsavory slurping sound, and when he looked inside he experienced an odd dizzying sensation at the sight of swirling water sloshing against orange plastic. It took him a moment to realize the water wasn't moving on its own, and for a flash he believed the boy had magical powers, or mystical ones—confirming, in either case, childhood suspicions that the world was far more complicated than he knew. Then he saw the wriggling creature at the bottom, about six inches long, a black streak turning circles and figure-eights, at once frantic and graceful.

"It's an eel," Paul said, though even as he spoke the word it sounded like the name of an imaginary being, no less magical for having been identified.

"It really is beautiful," the boy said. "And a little scary, don't you think?" Paul had an urge to pick the eel up and feel its scales slipping against his skin. He could have kept staring at it all afternoon as it searched for an exit that didn't exist. But he knew he had to be the one to say they should let it go. "Yes, of course," the boy replied, without hesitation. "I've kept it long enough."

He was already barefoot, but he waited for Paul to slip off his loafers and socks and tuck them behind the big rock. Then together they walked into the shallows, up to the boy's knees and Paul's shins. The boy let Paul hold one side of the bucket as they lowered it to the water. He peered over the rim but didn't see the eel slip out. He thought he felt something brush his ankle, but it might have been a weed, or more likely an imagined sensation, one he wished he could imagine again. When the boy lifted the bucket, only a scummy film of water covered the bottom, now perfectly still.

"I don't suppose I'll ever forget that," the boy said, and Paul agreed, though whenever they met afterward—at Joy's bat mitzvah, at her sweet-sixteen party, again at her high school graduation—neither of them mentioned it. Instead Paul would ask Aziz about school, about living in the city—his family had a house in Jackson Heights and a storefront and warehouse in the rug district of lower Midtown—and Aziz would talk about teachers and friends and sports teams without any awkwardness or embarrassment, any sense that he was putting on a show. "He wants to be worshipped," he'd say of a basketball coach who tried to model himself after Red Auerbach, chewing on a Sharpie instead of a cigar. "So we only laugh at him when he's not looking." His accent added a formality to his breeziness, and only afterward did it occur to Paul that if he'd heard Kyle talk to an adult so casually, without restraint, he would have cringed. "It's a pleasure catching up," Aziz always said after they'd chatted for twenty minutes, and then joined the kids his age flailing on the dance floor.

He'd since gone on to Columbia, where he studied music and world literature, and then to the Berklee School in Boston, where he earned a master's in composition. For several years he played in experimental jazz and new music combos whose CDs Paul found unlistenable—nothing but squeaks and groans—though Cynthia showed him reviews that claimed they were "important," "cutting-edge," and "brilliantly anarchic." Recently, however, Aziz had given up music to learn his father's business, which he would take over in a few years. During the day he oversaw operations at the warehouse, and in the evening he was taking classes toward his MBA. How he found the time to court Joy, who'd been living in San Diego for the past six years, Paul had no idea. He might have been grateful to Aziz for bringing her back to the proper coast—they'd put a downpayment on a house in Stamford—but his first thought on hearing the news was that the boy had tricked him. All this time his friendliness had been a ruse, his easy confidence a mask for unbounded arrogance. Had he been laughing at Paul, too, every time he turned his back?

The previous night, when they'd gathered at the groom's father's house in Queens for a rehearsal dinner, Paul had kept his distance from Aziz, who at first seemed happy to ignore him, laughing with his musician friends, an arm in shirtsleeves draped over Joy's bare shoulders. And Paul thought Joy looked unusually small under that arm, diminished and fragile in a strapless purple dress. She'd always been self-possessed and quietly forceful, though languid when surrounded by those who put her at ease, with a look of just having woken up from an unplanned nap. Maybe with Aziz she'd gotten too comfortable. She'd let her guard down, and he'd taken advantage of her trust. Or maybe he had magical abilities after all, though Paul had made a mistake in believing them to be benign.

In this house, too, richly colored rugs covered all the floors, and more hung on the walls. Only here there was no backyard to speak of, no lake to stare at, and he couldn't escape the patterns that made the room dance even as he sat still on a hard sofa, gazing into a cup Aziz's mother had handed him. Inside was what looked like watery milk and tasted like carbonated toothpaste. A traditional Person drink, she'd said, and then added, Joy's favorite. She and Cynthia had since disappeared upstairs to coordinate jewelry for the wedding.

Aziz's father, thick-bodied, with a white pompadour and a mustache that covered both lips when his mouth was closed, stood inches from Russell Demsky, who'd had his left ear re-pierced some years ago, right after Kyle had come home from his first semester at college wearing a gold-plated hoop. He'd done it ostensibly to bond with his son, though Paul knew better: Russell couldn't let anyone in the family out-bohemian him. Kyle had long since taken his earring out. He'd survived medical school and become an orthopedic surgeon. Even now he was still in D.C., on call through Saturday morning, though he'd promised to make it back in time for the ceremony. To

Paul's surprise he'd begun to turn into something of an adult, while his father remained a child, a diamond stud glinting on the side of his head. Russell and Aziz's father spoke in whispers—co-conspirators, Paul thought, who'd arranged to shut him out of Joy's life.

He took another sip of the toothpaste drink, which left a pleasant tingle on his tongue, and then Joy was standing in front of him, the hem of her dress brushing his knee. "What's your problem?" She kicked his foot as she said it, the point of a silver pump jabbing his toe. Her hair was pulled back to reveal ears that seemed hardly to have grown in the twenty years since he'd first seen them, tiny little disks with silver baubles dangling down. "Eat too many kebabs?"

"Just enjoying watching the happy couple," he said.

"You're such a sap." She reached down to pull him up. When he was standing, her eyes, raised by heels, were slightly higher than his. "Mom told me you've been on the phone with the caterers."

"They always try to skimp on the hors d'oeuvres."

"And she's making you pick up the cake?"

"I've got a lot of time on my hands."

"Better save some energy. You're dancing with me on Saturday, whether you want to or not."

Then, just as he was about to put his arm around her, there was Aziz's again, landing in its place. And again she seemed to slump beneath the weight of it, her head tilting forward, as if his touch drained her strength. Aziz didn't remove it to shake Paul's hand, instead giving him an awkward bump on the shoulder with his free fist. "She's not telling you secrets, is she?" he asked. "Confessing that she's getting cold feet?"

He smiled as he said it, but this wasn't his easy, confident smile. His dark cheeks looked plastic and strained. "Will you quit already?" Joy said. "I'm not getting cold feet."

"She's been freaking out all week," Aziz said, and pulled her closer. Over the years his accent had faded, and now he sounded hardly better bred than any of the kids Joy and Kyle had grown up with, exotic only because of his name and the shade of his skin. "Yesterday she said she didn't think she could go through with it."

"It's the whole production," Joy said. "Mom, Dad. They're making me crazy. Questions every two seconds. Everything's got to be equal. Same number of guests, same number of toasts from each side. Do they think I care who makes the stupid jokes?"

Aziz gestured at their fathers, still huddled together. "For them, it's just another chance to sell rugs."

"Maybe you should postpone," Paul said, somberly, working hard to keep a hopeful note out of his voice. "Take some time to think it over."

Aziz shifted his arm, which now seemed to have a hypnotic, pacifying effect. Joy leaned into him, pressed her cheek against his neck. "I just want you to myself," she said. "Our families," she added, and glanced at Paul, "they can all go stuff it."

To change the subject, Paul asked Aziz about the musicians, who now crowded around the buffet table, scarfing dates and squares of salty cheese. Had they played on the CD he'd sent Cynthia? The one with the bird on its cover?

"That's right," Aziz said, loosening his hold on Joy's shoulder. "*Shoot the Albatross.*"

"I enjoyed that one," Paul said.

"They're playing for us on Saturday. Before we walk in, and while everyone's heading into the reception."

"Oh," Paul said, imagining how quickly the hotel's courtyard would empty as it echoed with screeches and hums. "What a treat. Another thing to look forward to."

"You're the worst liar I've ever known," Joy said, sounding less annoyed than beleaguered, as if Paul were one more person trying to oppress her. But when they excused themselves to talk to other guests, she gave him a look—a familiar one, meant to forgive him, he thought, or else to let him know he meant something to her. Why, then, did it so unsettle him? After they were gone he had to stare hard at the rug on a nearby wall—a grid of diamonds inside of diamonds inside of diamonds—to shake the sight of her eyes passing over his.

•

The cake box was bigger than he'd expected, three feet wide and two and a half tall, but still it fit with no trouble into the back of his Jeep. One of the baker's assistants wheeled it out on a cart and eased it onto the blanket Paul had laid out to keep it from sliding. Through a plastic window on top he could see swirls of white and peach icing, the stem of a sugar rose.

His own wedding cake had been far simpler—two rectangles of angel food with a layer of fudge between—but so had been the wedding generally. For the children's sake, Cynthia wanted to keep it understated. The less fanfare the better. It was confusing enough to have their mother remarry, she said at the time. Plus, you weren't supposed to make a big deal of a second marriage; throwing an elaborate party to celebrate risked linking its fate to the first. And of course Paul had agreed. He didn't bother reminding her that this was his first wedding and, with luck, his only. They held the ceremony in the synagogue's smaller sanctuary, the reception at the house. Only two dozen people came: on Paul's side, just his parents, Reggie and her then-boyfriend of two weeks, and a pair of co-workers. There were too few people to dance the horah. As she was leaving, his mother said, as if to comfort him, "It still counts, as long as you signed the papers."

He had to remind himself to drive slowly on the way home, though every time he looked down at the speedometer, he was five miles an hour over the limit. The twinge in his groin threatened every time he touched the brake, and again when he made it to the driveway and stepped out of the car. The nearest shade at this time of day was in front of the house next door, beneath an old oak whose branches stretched all the way to his bedroom windows. Parking there would have meant walking uphill, and worse, getting trapped by a chatty neighbor who last week had cornered him as he was heading out for a jog. She, too, had recently retired, from selling real estate, but unlike Paul she had nothing better to do with her newly open days than harass innocent passers-by. For twenty minutes she talked to him about recent proposals to install sidewalks on their side of the street. Did he know the township had an easement on the first ten feet of his yard? Did he think they'd cut down her tree? He tried to excuse himself by saying he had an appointment, and then because nothing else came to mind, added, "I'm getting fitted for a tuxedo."

She didn't know, of course, that he owned a tux already, but it was a mistake anyway. As soon as the neighbor heard about Joy's wedding, the questions multiplied. She wanted to know every detail about the groom—what an interesting name! is he Algerian?—about the reception, about the honeymoon. "I never expected her to settle down. All those different boys she'd show up with. She's not, you know," she said, twirling a hand over her belly, "is she? You'll love being a grandparent."

He finally managed to extract himself by saying, yes, he thought the oak tree was likely slated for the chainsaw. "If I were you, I'd get over to the mayor's office as soon as possible."

Now, with the Jeep out in the open, he pulled the blanket over the top of the cake box to keep the sun off. He took his time clearing out the basement fridge and removing its shelves. Joy and Cynthia were due to arrive any minute from their appointment at the nail salon, but when fifteen minutes went by, and the sun rose higher, he maneuvered the wheelbarrow from the garage to the back of the car. Before attempting to move the box he pulled up the corner to test its weight. It wasn't any heavier than the bags of newspaper, really, so he spread his feet apart, bent at the knees, and lifted.

What he experienced first was a simple physical sensation, the feeling of something inside him giving way, isolated for a moment before the pain arrived. And in that moment the image that sprang to mind was of the little black eel, back fin rippling as it turned circles in the bucket, and of Aziz's serious expression as he lowered it into the lake. Only somehow the eel was Joy, and she was slipping into the water, and he didn't want to see her go.

And then he was on his back, the box on top of him.

He learned what had happened only later, in the hospital, and for weeks after he kept picturing it: a piece of his lower intestine slipping through a weakness in his abdominal wall like an elastic knuckle, snapping down into his scrotum, smack against his right testicle. The label for something so outrageous seemed far too ordinary. Hernia. He wanted a more drastic word, something with gravity, but when he asked the doctor if his condition had a Latin name, he received only a raised eyebrow in response.

Even while he was in the middle of it, though, when he didn't yet know what to call it, he recalled an incident when he was ten years old, following a dispute with a neighborhood kid over stickball. They'd been arguing for most of an hour. Then the kid, fed up, cried, *catch*, and from a few feet away, threw the ball as hard as he could into Paul's crotch. All the breath left his lungs, tears flooded his eyes, snot exploded from his nose, and he writhed on the gravel and weeds of the empty lot. He kept doing so even as the pain subsided into a dull throb, mostly because he didn't want to have to stand and wipe his face while people were watching. Only when all the other boys left him alone did he pull himself from the ground.

It was being conscious of the snot on his face, and of his embarrassment at the thought of other people seeing it, that assured him he wasn't dying in the driveway. But he stayed where he was in any case, afraid to move, until he heard Cynthia's car pull up behind him. He kept his eyes shut as he heard doors open and close, plastic soles slapping pavement, gasps and shouts. "I'm okay," he managed to call out, "sort of," and then groaned in spite of his effort not to. He was aware of them moving the box from his chest, of being helped into the car and driven away. At first he thought Cynthia was driving and Joy was beside him in back, with her warm hand on his forehead, and tried not to be disappointed to discover it was the other way around. In the darkness behind his tightly shut lids he focused on the pain, which he visualized as a flame that enlarged or contracted with each breath, and on the hushed voices of his wife and stepdaughter, distinguishable only by a slight difference in pitch, a nearly identical rasp sounding somehow youthful and sultry in Joy's but haggard and put-upon in Cynthia's.

"Do I turn here?"

"Look at the sign."

"Jesus, this isn't it."

"There! There! The goddamn sign. Are you blind?"

He wouldn't let himself look at either of their faces as the car jerked to a stop. He knew he would see fear in them, and even more, anticipation: even if they, too, realized he wasn't dying, they'd also realize it might not be the case next time. And maybe that was what made him say, without having been conscious of thinking it, "The key to the safe deposit box. Taped to the underside of my sock drawer."

"We should have eloped," Joy said from the front seat.

Cynthia said, close to his ear, "Shut up, both of you."

When he finally did open his eyes, flat on his back in an examination room, lights scorching overhead, a doctor bent over him, gloved hands probing his groin, he wished he'd kept them shut. He'd imagined only Cynthia had followed him in, but there was Joy standing beside her, staring openly at his exposed middle. Instinct made him try to cover himself, but the doctor batted his hand away. Both Joy and Cynthia wore tank-tops, shorts, flip-flops, their nails— finger and toe—painted the same burgundy shade as the bridesmaids dresses hanging beside the tux in his closet. Even without Aziz's arm around her, Joy looked smaller than she should have, and he wondered if she'd lost weight. Or was he simply seeing her now as she'd always been? Cynthia, too, looked shrunken, though she was rounder, her bare shoulders meaty next to Joy's bony ones. Paired together they produced an odd effect on his vision. Not that he thought he was seeing double, exactly—Joy fair and slim, Cynthia dark and stout—but that he was seeing simultaneously into two different periods of time. His past and present, maybe, or a past he might have had and a present he might lose at any moment. The doctor prodded and shifted, and despite the discomfort, something began to stir between his legs.

An erection? Now?

And still Joy didn't avert her eyes. Maybe this was her way of getting even: once, when she was home from college for the summer, he'd accidentally walked in on her in the upstairs bathroom, where she stood in front of the mirror in nothing but underpants, picking at something on her face with tweezers. Of course he hadn't stood there gawking, instead muttering apologies and asking why no one used locks anymore as he stepped out and slammed the door behind him.

The doctor pressed something—a thumb?—under his scrotum, sending another shock of pain through him and cutting short the embarrassing flow of blood. "Incarcerated," he said, and Paul was delirious enough to believe he was being accused of a crime.

"Jail?" he asked, but the doctor ignored him, speaking instead to Cynthia. The herniated intestine was caught in the muscle and wouldn't retract. Very dangerous condition if left untreated. Surgery, right away.

"We'll prep him and move him up as soon as an OR's ready," the doctor said.

And because he didn't want to see the expression on either of the women's faces, one that would suggest he'd messed everything up, as they'd always expected he would, he stared straight into the ferocious light hanging above him. "I can't," he said. "My stepdaughter's getting married tomorrow."

A raspy voice answered. "Shut the hell up, Paul." This time he couldn't tell if it was Cynthia's or Joy's.

Only after he woke, still groggy from anesthesia, did he remember the cake, and he asked Cynthia about it as soon as she came into the recovery room. She shrugged and said, "A little extra icing, and it'll be fine." And then he found himself astonished to hear that the wedding was going on as planned. Why would he have imagined otherwise? Guests had already flown in from California, from London, from Iran. "We've got to get that girl married before she flips out and runs away with a busboy," Cynthia said.

He was equally surprised to find out he was being discharged in a few hours. He wouldn't even spend the night in the hospital. They'd send him home with a wheelchair and pain pills, he'd have to stay off his feet for a week, but soon enough he'd be back to normal. It was the most dramatic thing that had ever happened to him, and in the end nothing had come of it. Or almost nothing. When he asked if he'd be well enough to make it to the wedding, the doctor raised an eyebrow again and said, "Watch the video."

He was home by dinner time, though of course he couldn't eat. The painkillers kept him cloudy on the family room couch, where he watched a European soccer match he couldn't follow, except to keep track of the score; it was one-all when he dozed off and no different when he woke half an hour later. He heard activity in the kitchen, plates clattering, Cynthia talking quietly, and then Joy, loud, "Will you lay off already? It's not your fucking wedding." Then more muttering from Cynthia, footsteps heading toward the basement door, and Joy's voice again, even louder, "And unlike you, I'm not having more than one."

Paul wasn't aware of being brought up to bed, but that's where he woke the next morning, just before dawn, birds clamoring in the branches of the neighbor's oak. Were they always so loud? If so, he didn't know how he'd ever managed to sleep past sunrise. A dream lingered just out of reach—something to do with water or light, and missing keys or a lock that wouldn't work—but it had had enough of an erotic cast to leave him hard, all the way this time, skin pulling at his stitches. He needed another pain pill, but he didn't want to wake Cynthia, whose face was turned away, her thick hair still so black that every errant white strand stood out as an absence, as if a tiny sliver of her head had disappeared in the night. If he thought he could have done so gently enough he would have reached out to stroke it, for his own comfort, because when the erection deserted him, along with the vague, dreamy desire that had propelled it, what arrived in its place was the naked chill of fear.

Today it was his abdominal muscles. And tomorrow? Next week, next year? What would give way then? His heart? Blood vessels in his brain?

How he'd fooled himself, to believe retirement was a new beginning, that his life was starting over again at sixty. But then, maybe he'd always been fooling himself. Didn't life begin again every morning, when the birds raised this racket in the oak tree? If so, he'd slept through every new call to be reborn. He should have kept in mind all along: life began tomorrow and tomorrow and tomorrow. Until it didn't.

Tomorrow the township might cut down the neighbor's oak. Tomorrow Joy would wake up beside her new Persian husband, with his shining dark hair and gleaming white teeth. And if you believed the old stories, he might decide to behead her in favor of a new bride.

Yes, he needed the pill for sure. He eased his feet off the edge of the bed, and then his legs. As long as he propped himself on the nightstand, and then the wall, he didn't think he'd have any trouble standing or walking. Up you go, he thought, and then he was doubled over on the floor, each pulse of pain making him moan. Behind him, Cynthia said, "For crying out loud, Paul. Can't you just let me take care of you for once?" In the oak, the birds hollered and beat their wings.


All morning—or was it afternoon already?—people stopped in to visit. They hadn't come to see him, of course. They were already in town for the wedding, and he happened to be an interesting side show, a way to kill an hour before heading to the hotel. First came Kyle, who walked in wearing rubber gloves and carrying a medical bag. He'd finished his residency a year ago and had been practicing at a private hospital for more than nine months, but still Paul couldn't imagine anyone calling him Dr. Demsky. Nor could he see the little van dyke beard as anything more than a flimsy mask for his boyish face, a costume that hid nothing. "Most surgeons are lazy," Kyle said, insisting on taking a look at the incision. "If I don't know him, I don't trust him."

"Does everyone in the family have to see my balls?" Paul said, and before Kyle had covered him up, Reggie walked in, carrying a vase stuffed with greenery and dark branches, a few wispy white flowers at their tips.

"At least they didn't cut it off," Reggie said. When Kyle went to hug her, she took a step back and put up her hands. "It's nice to see you, sweetie, but you better take the gloves off first."

Reggie's face was tan for the first time in her life, as far as Paul knew, and her hair was longer than he'd seen it since they were kids. She had it pulled back tightly, so that her long nose was more prominent than usual, and it made her look so much like their mother that Paul wondered if she'd stopped looking in the mirror. When they were alone, she moved the vase from the nightstand to the dresser and fiddled with fern leaves, and only after she was quiet for ten seconds or so—a record for Reggie, he thought—did he realize she was crying. She covered her face, then ran to the bathroom, and when she came back she was flushed and smiling, proud of herself, it seemed, either for being overcome with emotion or for getting it back under control. "I was so scared when I heard," she said. "We're all we've got left."

This was what happiness did to people, made them sentimental, delusional. She now talked about the past fondly, as if she'd appreciated it while it was here. She recalled stories about their parents Paul had forgotten or never known, at least one of which he was sure she'd made up: the time, to cheer up their depressed mother, their father put on her wedding gown and danced through the apartment to a Benny Goodman record, cigar clamped between molars. She talked about shops on Utica Avenue, the pool club where they'd spent summers splashing water into each other's eyes, the shul where fifty years ago she and her boyfriend Larry might have dozed a few feet from each other during services.

"No wonder we understand each other so well," Reggie said. "Why you'd marry someone from a totally different background—and an Arab?—I don't get it at all." She and Larry were driving out to the old neighborhood tomorrow, she said. She dreamed about those streets every night and wanted to see them again, even if they were full of Haitians now. And then they'd go out to the cemetery, the big family plot where dozens of Habermans were buried: grandparents, uncles and aunts, a cousin who'd died from polio at thirteen, another, at twenty-nine, from an unfortunate combination of vodka and sleeping pills. "I want to make sure they're taking good care of Mom and Dad."

"You should bring these," Paul said, gesturing at the vase. She could look back all she wanted. But from now on, he decided, his sights were set firmly ahead. Tomorrow's a new beginning, he wanted to tell her. And the day after that, and the day after that. Until, one day, it isn't.

Later, after he slept again, Russell Demsky poked his head in and said, "This is what happens when you're married to a ball-buster.

Would've been me if I didn't have the sense to cut loose." Then he winked and added, "The first need of a free people is to define their own—"

Before he could finish, Paul coughed, then winced. "About the interest on your loan—"

"Feel better, champ," Russell said, and left.

Only when the room darkened, the sunlight now partially blocked by the neighbor's oak, did he admit to himself he'd been waiting all day for Joy. He had the feeling that he had important things to tell her, though with the pain medication fogging his thoughts again he couldn't remember what those things were. Maybe she'd come to see him already, and he'd been sleeping. Or maybe he'd been awake but so groggy it had since slipped his mind. She couldn't simply have forgotten him, could she, even on a day like this?

When he heard footsteps outside the door, he ran fingers through his hair and tried to sit up but couldn't manage to wedge the pillow under his back. Then came a soft tapping on the doorframe. Not Joy. She would have knocked harder, or more likely just blown in without waiting to be invited. Here instead: obsidian hair, skin the color of wet sand, porcelain teeth. Aziz. He didn't look like someone who was getting married in a few hours—or else he looked like someone who might always be getting married in a few hours, who, on a moment's notice, could throw on a tuxedo and walk straight into the most important event of his life. He wore loose blue jeans and a V-neck shirt that showed off a surprisingly smooth chest, not a single hair in view. What was it about him that made Joy look so small under his arm, when he himself wasn't more than a few inches taller than she, only an inch or two taller than Paul? To his credit, he was nothing like Russell Demsky: dainty, almost feminine, with long eyelashes and a dimple on his left cheek when he smiled and sat on the edge of the bed.

He was carrying something. Not a bucket with an eel inside, but a small rug, maybe two feet square, with a pattern of abstract shapes that resembled birds and others that resembled goats. Aziz held it up, and then his hand disappeared inside. Not a rug but a bag. Or a bag made of a rug. What came out of it was a flat black box, just bigger than his hand, with a split wire hanging from one side. "In Persian culture," he said, "it's traditional for the groom's family to heap gifts on the bride and her people. My dad wants to stay on Russell's good side. But I know you're paying for everything. So, anyway, just a small token. Stuff for the gym. Cynthia said you've been going." He held up the bag. "To carry your things." Then he set the box on Paul's chest. "And something to listen to on the treadmill."

"I don't think I'll be on the treadmill for a while."

"For relaxing in bed, then."

At the ends of the wire were two little pads for his ears. Paul slipped them on, and Aziz pressed a button on the box. A compact disc player, yes, he could see that now, though he couldn't shake the sense that Aziz was handing him occult objects, ancient, unidentifiable, possibly dangerous. He expected to hear more squeaks and groans, but when the music came through there were sounds he recognized: a violin, a piano, even a melody, though not a familiar one. He let his head sink down into the pillow. Aziz didn't move from the edge of the bed. They'd stay this way until the music finished, he thought, or else the music would continue until *he* was finished, and Reggie, too, and Cynthia and Russell, and even Joy and Kyle. It sounded like a tune that had been here long before they'd arrived and would remain long after they'd gone. And it was carrying him somewhere with its extended simple lines, its gradual changes of pitch, somewhere beyond thought, where he could simply lie and listen.

But before he made it there—his eyes still open a crack, though blurred—Aziz was moving to the door, half turned away, smile faltering. When Paul slipped one of the earphones off, the tune in his head mixed with the sound of Joy shouting from below. "Z! Do you hear me? Come on, already. It's time to go."

"She's losing it," Aziz said quietly, without turning to face Paul, without knowing for sure, it seemed, that Paul could hear him. "Still four hours to the ceremony. It was her idea to wait for sundown. She'll be sitting in that dress with her makeup done all afternoon."

When Joy's voice reached them again, it was from outside, in the driveway. "If you're not down in five minutes, you can find your own way there."

Paul wanted to know the name of the tune, but Aziz was already moving to the window. His hair was as luxuriously black as Cynthia's, shoulder blades pushing out the back of his shirt like chicken wings. He didn't look like anyone's husband. Certainly not like a husband who'd behead his bride the morning after their wedding. Of course there were other old stories, too. Strange that he remembered them only now. One about a Persian king, for example, so devoted to his lovely Jewish wife that he spared her people from the gallows.

"On my way," Aziz called down, but made no move to leave the room.

Paul pushed aside the sheet that covered him. He had only an undershirt on, nothing below. It was the least dignified outfit a man could wear, but for some reason he didn't mind. He swung his legs off the bed, set his feet on the floor, and waited until he felt the strength to stand. And if it never came?

"Be right down," Aziz called. He, too, seemed to be waiting, gathering strength or patience or nerve. When he saw Paul sitting, he came to him and helped him up. Together they shuffled to the window. In the driveway, Cynthia and Kyle carried the cake box to the back of the Jeep while Joy watched, or rather, directed. "Keep it flat," she said. "Bring your corner up." She was in the same shorts and flip-flops and tank top as yesterday—had it only been yesterday?—but her hair was different. New bangs, the rest twisted and pinned to the sides of her head, so that curls fell over her cheeks and ears and left the taut skin of her neck exposed. The skin who knew how many men had touched, that Aziz had touched who knew how many times. The same skin Paul had seen when he'd surprised her in the bathroom—when, in that frozen moment before he'd closed the door, she'd hardly moved to cover herself, instead giving him the very look she'd turned on him at the rehearsal dinner, direct and unabashed, mouth open.

"Keep the end up, goddamnit," she cried, out of sight now behind the Jeep's open back door. "It's already mangled enough."

He knew now, what kind of look it was. Maybe he'd always known. One of understanding, of pity. One that recognized shame and longing and heartache.

"You'll be stunning," he called down. "Just remember to have fun tonight." To Aziz, he said, "Your kids. They'll be something to see."

He hoped she'd come around the car and look up. Kyle did, and then Cynthia, who shaded her eyes with a hand and yelled, "Stay off your feet. And don't even think about going downstairs. Gail, from Hadassah? She's bringing food up later." Her hair, too, was pinned up, and he wanted to experience a similar pang for the skin of her neck, though it was looser and ruddy. That he couldn't was something for which he'd have to try to forgive himself. How could he long for what he already had? And without something to long for, what did it matter that tomorrow was a new beginning, and tomorrow and tomorrow and tomorrow? "I'll take extra pictures," Cynthia said. "You won't miss anything."

When Joy finally came back into sight, her hands were on her hips, face red. All he wanted was a single wave. "Z!" she called. "Last chance. If you don't come now, I'm marrying the first guy I find in the hotel."

Paul let go of the window sash. He wanted to stand on his own, even for a moment, feeling the throb between his legs and in his chest. She wouldn't acknowledge him, he knew, but he waited anyway.

Beside him, Aziz made a strange noise, something between a gasp and a guffaw, and when Paul glanced at him he wore a strange expression, frozen smile, stricken eyes, a combination of amazement and alarm. His dark face seemed oddly pale beneath the surface of his skin, as if it had thinned and gone translucent. "My God," he said, and blinked several times, leaning backward on his heels. For a moment Paul thought he was going to faint, but instead he hugged himself. "I never thought I'd—"

He broke off and turned away from the window. His posture was one Paul recognized—that of a man overburdened, crippled by love.

"I think I'm going to hurl," Aziz said.

And Paul surprised himself by taking the boy's head between his hands and kissing him, firmly, once on each cheek.

# ACKNOWLEDGMENTS

I owe huge thanks to Victoria Barrett and Andrew Scott of Engine Books for all their selfless work to bring this book into the world; to PJ Mark for essential suggestions; to Willamette University for research support; and to Alexandra and Iona for making life so sweet.

I'd also like to thank the editors of the following journals, where some chapters first appeared:

*Passages North*: "Girl Made of Metal"
*Harvard Review*: "The Measure of a Man"
*PRISM international*: "Four Nocturnes for Left Hand"
*Four Way Review*: "Could Be Worse"
*Arts & Letters*: "Some Macher"
*Jewish Fiction*: "Grow or Sell"
*The Laurel Review*: "Around the Cape of Good Hope"
*Fifth Wednesday Journal*: "Between You and Me"

Finally, I am grateful to the University of Nebraska Press for permission to quote Wright Morris in the epigraph:
Reproduced from *The Works of Love* by Wright Morris by permission of the University of Nebraska Press. Copyright 1949, 1951 by Wright Morris.

# ABOUT THE AUTHOR

SCOTT NADELSON is the author of three story collections, most recently *Aftermath*, and a memoir, *The Next Scott Nadelson: A Life in Progress*. Winner of the Reform Judaism Fiction Prize, the Great Lakes Colleges Association New Writers Award, and an Oregon Book Award, he teaches at Willamette University and in the Rainier Writing Workshop MFA Program at Pacific Lutheran University.

CPSIA information can be obtained at www.ICGtesting.com
Printed in the USA
LVOW06s0815131015

457943LV00003B/3/P